HER THIN BLUE LIFELINE

A.J. DOWNEY

COPYRIGHT

Book design by Maggie Kern

Cover art and Indigo Knights Log by Dar Albert at Wicked Smart Designs

Photo by Golden Czermak
Model Julio Elving

Dedication

To D.C., J.S, and P.L.J. never would have thought of this without you. Thanks for the inspiration.

I'm hurt,
And tired,
And battered,
And bruised.

I've been used,
And bullied,
And scarred,
And abused.

But I'm not broken,
Or shattered,
Or beyond repair.

I just need time,
And patience,
And tender loving care

PROLOGUE

*C*hrissy...

"Seriously! I wouldn't worry about it. It's not like anyone's actually going to *do* anything with it. I mean, who *does that* anyway?"

I refilled my best friend's glass and added a touch of wine to my own. Setting down the bottle and leaning heavily on the edge of my kitchen counter, I looked into the living room through the portal left between my cabinets and countertop. Sam was on my couch, looking at me over the back of it, lounged comfortably against the arm. She was blonde, bubbly, and perfect just like she'd been all through high school and college and I couldn't help but smile with affection.

It was a casual night in after wrapping the biggest defense case of my life. I'd won and couldn't believe how relieved I was that the jury had seen what I had. Miranda Maguire had been systematically abused by her husband, baseball legend Skip Maguire. Even though she had killed him, it hadn't been for his money like the prosecution had claimed, but to save her own life.

That wasn't what we were talking about, however, and it wasn't the celebration I had expected it to be. No, this one was a hard-won victory and was thoroughly tainted by the utter vitriol of Skip Maguire's rabid macho fan base. The same fan base that had spawned the total creeper who had published my home address online with the ominous message to go ahead and come let me know about their displeasure with me... of course, I was being polite phrasing it like that.

"It's creepy and really uncomfortable. They don't know what happened, Sam..."

"He's their big damn sports hero, Christina. It doesn't really *matter* to them what really happened. The only thing that matters to them is that he's dead, and *you* got his killer off. The blame has to land somewhere," she shrugged, "and Miranda has his fortune and has all but disappeared and so that leaves *you*."

I hung my head and shook it, picking up the wine glasses and coming around the kitchen island. I held out her glass to her, about to say *'you're so comforting'* when *bam!* My front door exploded inward, shards of wood flying, I dropped her glass, the stemware falling and crashing against the hardwood floor.

I spun, as a man loomed through the opening, he raised a gun, Sam was screaming, I think *I* was screaming, and the gun, it went off. Everything was happening in slow motion, the barrel of it belching fire and flame. Sam's head snapped back, blood arching from her forehead, her blue eyes staring, mouth dropped open. I spun, turning on the ball of one foot, dropping my glass.

Run!

My mind screaming, panic and terror clawing at the inside of my skull.

Get away!

Three loud reports, the sound as if everything was under water, the first shot deafening in the small enclosure of my one bedroom apartment. The man, he punched me, twice in the back. *Boom! Boom!* I started falling, as if my strings had been cut, the floor rushing up to meet me.

The world, the world went black, and disappeared until I was suddenly floating. Floating in perfect darkness...

ony...

"Homicide."

"Yeah, Tony, got a couple of fresh ones at two-two-one-six, east 53rd; apartment two-oh-six. You're up."

I finished scribbling the address he'd given me on a legal pad in front of me saying, "I think this damn city has had enough with the baseball references, Captain."

"Yeah, whatever, get your ass over there, this city has had enough with the homicides lately, too."

"You ain't lying; I'm on it."

I tossed the receiver back onto its cradle with a clatter. I sat up from where I'd been hunched over my desk and rubbed the back of my neck, giving myself at least enough time to indulge in a stretch before getting up. I picked up the pad of paper, my eyes roving over the address as it tickled the back of my brain.

I knew it, but couldn't place it. Something about all those twos and sixes was just niggling at me in the worst way, but I figured I'd see it soon enough. I needed to get over there before the bodies got cold. Before the medical examiner got any kind of time with them. It helped to see the scene before anything was touched or moved.

I got up and hauled ass, heading down to the garage and my assigned cruiser. It was a short drive from the 12th precinct to the apartment's address, and there was plenty of parking among the black and whites with their party lights that were already there. Hell, the coroner's van wasn't even here yet. Just a couple of uniformed units. *Lucky me.* I double parked, and then it clicked... *this was Chrissy's place.* She was a lawyer, a defense attorney that I'd taken out a couple of times. We were like ships passing in the night schedule wise, and after the fourth interrupted date, we had pretty much come to the conclusion that it was nice, but it wasn't going to happen.

That'd been over three years ago, pushing four; I'd always sort of wondered if our paths would cross again. I never imagined it might be on a homicide call in her building, that is if she still even lived here. *Who was I kidding?* I knew, deep in my gut from the minute I'd pulled up, it was the feisty lawyer's apartment I was headed to.

"Well you can definitely say there were signs of forced entry, huh detective?" a uniform, Johns by the nametag on his chest, said as I stepped carefully over the shattered debris that'd been Chrissy Franco's doorframe and lock.

"Jesus Christ," I muttered taking in the raw scene.

There was a blonde, draped back over the arm of the couch, a movie-perfect shot through her fuckin' forehead, right between the eyes. I walked carefully up to the second body and leaned down over my knees.

"Yeah, that's Chrissy Franco, alright," I said, heart heavy in the center of my chest. Regret weighed me down like a thousand pound boulder in the center of my chest. She was beautiful, even like this, body cooling on the floor. If ever there had been one that'd got away, it was Chrissy. I'd thought about her a lot in the intervening years since I'd last seen her. I'd even caught myself lingering in the corridors of the courthouse on the occasions I'd had to be there. Hoping to run into her, hoping to rekindle things; that she might happen to be single, maybe willing to give it a shot again... This was a-fucking-shame, and I was gutted that it had to be me to catch the call.

Damnit.

I pulled on a pair of gloves and went to trace some of her long dark hair away from the side of her face so I could get a better look at her when she gasped.

I nearly shot through the fuckin' roof.

"Call a bus!" I screamed and knelt down amid the broken glass and spilled wine, the sweet smell of alcohol and coppery tang of blood singeing my nose even as hope filled me up like a goddamn helium balloon.

"H-he-help me," she stammered out, and I took her hand.

"Ambulance is on the way, just hang on, baby."

"Tony?"

"Yeah, yeah, you remember me?"

"It hurts!" her tone was mournful, pain filled, and I deflated a little on the inside, but I wasn't willing to show it. Confidence, surety, that's what she needed right now.

Shit. Both of those things were the *last* things I was feeling right now. I wasn't used to live victims, especially not ones I'd had the occasional date with. I couldn't fucking help her except to wait for paramedics, and I hated it. I glared at the uniform who was spewing panicked words into the mic at his shoulder.

"Didn't you check to see if she was a-fuckin'-live!?" I demanded, needing to direct my helpless anger *somewhere*.

"I mean, who gives a shit, man? I didn't know! Just look at her!" he shouted, and I swore I was gonna have a quiet conversation with him and his CO later, whether or not she lived or died. That shit wasn't right. *You didn't get to pick the vic.* I strapped down my incendiary rage at the comment and stroked her hand, giving my attention to the wounded woman on the floor, the person that needed it most.

"Hang on, Chrissy, we're gonna get you some help." She squeezed my hand, and I could swear my heart squeezed down with it, a tight ball of sympathy for her pain.

Nobody deserved this shit. To have someone break down your door; shoot you up, and for what? I thought about it. *About the uproar over the Maguire case,* it was the likeliest conclusion based on what I knew so far... *Because you did your job?*

"Just hang on for me, baby. Stay with me..."

Rattled didn't even begin to cover how I felt about this one.

I STAYED on the scene despite how much I wanted to follow the living victim in this case. I couldn't do anything for her, it was all up to the EMT's, doctors, nurses, and probably surgeons - if she made it that far. What I *could* do was work the scene and speak for the blonde on the couch who didn't have a voice anymore.

I went through the motions, but everything here was just so damn *personal* like I'd never been on a scene before. My mind going over the little details.

She liked soothing, neutral colors, her walls a misty blue-grey, it was amazing that she'd found an apartment that'd let her paint the walls.

That, or she threw caution to the wind and didn't give a fuck about getting her deposit back. I smiled to myself; that sounded like the Chrissy Franco I'd known. *Knew,* I admonished myself. *She's not dead, not yet...* Fuck. I shook my head, dropping my chin to my chest and pulling on the back of my head in an attempt to ease the tension there.

"Got an ID?" I looked up and over at my partner and sighed.

"What took you so fucking long?" I asked.

"Cipriani case is going to court next week, it's all hands on deck at the DA's for witness prep."

"They act like you've never testified before," I said and sighed.

My partner, James McDonnell, was another Mick like me, only seventeen years my senior. Still a while from retirement, being only in his fifties, the world hung on him, weighing down his shoulders like the tired old raincoat that he had on over his equally tired suit.

He waved me off and looked over at where the medical examiner was doing her thing. He shook his head and asked, "Who's our vic?"

"Wrong question, what you should be asking is who're our *vic's*, plural." I stepped aside so he could see the blood, wine, and broken glass from where Chrissy had lain.

He grunted and said, "Alright, Youngblood, get me up to speed already."

"The blonde is Samantha Lynn Hayworth but the apartment belongs to our other vic, Christina Marie Franco."

"Aw Christ, the one that got Skip Maguire's ol' lady off the hook?"

"Yeah, that would be the one," I said heavily.

"So what do we know?"

"Not a lot yet. When I got here, there were obvious signs of forced entry." I pointed with my pen at the shattered doorframe, my tone ironic even though he probably wouldn't get the joke – the uniform did, barking a laugh.

Jaime eyed him and said to me, "No shit, Sherlock."

"And Ms. Franco was laying here on the floor unconscious." I finished, not missing a beat.

"Wait, you got all the way here, and no one checked to see if she was alive or not?"

"And I quote from our boy over there, 'who gives a shit?'"

Jaime reeled back, same as I'd done and said, "Really now?" he asked, the uniform finally cluing in and blanching. "That's some bullshit, son. What's your name?"

"Uh... Officer Johns, sir."

"Well, Officer Johns, from the," he squinted at the officer's collar pins, "11th... you go on and wait out front. Youngblood here and I will be having a quiet talk with you and your CO later."

The kid, who barely looked like he was out of being a rookie, turned red and nodded, ducking out the fucked up front door under Jaime's stern gaze until he was out of sight.

I chuckled and it was a dark one. No one gave good pissed off cop face better than my partner. It was never our favorite thing having a chat with another cop's CO about things. ICPD already had a bad rap with the public when it came to corruption and a whole host of other bullshit. The new community slogan that the Mayor's office was trying to impress upon everybody was *be the change that you want to see.*

Not only in an effort to weed out the corruption but also to get aspiring new recruits into the uniform. There were a whole lot more cops than not on the verge of retirement with all the baby boomers hitting their sixties. In any case, it was better that we have a quiet chat with him and his CO than it was to write him up and jam him up with IAD. No one liked to be a rat, but there was a difference between a quiet but stern talk; keeping it in-house, versus official complaints with the Rat Squad.

"You've got that look, Youngblood." Jaime said and I shook myself out of my funk.

"Yeah, what look?" I demanded.

"The one that says something about this case has got yah, and that you're gonna solve it come hell or high water."

"Ah, yeah," I nodded once.

"Mind letting me in on what's chapping your ass?"

"Later, right now we have a building to canvas."

"Fan-fucking-tastic, arrived just in time, did I?"

"Ah, yeah."

"Perfect." He sounded like it was anything but and I smirked. CSU had things here and I figured I'd pretty much-absorbed everything I was going to out of seeing it firsthand.

"Let us know when you have anything, Linda," Jaime called and the medical examiner raised her hand and waved us off.

We canvased the entire building, but aside from the little old lady that lived above Chrissy who'd called it in, nobody was talking or wanted to 'fess up to seeing anything. It was a dead end from the start and looking pretty grim. The only shot we really had at figuring this one out was if Chrissy managed to pull through, but she'd been in a pretty bad way.

"What now?" Jaime asked and I shook my head.

"She's gonna be in surgery for a long damn time. Might as well get started on the paperwork."

"Always with the paperwork," he grumbled.

"I like to have my bases covered."

"And that fancy law degree, too."

"Admit it, you like it," I said and he barked a laugh.

"When it's not being a pain in my ass."

"Dude, get in the car."

"Brought my own, remember? You sure you ain't too close to this?"

I gave him a hard look and deflected saying in a tone that brooked no argument, "See you back at the shop."

We went back to the precinct where I called over to Trinity General Hospital first and got some nurse who, it might as well have been their first fuckin' day.

"Yeah, this is Detective Anthony McCormick out of the 12th precinct calling about one of your patients, Christina Marie Franco. She was brought in with a couple of gunshot wounds earlier tonight."

"I'm sorry, I can't give out that information," she said dubiously.

"What do you mean? Did she pass?"

"I can't give you that information, sir. I can't even confirm or deny if a Ms. Franco is a patient here." I scowled at the phone and Jaime started laughing across from me.

"What the hell are you talking about?" I demanded.

"HIPAA dictates –"

"Woah, now I'm gonna stop you right there. HIPAA dictates that you're allowed to disclose patient information without said patient's consent to an officer of the law, such as myself, under extenuating circumstances, sweetheart. One of those circumstances is when I need to know, like I do now, what her status is in order to catch the bad guy that did what she's in the hospital for in the first place."

"I'll have to check with my supervisor..."

"Yes! Do that, put your supervisor on the line so I can see if my witness is alive and you can stop wasting my time." I was getting irritated.

"You don't have to take that tone with me!"

"Either you put your supervisor on the phone yesterday, or I'm coming down there and putting you in cuffs for impeding an active investigation."

Silence for several heartbeats after an indignant sound that sounded a whole lot like obstruction. Jaime leaned back in his desk chair and raised his eyebrows at me while Nurse Jr.'s voice became muffled. An older more mature woman's voice came on the line, one I recognized.

"Merlyn, is that you?" I asked.

"Detective!" She cried, delighted.

"Yeah, I need to know about the status of a patient, can you help me out?"

"Of course, honey, what's the name?"

"Christina Marie Franco, gunshot wounds to the back."

I heard Merlyn's long nails click against a keyboard before she made some investigative noises with her breath. Finally, she came back on the line and said strong, "Oh, Honey, she's still in surgery and will be for a while yet. That poor baby is in real bad shape."

"I know, I was there," I said and leaned back heavily in my own chair. "Any telling when she might be out?"

"Mm-mm, baby. No tellin'."

"Okay, I'll stay here and finish up what I'm doin' then. Can you call me if there's any change? Better yet, have Nurse Jr. do it."

Merlyn laughed, a deep belly laugh over the phone and said, "Nurse Jr., I like that. Sure thing, baby. What number are you good at?"

I gave her my cell and added as an afterthought, "Tell Nurse Jr. she better not *ever* try to impede an investigation again, or I'll have her up on charges."

"Mm, Tony. You ain't letting that detective squad change you, now are you?"

I scrubbed my face with my hands, "No, mama, I ain't," I told her, but Merlyn, she knew. She reached out over the line with that sense of hers, the one that made her such a good nurse.

"Then what's the matter?"

I picked up the phone off the cradle and sighed, pinching the bridge of my nose and turned away from Jaime, not like it would make a damn bit of difference.

"I know the vic, Merlyn. It's a little different this time."

"Oh, baby! I'm so sorry. If anything changes, I'll call you myself."

"Thanks, mama."

"You bet, I never will forget what you did for my Ernesto."

"Mama, we're even on that in spades," I told her with a chuckle.

"Now I know I ain't heard that right!" She declared. "We will *never* be even, you saved that boy's life."

"Just did my job."

"Mm-hm," she didn't sound like she believed me.

I laughed and said, "I've gotta go."

"I'll call you."

We hung up and I turned back around and Jaime eyed me seriously. "Rut-roh," I said, mockingly, aping the old Scooby-Doo commercials.

"You know the vic, Youngblood?"

"It ain't like that," I said. "Back when I first made detective, we went on a couple of dates but the careers, they just didn't jive. Never even made it past first base."

"Uh-huh."

"Seriously."

"Right."

I gave him a flat look and he cocked his head to the side, "Fine, I'll drop it for now, but I don't like what happened to those girls any more than you do. I want to find this animal and get him off the street before he gets any other bright ideas."

"What makes you think it was a 'he?'" I asked, and I was being a smartass.

"Yeah, like I need to rattle off crime statistics to you, do your fuckin' paperwork, jackass."

I laughed a little, glad he wasn't making a big thing about me knowing Chrissy, at least not yet. The investigation was still young, and if he didn't think I could remain objective, or hack it, he wouldn't hesitate to call me on my bullshit.

We spent the better part of the next four hours dotting all of our I's and crossing all our T's and making it so our reports would hold up in court later and the like. Finally, Jaime leaned back in his seat and let out a satisfied 'Ah!'

"What?" I demanded, fingers still flying across the keys.

"Quittin' time, Youngblood." I looked up at the clock, sure as shit, our time in the cubicle farm was up. I saved what I was doing and switched off the monitor before I got up, stretching.

"They're still serving over at Ten-Thirteen," he said and I chuckled but shook my head.

"Not tonight, man."

"No?"

"Naw, I'm going to head over to the hospital. I want to be there when she gets out of surgery, see if I can get anything to go on, because right now, we don't have squat."

"You sure that's the *only* reason you're going?"

I made a mock-disgusted noise, "Yes, *dad.*"

He put up his hands in surrender and said, "I can think of a hell of a lot more comfortable places to sleep than a hospital chair, but that's all you."

"Night, partner," I called to his lumbering back as he moved toward the squad room's exit.

"Night, Youngblood!" he called back.

I took my happy ass to the locker room to change and gear up. I didn't do combination locks, I used a burly ass padlock on my locker and I *never* not *once* locked my damn keys inside. I pulled the ring out of my hip pocket and stuck the key in the lock giving it a twist and popping it free. I opened up the sheet metal door to reveal my jacket and cut, motorcycle boots, and chaps.

I pulled my helmet off the top shelf and set it aside and pulled out the rest of my gear. I swapped shoes and instantly felt better about life, that familiar giddy energy that never got old starting up as I pulled on the chaps and snapped, buckled, and zipped everything into place. I stared down at my colors and sighed at the name flash on the front, '*Youngblood*' picked out in indigo thread against a dirty white patch backing.

I belonged to the *Indigo Knights*, a cop MC that'd been around going on fifty years, although it wasn't just specifically for cops anymore. We met and did charity shit out of The Cormorant Bar & Grill on Muller Street down in Old Town. It was what Jaime had called the Ten-Thirteen, which was a double play on words. One-zero-one-three was The Cormorant's address, but it was also 10-13 which was the radio code for 'officer in need of assistance.'

The Cormorant provided assistance to officers in a lot of ways, especially those of us who belonged to the Indigo Knights. It gave us a place to relax and unwind around guys like us. Not just cops, but other first responders, too. Some of the boys in fire hung there, as well as prosecutors and corrections. We even had some of the medics that we worked with on the regular come through. The Ten-Thirteen wasn't officially a 'cops only' bar. Civilians found their way in from time to time. The food and booze was pretty top-notch, the place run by a retired cop and his best friend, a retired fire guy.

Nobody knew their way around a bottle like a cop. Unfortunately, the same was true for Skids, one-half owner of the Ten-Thirteen. It was ironic as fuck having an alcoholic and dry dude as a bartender.

Reflash was his best friend; all the recipes that'd come from the firehouse made the Ten-Thirteen's kitchen what it was and had earned them both some pretty high accolades in a couple of fancy fuckin' food magazines. It was great for business, but every time one of the articles came out, the place filled up with yuppies, which made it a little uncomfortable for us blue collar boys for a bit until it blew over.

I'd found my way into the Indigo Knights by way of one of the fire guys some years back. Flashover had been a good friend, we'd practically grown up together – three houses down from each other. After I'd finished up with being a rookie, he'd ended up passing muster and had joined up with Indigo City's Fire Department. I'd always been ahead of him academically, and so there'd always been a gap between us measured by our successes and gains, but it'd never interfered with our friendship.

We'd lost Flashover a little over a year and a half ago to a warehouse fire down at the docks. It hadn't been my case, but it'd been ruled an accidental homicide. The owner of the warehouse had gotten in deep with the Cipriani crime family and had lit the place up for the insurance money. Indigo City had lost three good firefighters in that blaze, a fourth had been severely burned and forced into retirement. I'd felt Flashover's loss keenly just about every day since, but he'd given me one hell of a thing by convincing me to join up with the Knights.

I picked up my jacket and cut and swung them on. When it came to wearing our colors *that* had been a huge fight between the department and the union. For once, the union had actually done us a solid and had won us the right to wear our colors in and out of work. The higher ups had demanded a certain, and I'm quoting here, 'high level of standard' from its officers and had wanted to ban our ability to wear certain things to and from work. The union had argued on our behalf that unless the department wanted to pay us from the time we got dressed in the morning to the time we took our clothes off at home on our working days then they'd best let it go. The union had pushed it to the max and finally the department had relented, but it'd been an ugly win.

Now any of us who rode with the club had to mind our P's and Q's to a fuckin' T. It was a whole goddamn alphabet soup of good behavior. It's one of the reasons Jaime was on my ass about the Franco thing. I traded out my guns, leaving my service weapon in the designated holster built into every locker, retrieving my personal one. I tucked it into the hard holster riding on my belt, up under my jacket and cut. It was the same make and model, Glock 19. Dependable, reliable, and a straight shooter.

I shut my locker door with a metallic clang and retrieved my keys and the lock. I made sure everything was tight, adjusted my firearm one more time, scooped up my brain bucket and headed for the elevator to the garage.

"Oh Captain, my Captain," I greeted the man in charge. He was a beanpole of a man, balding pate shiny in the overhead lights, nose straight and sharp, brown eyes nondescript.

"You outta here?" he asked, stirring his coffee.

"Headed to the hospital, see if our surviving vic can give us anything to go on."

"She out of surgery?" he asked, taking a swallow of his coffee and grunting.

"Not yet, but I was there, looked bad. If she comes out of it, might only get a brief chance, gotta do my due diligence on this one because this? This was beyond the fuckin' pale."

"I read the report, doesn't look like you have shit to go on."

"Yeah, if she dies, this one might not get solved unless CSU pulls a Hail Mary out of the air."

The elevator dinged and the doors worked their way open.

"Not a thing from any of the neighbors?"

"Zip."

"Well, the investigation is still young."

"That's what I keep telling myself, boss."

The doors to the elevator tried to close on me and I stuck my helmet in the way. The doors halted, jarring violently and shuddering before opening back up.

"Shit, this fuckin' thing," my boss griped. "I'm going up, looks like you're its favorite." Sure enough, the elevator was going down, even though the boss is the one who'd called it. I got on and realized it was because someone had punched the wrong button. *Lucky me.*

"See you tomorrow, Cap."

"Tomorrow, McCormick." He raised his paper cup in salute and I gave him a chin lift as the doors slid shut. I hit the button for the garage and after one more stop on the next floor down I was underway to the garage.

The ride over to Trinity Gen was a meditative one. There was no telling when she would be out of surgery, but I knew enough about her to know that she didn't have a whole lot of people; at least she didn't three years ago. I also knew the blonde, Samantha Lynn must be her bestie who she'd always called Sami or Sami-Lynn. So, with that being said, I figured it'd be good for her to have at least one person she sort of knew versus nobody that she didn't when she came to. I felt bad I couldn't guarantee that I would be there when she finally woke up but I could do my best. I'd just have to see how it went.

2

*C*hrissy...

The bar atmosphere was nice, too bad I wasn't really here to soak it in. I was supposed to be on a date, but that had gone to hell with yet more mandatory overtime from the firm I was working for. I stepped into the Cormorant and scanned the room for Tony. I was pretty sure this was going to be our last date but I couldn't exactly blame either of us for it. We had something in common, he and I, and that was that we were both very career driven people.

It was too bad, really, because he was just so damn hot. Maybe just one inch taller than me at five foot ten, he had a set of shoulders to die for and a pair of arms to go with them. I'd sadly never gotten the chance to see under the clothes but if what I'd felt was any indication, maybe that was a good thing because if I had, I wouldn't go through with this.

"Rut-roh," he said, and I smiled as I slid up onto the barstool beside him.

"Uh-oh," I echoed with a long-suffering sigh added for good measure.

"Let me guess," he said taking a sip of his drink, "back to the office in a flash?"

"Sadly, yes..." I hung my head and he smiled, reaching out and tucking some stray tendrils out of my tired French twist behind my ear. The casual and familiar gesture set my heart to racing. It was one of the things I'd immediately liked about Tony, that he was so casual and comfortable with me right off the bat but it didn't feel off or skeevy at all.

"We're three for three," he said, a sparkle in his steely blue eyes.

"I know..." I said, tone mournful, and while in all fairness all three of those weren't my fault, I saw the writing on the wall. With weeks going between dates and something coming up for either him or me just about every time... God it killed me to say it but... "Maybe this just isn't meant to be." I sounded hopeless even to me.

"I really hate to agree with you, gorgeous, but I think you and I have to face it; the timing just ain't right for either of us." He sighed heavily and signaled the bartender who drifted down this way.

"You know what? Fuck it," I said and ordered a glass of red for myself. Tony chuckled and sipped his whiskey.

"To second chances," he said when I took my glass in hand.

"Thank you for understanding," I murmured, clicking my glass against his and taking a sip. He savored a sip out of his own glass, eyes traveling over me.

"I get it. We're both all about the job, right now."

I smiled and took another drink of the deep red liquid in my glass, swirling it across my tongue before swallowing it down.

"Yeah, well, let me add to that toast. 'May the next time we meet, have us both on the same side of the aisle.' I would hate to run up against *you in court. You're making quite a name for yourself for being such a new detective."*

"Likewise, for you being such a new lawyer. We cops aren't dumb, gorgeous. Anytime you walk up to the defense table and start your whispering bit, the boys say they can expect a curveball. Still, they also bitch nine times out of ten that even when they see it coming – they don't see it coming, if you catch my drift."

I smiled to myself, the wine going to my head a bit, the blush being a bit deeper and the smile a little looser at the praise. I needed to grab something to take back to the office. I signaled the bartender and asked, "Can I get something to go?"

"Sure thing, sweetheart. Here's a menu."

I looked it over and made my selection. Tony raised his eyebrows at the bartender and said, "Put it all on my tab, would you Skids?"

I smiled at the bartender, a man in his early fifties. He was a big bear of a man, gone soft around the middle, but in that way, that reminded me of a fitter version of Santa Claus. I was betting the steel grey and white beard had something to do with that, though. His hair, close cropped like his beard with just a bit of length gelled on top to keep him in line with the times. Dare I say? The man was a silver fox of sorts. He smiled over at us winked one blue eye at me saying, "You got it, Youngblood."

It was my turn to raise an eyebrow, "Youngblood?" I asked.

He looked a bit uncomfortable, but he answered me anyways, "Yeah, it's what some of the older cops have been calling me since I made detective. Youngest in the department."

"Ah, I see."

Damn. I was really going to miss out on learning more about this man, but it just wasn't plausible anymore. It wasn't fair to him, or really even to me, the way the firm was working me like a dog. Still, if I wanted to defend my own cases as first chair, I needed to prove myself.

"Gonna miss our little talks," he said with a wink and I bit my lower lip and smiled.

"Regrets?" I asked.

"Fuck yeah," he said laughing. "But I think I'd regret it more if we went there and I couldn't anymore."

"Better to have loved and lost than to have never loved at all..." I quoted, and I would be lying if I said I wasn't hopeful.

"Hey now, Tennyson isn't going to help your case with this one, baby. As much as I would love to go there with you, you're a classy woman, Franco. It kills me to say it, but you're so much better than a one night stand."

Damnit he was smooth and I said, "Twist the knife, why don't you?" with a wry smile to hide my disappointment.

He laughed and said, "It's not all on you. You were just ballsy enough to say it first. It's been over a month since we had a date that wasn't interrupted by one or the both of our jobs. That says something. I'd rather stop here with you and have a real shot down the line if I'm lucky, rather than keep trying to cram a square peg in a round hole and get one or the both of us hurt." I nodded and sighed but before I could say anything he said, "Would still love one last kiss for the road."

"I think I can manage that," I said and the smile he gave me damn near melted me into my pumps.

The dream-memory shattered and my eyes flew open. I sucked in a startled breath and froze every muscle as the pain radiated through my back and into my chest. I blinked several times and stared at sterile and bland ceiling tiles and went to turn my head in the direction of the curtained sliding glass door that led out onto the floor.

Agony ripped through my back and shoulder and I let out this god awful strangled noise. The shift and creak of leather, the rattle of a metal buckle.

"Easy, Chrissy. Take it easy, I'm gonna get a nurse."

My vision blurred with pain and tears as a back clad in black leather, a silver shield and indigo blue knight's chess piece went past. He swatted back the curtain and slid open the door, his familiar voice whisper-shouting, "Hey Merlyn! She's awake and in a lot of pain."

A strong female voice called out gently, "Right with you, honey."

He stepped back in and turned around, just as I squeezed my eyes shut against the hurt. Hot tears trickled out from under my lashes and down my cheeks but I didn't dare try to move, the pain was bad, but moving? I didn't want to think about it.

"Easy, Chrissy." Maddeningly familiar voice! A tissue gently wiped away the tears and I opened my eyes to a pair of steely blue ones that radiated concern.

"Tony?" I whimpered.

"You're okay, you're safe now." More fresh, hot, tears leaked out of my eyes. "Shh," he soothed and I realized I was babbling.

"What happened; why am I here? What happened to me?" My mind tried valiantly to cling to anything but it was like as soon as I grasped it, it was gone, swirling into the murky haze inside my skull.

"You were shot, baby. In the back, you were shot twice."

"It wasn't a dream? It wasn't a bad dream?" *Of course it wasn't, stupid! You were just dreaming of Tony before you woke up.*

But *why? Why* would I dream of Tony, and *why would he be here?*

It finally came to me. *A cop. Tony is a cop... tell him I have to tell him.*

"They put my address up on the internet." I swallowed hard, my voice a little warped but whether it was from the pain or soggy from my tears, I couldn't tell. One thing I *did* know was that I had to tell him. I had to tell him everything I knew, because I hurt so bad I surely must be dying and he had to know in case I really was...

"Jim. Jim Parsons from my office found it. They put my address on the internet, told them to come to my apartment. Sam, Sami said that it was nothing, but I asked her to come over – oh god, is Sam okay? Where's Sami Lynn?"

I wanted my best friend, I wanted to know that she was okay, but I didn't think she was and he wouldn't answer me... instead, he was holding his phone out in front of himself looking at the screen and I cried, "Why aren't you listening to me!?"

"I am, I am, I promise, Chrissy. Can you tell me what he looked like?"

"Sam, where's Sami? Is she okay? Is she alright?"

His steel blue eyes held a deep pity in them but he wouldn't answer. He was saved from having to by the nurse. A buxom black lady with long thick braids to the middle of her back, came into the room in green scrub pants and a floral print scrub shirt. *Buxom*, that was a word you didn't hear anymore but it was the best one used to describe her.

"Ms. Franco, honey. Do you know where you are?" she said and her voice was loud.

I ignored her, focusing on Tony, sweat popping out on my brow as I gritted my teeth against the pain and tried to fight back the only way I knew how. Through the system and by being a good witness.

"Sweatshirt, one of those ones that zip up with a hood, he had one of those on. A red one," I said.

"Good, that's good, baby."

"Ms. Franco, honey, I need you to tell me where you're at," the nurse called again and I looked at her and tried to focus.

"Hospital, right? I'm in the hospital." I flicked my eyes back to Tony and gritting my teeth through another grinding, burning, tearing wave of agony gasped out, "His gun was big, and black... he wore gloves. The plastic kind, but white. Not like those." I flicked my gaze to the nurse.

"I've got to give her some medicine, Tony. She's getting distressed."

"Okay, okay, Chrissy, what about his face? Can you tell me what his face looked like?"

I closed my eyes and whimpered and the pain eased off and so did I. As if gravity had ceased and I was suddenly floating.

"Shit, Merlyn... what did you give her?" he demanded.

"Morphine, look at her face, you can ask your questions when she's more stable."

"Damnit," he cursed and leaned down.

TONY... *don't leave me!*

I tried to speak, but couldn't. Gentle fingers tucked some stray hair behind my ear and I realized I couldn't see and then, a heartbeat after that, I didn't care.

3

ony...

"Shit."

"Had to be done, sugar."

I didn't take my eyes off Chrissy, willing her to come to, willing her to be lucid and give me more information even though she'd done great and had given me a solid lead.

"How's she holding up? Give it to me straight, no bullshit," I told Merlyn and she sighed.

"You love this girl?" she asked frankly, and I smiled, smoothing some of Chrissy's dark hair off from where it was plastered to her forehead. I loved her hair. Thick and silky, like it was some kind of living thing of its own. She was still rocking it long, but it was a different style than the last time I'd seen her.

"No, we just went out a few times a few years ago... She ain't got nobody."

"Mm-hm," she sounded like she didn't believe me, and I huffed a bit of a laugh but what she said next was pretty profound and one of the reasons she made one of the best foster moms this city had ever seen. "Looks like she has *you*, baby."

Fuck.

I guess she had me there. I didn't answer, instead I put one hand against the thin hospital mattress by her head, glad she was propped up in a sort of sitting position and I leaned in, pressing a light kiss to her forehead. Merlyn left the room, sliding the door closed behind her.

I knew that Chrissy wouldn't know I'd done it and that it could be considered creepy, but I seriously couldn't help it. My heart went out to her. She'd sounded so scared and so lost as the drugs had taken her under with her pleading, "Tony, don't leave me!" but I had to leave. I had to catch whoever had done this to her; before he could to it to anyone else, sure, but also to bring him to justice. Although, I didn't think for a minute that whatever the criminal justice system did to him would come close to making him actually pay.

"I'll be back, I promise," I murmured to her and just took a moment to listen to her strong, deep and even breathing between the blips and beeps of all the monitors and shit they had her hooked up to. I made sure her oxygen tubes were on and comfortably tucked up and over her delicate ears before I straightened up and went back out. I waited for Merlyn who was with another patient and when she came out, I made her promise to let Chrissy know I'd be back with more questions and to call me when she was awake again.

"Might be hours, might be a couple of days before you get any kind of coherent outta her, honey. Morphine is a hell of a drug."

I nodded and asked her point blank, "She gonna make it, okay?"

"Surgery was rough, but they got it all. Her body's under some serious stress and everybody reacts differently. You never can tell with these kind of injuries, baby. Anything could happen, secondary infections, all manner of complications. The way she looks now, I wanna tell you she's gonna be fine, but I can't tell you how many patients I thought that and we lost them the next day. All you can do is what any of us can do, wait and say those prayers."

I leaned in conspiratorially and said, "That's why I like you Merlyn, you always give it to me straight."

"I know you cops, there ain't any other way to be with your kind."

"Smart lady."

She smiled and said, "Go on and get that animal. I'll call you if there's any change."

"You're her guardian angel," I said walking backwards towards the ICU's exit.

She looked me up and down, her brown eyes sparkling, but still full of criticism, "Huh! Looks to me like that position is already filled, but I know something else about you cops."

"Oh yeah, what's that?" I asked stopping.

"You never can have too much backup."

I barked a laugh and she shooed me off, fingers sparkling with rings, her long purple nails with rhinestones. The woman sure had some fabulous class to her. God love her.

I went down to the garage and got onto my bike, replaying the video of Chrissy that I'd taken with my phone. When someone was in that bad of shape, you video documented everything – thankfully cellphones made that possible – because if they died, the video could still be admissible as evidence and even testimony if you had the right district attorney who knew the ropes and could get it past the defense.

She looked both sallow and wan, which was a feat; and spoke of just how fucked up on the inside she was. Her eyes were sunken, haunted, and exhausted, her expression hampered by drugs and pain, but she was a fighter. A real fighter, trying to give me everything she could.

"They put my address up on the internet." I watched as she swallowed hard. *"Jim. Jim Parsons from my office found it. They put my address on the internet, told them to come to my apartment. Sam, Sami said that it was nothing, but I asked her to come over –"* Her face crumbled and it was a different kind of pain. Even if she didn't remember with the front of her brain, her subconscious knew what'd happened to her friend. *"Oh god, is Sam okay? Where's Sami Lynn?"*

I didn't have the heart to answer her as it was happening. Now, I didn't have the heart to watch that bit over again. Instead, I stopped the video, clutching the phone in my hand and bracing it on top of my leather and denim clad thigh while I thought some things through.

She needed time enough to heal before dealing with all of that shit. I felt bad as it was that I'd had to push her right after she'd woken up, like that. My reasons may be noble and justified, but I still felt like a steaming pile for doing it. The job at hand wasn't always a bowl of roses and this case was going to be even uglier than what I typically dealt with. Survivor's guilt was a hell of a thing.

I shook my head and put my phone inside my jacket before firing up the bike. It was just after six in the morning. I had just enough time to ride back to the precinct, take a shower, and use some of the clean clothes I had stowed in one of my saddlebags for just one of these occasions. When I got off the elevator on my squad room's floor, my partner was waiting for me with a cup of coffee that he shoved into my hand.

"The Lord bless you and keep you," I muttered testing it carefully before taking a sip.

He ignored my Mick blessing and said, "Y'know, I was thinking about something. Had me up all night."

"How did the shooter know it was Chrissy's apartment?" I supplied.

"Yeah, great minds think alike," he said and I shook my head and took another careful sip of the coffee. Still too hot but it'd be just right after I got done in the locker room.

"Yeah, well, Chrissy woke up long enough to supply us with an honest to god, solid goddamn lead. C'mere, I'll get you up to speed."

"Heh, your momma raised *you* right," he commented. "Praise the lord one minute and use his name in vain the next."

"Shut up," I groused and went over to his desk and sat my happy ass on the corner of it, digging out my phone. He sat down in his chair and waited me out and I cued up the video and handed it to him.

"Gonna grab a shower and a change of duds, be right out." I set the offering of the sacred bean down at my desk and hitching the knapsack I'd dragged up here out of my saddlebag higher onto my shoulder, I headed for the detective squad's locker room.

A quick, cold shower to wake me up, and because the pipes in this building were old as fuck and the hot water heater as far away as it could get, and I was halfway ready to start the day.

I had *detective casual* in the knapsack. A crisp pair of jeans, devoid of any holes or wear on the cuffs and pockets, came out right after a pair of clean boxers and a tee shirt.

"Jesus Christ, gimme that." I smirked and handed the button down shirt and tie over to Jaime. "This is why you should drive that truck of yers instead of that moped," he said shaking it out and pulling down the ironing board from the wall.

I laughed and pulled on my boxers under the towel I had around my waist. I dropped it and pulled on my clean socks and jeans, next.

"So what'd you think?" I asked and Jaime tsked.

"I think she'd better live so we can nail this bastard dead to rights. You know a breathing witness is always the best witness."

I snorted, "There are no 'good' witnesses; you know that."

He picked up the shirt after whipping the iron over it, squinted at it, and laid it another direction resuming bullying the wrinkles out of it with the steam.

"Woah, aren't you two all domestic and shit." Riley Adams, another detective from the squad walked in to drop his shit at his locker.

"Man, fuck you," I said laughing.

"Mm, no... that's all your partner," he said shutting his locker door and backing out of the room.

Jaime ignored the exchange like it never happened and sighed saying, "You need to leave this cynical cop shit to me."

"So, you were thinkin' what I was thinkin' last night," he looked up at me and I said, "That this Jim Parson's needs to be our first stop."

"Yeah, I think that's about right."

I tucked in my tee and threaded my belt through the loops of my jeans. He handed over my light blue shirt and I shrugged it on, buttoning it up and tucking it in. By the time I was done with that, clipping my badge to the front of my belt, and holstering my duty weapon after checking the serial to make sure it *was* my duty weapon, he had my tie pressed and was holding it out to me. I flipped up my collar and looked into the small mirror held onto the inside of my locker door by magnets to get the damn thing right.

Jaime put the iron in its rack on the wall by the board and made sure it was unplugged. When he folded up the board into its upright position, I had my locker door shut and the lock latched, my keys around one finger and tucked into the palm of my hand.

"Grab yer phone and yer coffee, meet you by the elevator."

"Copy, that."

I swung into my blazer I left hanging in the back of my locker and shoved my feet into my street shoes, a pair of good, old fashioned, sturdy Rockport Oxfords in black. I went out into the squad room and swept my phone and my coffee up off my desk and made it to the elevator just as the doors shushed open for Jaime. He stood aside and waved me in and I said, "Age before beauty," before sucking down some more of the elixir of life he'd brought me.

"See if I buy coffee for you ever again, Youngblood," he grated.

I grinned behind my cup and got onto the elevator behind him. "That was self-preservation and you know it," I cracked but I damn sure wasn't feeling it. The coffee wasn't even coming close to making up for a night of shitty sleep in a shitty chair at Trinity Gen's ICU.

It was going to be a long fucking day.

It was almost a relief to get back to the hospital and that shitty chair to put my feet up after the amount of pavement pounding, warrant gathering, and hurry up and wait we'd had to pull. The problem was, we didn't know if a crime had necessarily been committed when it came to Chrissy's personal info having been published online. We'd had to do some research. Lo and behold, there was actually a name for it. It was called 'doxxing' whatever the hell that meant, and it *was* a crime, but typically at a federal level.

Parsons, a paralegal at Reardon, Colfax & Price, the firm that Chrissy worked for, was something of a computer geek and ran the firm's Facebook page. That's where the hateful explosion over the verdict had started. He said that it began as a bunch of one star reviews of the firm full of a bunch of typical angry keyboard warrior bullshit. But then, this one guy let slip in one of those reviews that the whole thing started on some fanboy forum for Skip and the Indigo City Anglers, our baseball team.

Parsons followed the proverbial rabbit hole down into a fucking sewer of the worst kinds that humanity had to offer. Page after page of angry fucking diatribes and threats of everything from torture to rape, to gang rape, to murder. Some of it the grisliest shit I've ever read. Enough that Jaime had to bust out the Rolaids all the while Jimmy-boy sat to one side and wouldn't make eye contact with either of us.

It'd made me damn uncomfortable too, but my visceral reaction? It'd been more along the lines of being torn between wanting to do two things. Find the son of a bitch who'd done this to her and deliver some street justice by way of a wood shampoo, and the other? Go to Chrissy and never leave her side again, because I don't give a fuck who you are or what you did or did not do – no one deserved what she'd gotten or what she was getting by way of this fucking bullshit.

I stared at her and was grateful that she looked better already, her complexion less pale than it'd been before and the ghastly sallow brown shadows beneath her eyes diminished. She was sleeping peacefully now, the line of pain between her eyebrows smoothed out. She was on some seriously good shit, and I was afraid of what that might be like for her when she had to come down off of it. The last thing she needed was to cross the circle of hell that was an addiction to painkillers. Good Catholic boy that I was, I prayed for her, crossing myself.

Anyways, our next stop had been across town to the precinct that housed Indigo City's TARU, or Technical Assistance Response Unit. We needed their brain-trust to get our warrants for the information from the forum owners on the ISP belonging to screen name 'HoM3RUN_H3Ro' which then had to spawn another warrant to the Internet Service Provider themselves to cough up the information on a real name and address for whoever was behind the screen name. It was a convoluted mess for sure, and was seriously grinding my gears.

We'd gotten our warrants, and lucky us, dude was in the city – which we'd figured – but him being in the city took the doxxing charge out of the fed's hands and put the ball in our jurisdictional court. We just had to figure out what to charge him with on a local level. We had until tomorrow to figure it out, and I wasn't worried about it. I figured between me and Jaime sleeping on it one of us would have one of our strokes of genius, I don't think that there'd been a precedent set for this kind of a thing. I could always run it by Yale, one of the prosecuting attorneys for the city who happened to be a Knight like me, before pulling any triggers on making an arrest.

Chrissy whimpered and shifted slightly and I sat up. She sucked in a long, deep breath and opened those dark eyes of hers and I stood up and went over to the side of her bed, where her arm wasn't in a sling and propped up on pillows.

"Hey," I murmured and her gaze finally fixed on me.

"You came back."

"I promised you, didn't I?"

"I... I don't remember."

"You're on a lot of drugs, that's to be expected."

She tried to shift and gasped and I told her, "No, don't move. I'll get the nurse."

"No, wait!" I stopped and she breathed in through her nose and out through her mouth a few times, getting a handle on her pain. "She'll give me more and I won't be able to answer your questions."

"You gave me quite a bit the last time I was here. A solid lead."

"Good, that's good, but you need more, right?"

"Yeah," I rolled the doctor's stool over and sat down, reaching between the bed rails, and holding her hand on her good arm, careful of the IV running into the back of it. "What can you tell me about the guy that broke into your apartment?"

She started to shake her head and gasped, "He had on a red hoodie, white, um... brown hair, I think." She winced and sighed out, frustrated. "I can't remember everything. I want to, but it's like it's just not there." She looked at me, a pleading look on her face and in her eyes and asked, "What's wrong with me?"

I didn't have to call a nurse. Something about Chrissy's monitor must have tipped them off at the nurse's station because one came in all on her own and went around me to the IV stand, punching buttons on the front of it.

"I don't know," I answered her truthfully. "Maybe because of the trauma or something, I'm a cop, not a doctor but it's okay that you can't remember, you just take it easy now and rest."

She closed her eyes and pressed her lips together and it was pretty clear the nurse had upped her drugs. She turned to me, a blonde girl probably fresh out of nursing school, young and determined and said, "You might want to try in another day or two. It might take longer than that. Sometimes, when something this traumatic happens they never get their memory back but only time will tell." I wondered if she was Nurse Jr., but didn't comment.

"She doing good?" I asked, swallowing hard, and the nurse smiled.

"As well as can be expected. The doctor could probably tell you more."

"Thanks."

"You're welcome." She smiled and went back out into the ICU's hub. I wanted to stay with Chrissy, but I was out of clean clothes and needed my own damn bed tonight.

"I'll be back tomorrow," I promised quietly and looked at her tray of uneaten food. "And I'll bring dinner."

I think she heard me, letting out this broken little whimper, but her eyes didn't open and her hand was lax in my own.

It came to me on the ride home, what charge to pick up and hold HoM3RUN_H3Ro on. Inciting violence, possibly with a hate crime qualifier. It was barely into felony territory, but even a third-degree felony carried some scary time out here; about five to ten max. Add the hate crime qualifier it made it even scarier, upping things to ten to fifteen years if convicted. Maybe one of his internet homeboys had done some bragging to him after the fact, if he had, and we could get HoM3RUN_H3Ro to give them up, well then jackpot – that qualified the internet troll for a hefty charge of conspiracy to commit murder and attempted murder.

If he were the reason someone had beat down Chrissy's door, then I would work with the DA to get everything needed to nail his ass with that conspiracy to commit murder charge and slap a hate crime qualifier on that, too. With how much the happy bastard had waxed eloquent about his pure, seething fucking hatred of women, getting the hate crime qualifier added on was going to be a breeze.

I was feeling pretty good about myself by the time my garage door was trundling open and feeling even more confident than that by the time I got off the front of my bike to head in. As always, my paranoid-self waited for the garage door to completely close before I went inside.

Roscoe, my cat, came trotting up like he always did yowling loudly and rubbing up against my legs demanding pets and food. I never could figure out which one he wanted first.

"Hey, buddy." I bent down and scooped him up and went into the kitchen, setting my helmet on the countertop. I pulled out a can of his favorite cat food out from under the sink and he started squirming in my arms so I set him down. He ran back and forth in front of me as soon as I peeled back the lid, losing his goddamned kitty mind.

I laughed and shook the gelatinous meat-glop onto his clean, waiting plate by his gravity feeder and water bowl.

"I promise, it was a good reason this time." My thoughts drifted back to Chrissy lying in that hospital bed back at Trinity Gen's ICU and I sighed. I don't think I'd ever seen anyone so alone, so afraid, or just so *hurt* before in my entire career. That being said, though, I have to say I was over the moon; just fucking glad it wasn't the usual *dead* that I did see.

I listened to Roscoe purr and eat and decided I needed to get some sleep and hit it hard the next morning.

THE NEXT EVENING I was dragging ass up to Chrissy's room. We'd gotten the information back on HoM3RUN_H3Ro's IP address and had it traced back to a Miriam Cohan along with her home address. My partner and I had gone there with a couple of uniforms, dragging a pretty disgruntled Officer Johns along with us after a closed door meeting with his commanding officer.

Johns didn't have to be happy about it. He knew we'd done him a solid by keeping it in-house, so all he had to do was suck it up and toe the line. I'd been pretty sure, when we'd knocked on the old townhouse's door that Miriam Cohan would be Mommy HoM3RUN_H3Ro and I was right. The second she opened the door, cigarette dangling between her lips, she asked, "What's he finally done?"

"Excuse me, ma'am?" Jaime'd asked, and she'd rolled her eyes.

She'd screamed back into the house for her 'delinquent' son who turned out to be a fifty-two-year-old man well beyond the age of fuckin' knowing better. She'd even helped us out by squealing on him that he'd been the only one home with her the night Chrissy's address went up under his username.

Apparently, mom was sick of Kevin mooching off her social security and living in her damn basement. Kevin, on the other hand, was sick of rejection from the opposite sex, but considering his attire of sweatpants, holey tee shirt with what was probably days old food stains on it, with a grimy Skip Maguire baseball jersey over it all, I could kind of empathize with the fairer sex on that one. Dude had let himself go hard, and was pretty much all balding pate and ridiculous beer gut with a pair of glasses that went out of style sometime in the early nineties.

He kept screaming and squawking about how Chrissy deserved everything she got and he was glad she was in the hospital and mad as hell she wasn't dead. We just Mirandized him and let him go, letting him rack up and solidify the charges against him. The damn idiot too stupid to realize that hate speech wasn't free speech and for once, I was glad most of America either didn't take or didn't pay attention in their civics classes.

Still, we'd been the ones to end up flat busted for our efforts at the end of the day, the dude that'd shot our victims hadn't done any bragging, at least not to Kevin, and we were no closer to making an arrest when it came to the perp who'd actually pulled the trigger. It was a solid stonewall dead end.

Still, at least I had a little good news and some way better food for Chrissy when I showed up. That was, until Merlyn stopped me in the ICU's main hub.

"I've got all kinds of news for you, honey," she said.

"Shit. Let me have it," I said steeling myself for the news that Chrissy had coded or some shit.

"Bad news is, you can't have that up here," she indicated the bag of Chinese take-out in my hands, "Good news is, you *can* have it on the fourth floor, which is where your damsel in distress got moved this morning."

"What's on the fourth floor?" I asked.

"General care, honey. Your wounded bird is on the mend and got sprung from up here a few hours ago."

I felt a flood of relief, "That's good, no that's *great*."

"Mm-hmm, and I hate to rain on the parade, but I figured you needed to know. They tried bringing some flowers up here, had to reject them, not allowed, but it was a big bouquet of white lilies, pretty as can be."

"How are flowers bad news?" I asked.

"Because this was with them," she pulled a little white envelope from her scrub pocket and handed it over. I set the food on the nurse's desk and turned it over, opening it up as she was saying, "Now I know I was being nosey, and I shouldn't have opened it but I just had a feeling. I mean lilies I get, but *white ones?* Something was just all wrong and then I remembered why..." I read the card inside and shook my head.

For your casket. I'm coming for you, bitch.

"What tipped you off?" I asked, reading and rereading the card.

"Last time I saw white lilies was at my grandmama's funeral."

"What'd you do with the flowers?"

"Got everything back here, honey." She indicated the door behind the nurse's station leading into a supply closet or whatever the hell they had back there. I nodded.

"Hospital got your prints on file?" I asked.

"You know they do, but why?"

"Gonna need them for elimination purposes."

I called Jaime to see if he'd left the precinct yet. He said he'd be right over and I told him; cool, and that I would be here waiting. Chain of custody in an active investigation and all that.

This girl just couldn't get a break.

4

*C*hrissy…

I had been moved to a different room, and I worried that Tony wasn't going to be able to find me. If I was even remembering things correctly, he'd been here every night since I had been admitted. The hospital had brought my dinner and the nurse had helped me by un-lidding everything so that I could eat. I guess I should be grateful that when the man who had shot me had aimed, that he'd shattered my *left* scapula or what people more commonly referred to as a shoulder blade. My left side was my non-dominant hand, but you never really appreciated how much it did for you until, well, it couldn't anymore.

Right now it was in a navy blue sling that hugged my arm close to my body, cross ways over my chest and had another strap that buckled around my waist. It kept it pretty immobilized and I was told when I began occupational therapy to relearn both how to use the arm and how to walk because of my right hip and leg damaged by the other bullet, things were going to be tricky, but doable.

All I could focus on at the time was that I had to relearn how to *walk* and relearn how to use my arm to do things that I'd otherwise taken for granted until now. Things such as brushing my teeth, or stirring a pot. All I could think right now, with my thoughts still muddy and hazy from pain management was *what did he do to me?*

I went to raise a careful spoonful of soup to my mouth when someone shouted, "Ah! Hey! Put that down!" I jumped and immediately cried out in pain from the involuntary startle response reflex, my spoonful of soup flying and painting the napkin the nurse had laid over me orangey-red.

I froze and held still, breathing through the pain, a wall of black leather and blue denim approaching out of the corner of my eye saying, "Shit, I'm sorry. I didn't mean to scare you, I was just trying to save you from yourself there. I brought you dinner."

I forced myself to relax a muscle group at a time, turning my head slowly and at an awkward angle to look up at who'd spoken.

"Hi," I said faintly, and Tony smiled. Those dimples of his that just made my heart flutter every time they appeared, flashing out at me.

"I am so fucking sorry," he said, setting down the bag of take-out on my tray table and picking up the hospital cafeteria-style dinner tray. He moved it out of the way over by the sink. He pulled paper towels from the dispenser and came back to me, lifting the napkin off and gently dabbing at me where the soup had hit me where the paper hadn't covered.

"It's okay, I guess I just startled easy... I'm fine, really."

"Well, I'm glad to at least see you're with it today."

"Yeah, it hurts and I'm still medicated, but its pills now. A little easier to deal with than whatever they were putting through my IV. I just feel awful, though... like I ache all over."

"Morphine will do that to you," he said and began unpacking the takeout bag. I blinked and looked at the white paper containers with the red printed battling Chinese dragon and phoenix on them.

"Is that Wah-Kue café?" I asked, perking up a bit.

"Yeah, you still go there?" he asked.

"Only the best Chinese food in the city," I said, "This guy I used to date had me meet him there for our first one."

He grinned and those dimples came out again, "Aw yeah? What happened to you two?" he asked, playing along.

I gave a mocking light sigh, "Well you know, he'd just made detective and I was clawing my way up the ranks as a defense attorney at this prestigious firm and sadly, it just didn't work out."

"Yeah, I dated a chick like that once. A real go-getter, I liked her for that."

"Yeah?" I asked, surprised. I hadn't known that was one of the qualities he'd liked about me.

"Yeah," he said and went back over to the tray and grabbed my fork. "Can you hold this or are you going to need a hand for the time being."

"I think I can manage," I said, opening my hand in the sling. "If you can just put it there."

He put the carton in my hand and let me close my fingers around it in my lap, moving the tray table back some so I could manage better.

"Ah, hold on just a second." He went and pulled more paper towels and laid them over me and I grimaced.

"Afraid I'm going to be eating like a toddler or an old person for a while," I confessed. "Wearing more than I actually manage to get in my mouth."

"You got shot twice and in a real bad place. All that really matters now is that you're still here."

There was no joking, no more clowning to his tone. If anything I swore I could hear relief in his voice and it very nearly brought me to tears. Of course, the tears *did* start to flow when I thought about Sami... guilt swamped me and I hated that I was here while she was gone. I swallowed hard and Tony just sat patiently beside me while I cried into my Shrimp Foo Young.

I was glad he was here. I mean, the nursing staff had been wonderful to me. All of them had been really great, the doctors, too, but that was their job. No one other than Tony had come to visit me from the outside world yet, and it meant a lot that I could hear it when he spoke, the gladness that I was still alive; the fact that someone would have missed me if I were I gone, too.

"Thank you," I murmured, voice cracking and he smiled and wiped my tears.

"No crying into the Wah-Kue's Shrimp Foo Young. I think it's perfectly seasoned and doesn't need any more salt."

I laughed and bit down on the resulting moan. I said, "Don't make me laugh please. It hurts to laugh."

"Sorry, I'll try to take it down a notch."

He pulled up a chair and picked one of the containers, popping open the top and sliding a pair of chopsticks out of their paper wrapper. He snapped them apart and I smiled, remembering.

"You know that date was the first time I learned how to use chopsticks?"

"Oh yeah, I remember." He laughed. "You got the hang of it pretty quick."

"I did, didn't I?"

He popped a bite of food into his mouth and said, "Mm-hmm," as he chewed politely with his mouth shut.

We ate in silence for a bit, and I think that had more to do with him being polite and wanting me to get some food down because I could just tell he was burning to say *something* to me. To be honest, as good as the Chinese was, even if it was a bit cold, I wasn't terribly hungry. I was pretty sure that had to do with all the medicine they had me on, though.

I asked, because I wanted to know, "Anything on my case, yet?"

He lit up and eagerly launched into telling me his news, "Actually yeah, we made an arrest today."

I perked up, "Really?"

"Ah, yup. We got the guy who posted your address online, he's being held on inciting violence in the third degree. Did a great job incriminating himself, despite being Mirandized, and the ADA is not only willing to prosecute, he's pretty sure that the hate crime qualifier he's dropping as the cherry on top is going to stick. Dude is looking at a ten to fifteen year bid for this with more charges potentially pending."

"Let me guess," I said quietly, appetite completely fled. "Those additional charges would be in relation to whoever killed Sami and shot me if it's discovered that they acted on his posting my address..."

"Yeah." He looked me over. "Look, I know it goes without saying, but we'll get that guy, too. We just..."

"Have nothing to go on..." I said and nodded. "I didn't know him. I mean, I could talk to a sketch artist, but that's the best I could do."

"You remember more of what he looks like?" he sat forward in his seat and set his Chinese food aside, whipping out a pad of paper and a pen from his inside jacket pocket.

"He was white, and skinny. Almost nerdy looking with light brown hair, I think."

"You think?"

"Yeah, I mean, he had his hood up on his sweatshirt, and I only saw his eyebrows. I know that's silly, that sounds so stupid..."

"No, give me everything you've got Chrissy. You're doing great."

Bolstered by his small words of praise, which was silly when you stopped to think about it, but much needed given my awfully fragile psyche. I hated that I was this fragile and this vulnerable, but I also had to admit to myself that it was okay to be that way right now. That anyone in my position would be.

Still, I hated it. I was a successful defense attorney, defending my clients to the best of my ability and I was angry that I was judging that in a negative light all of a sudden. That I was questioning everything about it, because even though I knew in my heart that Miranda Maguire was innocent, that Skip really had abused her, and awfully so, I was the one lying here and Sami... It felt like *I* had killed my best friend. The guilt of that was overwhelming, a cloying, thick and choking thing that welled out of the center of my being like blood from a cut.

Tony was incredibly patient at the second sudden and fierce onset of tears when they came. Stopping, waiting them out, and snatching fresh tissues from the dispenser by the hospital room's sink and bringing them to me as they were needed.

Did you know that you really needed both hands to blow your nose? I mean to get a really good blow in to clear things up. I found out, but only by virtue of being limited to the one. Tony didn't judge at all, or even call a nurse when I tried to laughingly complain about it. He just went over by the door, put on a pair of the blue gloves with practiced precision and came over and helped me.

I wondered to myself why I hadn't tried harder back then, while at the same time tried really hard not to think too much about where he'd learned to put on those gloves with such practiced ease because when I did? A fresh storm of survivor's guilt raged and I hated myself even more for having been so selfish in asking her over, for having been so afraid and it turns out, for good reason.

"Thanks," I said as he stripped the gloves off and into the trash. He used hand sanitizer from the wall and winked at me.

"Don't mention it."

"Afraid all the other cops and detectives will make fun of you for being a soft touch?" I asked.

"Something like that," he agreed and came and sat back down.

"I... I don't think I can do anymore today," I confessed and he shook his head.

"Wasn't going to ask you to. You've been at it the better part of an hour and you've given me way more to go on than most witnesses give me in twice that time. I'll go back to the station and type up your witness statement and bring it back here tomorrow. We can go over it, you can make any corrections you need or want to it and when you're satisfied, I'll have you sign off on it."

I nodded, "Sounds good."

We were quiet for a time and I finally broke down and said, "I never thought I would ever see myself on this side of the process."

"No one ever does, but you're taking it like a champ."

"You think so?"

"I do."

I didn't know why that meant so much to me, but it did, so I said, "Thanks for saying..."

"Just telling you the truth."

I nodded and sniffed and he asked, "You done eating?"

"Yeah, thank you. I'm sorry I couldn't eat more, I mean, it was good I guess I'm just not that hungry."

"I wouldn't be either if I were you, and it's fine. It really is."

"Thank you for bringing it. It was a nice change from the hospital's food, which really isn't all that bad, honestly."

"Jesus, if you don't think this food is bad, then I should really get the doctors to reexamine that head of yours."

I laughed and it broke off into another moan. "Don't make me laugh!" I admonished and he smiled, those damn dimples in full force.

"Sorry."

"Yeah, not sorry," I accused and he smiled bigger.

"Yeah, not that time. Sorry, it was worth it to see you smile."

I couldn't help it, I smiled again and said, "Now for some reason *that* I believe."

5

———

*T*ony...

"It's a brick fuckin' wall, McCormick and yeah, we can release it to the media, but I need to put you guys back in rotation unless something breaks. We got more cases that need handling than we do detectives."

"What about the threat?" I asked.

"Did it pan out?" Captain Roberts looked to Jaime which pissed me off, but Jaime had to tell the truth and the truth was...

"No. It was a dude in a black jacket and grey hoodie, but he kept his hood up and his head down. Paid in cash, and the clerk at the florist said the guy wrote the card right in front of her and that the card said 'Get well soon, we miss you' not the actual threat. She swears by it, but he could have slipped the threatening message in when she wasn't looking. Wouldn't be that hard."

"Prints?"

"On the envelope, just the nurse's, the florist's and Tony's. On the card, just the nurse's and Tony's."

"Goddammit."

"My thought's exactly, Captain," I said grimly.

"So we don't even know if it's the same guy?"

"Both are white males, similar descriptions but not exact," Jaime said.

"Similar, what's that mean? Be more specific." The Captain was glowering at me and I sucked in a breath to answer him but Jaime, ever the good partner, drew the captain's fire off me.

"Both around the same height, same build, but different hair and eye color."

"That's not exactly similar."

"You know how ID's from witnesses can be, and the surveillance video at the florist's was in black and white, so no help there."

The Captain shook his head, "It's not enough. Look, I know the guy is still out there but this department has nothing to go on, nor does it have the resources to keep at it. I hate to say it, but we can't do anything until somebody fucks up. You know what I mean?"

I did, but I didn't have to like it. It'd been three days since I'd seen Chrissy at the hospital over shared Chinese. I'd been working every angle of this hard, hoping something would break, but no dice and here we were, predictably, having the plug pulled on us and I couldn't say I blamed the Captain for doing it. The case was cold and impossible to follow up on. He was right, we just had to wait for some other shit to happen and hope this guy fucked up. He was also right in that we didn't have the manpower to devote to protecting Franco. At least not on the clock.

I had a couple of ideas on that front, but nothing I could or would share here or with Chrissy. She didn't know about the threat and I didn't want to tell her unless I had to. I didn't like it, but one of the unfortunate bits about our criminal justice system and society as a whole was that it was, and probably always would be, purely reactionary. You couldn't do shit to prevent shit – it had to happen and *then* you could move in and deal with it.

The shitty thing about that, is even with how horrible and catastrophic the thing that'd happened to Chrissy was, we'd gone as far as we could go with it. We were at a solid dead end with no leads and nowhere to go, which meant we had to hurry up and wait for something to happen somewhere or to someone else.

This was the part of being a cop we never talked about because we loathed it just that damn much. The hopeless, helpless, and powerless feeling didn't jive with being the great white knights we all secretly were proud as hell of being. It felt good to get out in the community and do some real good but this part was becoming all too prevalent and we could all agree across the board it sucked hard. Especially when the vic was genuinely a good or nice person who deserved justice. Despite her field of defending the scumbags, like us and not being able to choose the victims, Chrissy didn't always get to choose her clients. It was how the system worked and as much as she was reviled for some of the douchebags she defended, she was still one of the good guys, like us.

I could see that. I knew it from the talks that we'd had on the subject. Chrissy had gotten into criminal justice for the same reasons I had, and I'd liked her for that then and I could tell, she was one of the rare ones, one of the ones that'd held onto her morals and her ideals. Who clung fiercely to the tenets of her profession; *everybody deserved legal counsel. Everybody deserved the best defense she could provide.*

My tenets were much the same, to protect, to serve, to bring justice by executing my duties and much like the lawyers further along in the system, I didn't get to pick the vic. The street thug who spent his life bangin' deserved just as much justice as Samantha Lynn Hayworth. Justice was blind, and so we had to be. It was one of the things we understood, both as cops and as Indigo Knights.

I couldn't wait to get out of the Captain's office once his edict that we had to refocus our efforts had come down. We were almost done with the day and I needed to head to the Ten-Thirteen and call together what club could make it in. I sent a mass text on my way back to my desk and Jaime looked me over appraisingly.

"What?"

"Coloring outside the lines on this one, eh?"

"I was never very good at staying in 'em when I was a kid, either."

He leaned in and whispered harshly, "You watch your ass with that shit, Youngblood. That's the kind of thing that gets IAB sniffing around."

"None of us are on the clock, you old dog. None of us are doing any investigation into things we shouldn't, either."

"Eh? So what are you thinkin'?"

"Protective detail."

"Think she needs it?"

"You watched the news or looked at Facebook or Twitter lately?"

"Fuck no, I like my sanity intact and I ain't got anger issues. No need to start that shit now."

I huffed a laugh, "Good point."

"You headed to the hospital?" he asked, already knowing the answer.

"Nope, headed to the Ten-Thirteen, first. Figured the lady could use a decent dinner. Trinity Gen ain't known for its gourmet food."

"Hmm, well, I figure that you've broken enough bad news for this investigation. I think I'll head over to Trinity Gen and be the bearer of the bad news so you can try and cheer her up with some decent chow. She seems like a nice girl."

"Yeah, it's a hell of a thing happening to her."

"Ain't that the god's honest truth?"

I rode to the Ten-Thirteen, and watched Jaime turn out of the garage in my side view in the opposite direction heading for Trinity Gen. I didn't think I could get her exactly 'round the clock coverage, but we could do our best. I'd see what the guys would have to say about it when I got there. I pulled into the alley by the bar and felt pretty good about the number of bikes lined against the side wall of the place. I went around front and into the bar to a packed floor.

Skids caught my eye from behind the bar and gave me a hearty chin lift and then jutted it towards the back where the room typically reserved for private parties of ten or more was. I nodded and headed that way, pushing past a few couples waiting to be seated.

I opened the glass door to the fishbowl to just about everyone here. Seven men sat around the table. Four in leathers and colors like me and three still in their work wear.

"Any of you boys on meal break?" I asked.

"Yeah," Poe said raising a hand.

"Kay, I'll try and make it quick as soon as Skids and Reflash get in here."

The door opened and Skids slid through saying, "Reflash'll be just a minute."

"Reflash is right there," Golden said, thrusting his chin at the door.

Skids got the hell out of the way and Reflash, a short and stocky

Hispanic dude with curly hair shorn short on the sides and back pushed into the room and demanded, "Where's the fire at?"

He was in his fifties, but barely looked a day over forty-three, he just aged real damn well that way. His medium brown eyes were sparkling with good humor, but shrewd at the same time, and even though he'd been fire, he might as well have been a cop. He didn't miss a damn thing.

"Ha, ha, fucking, ha," Backdraft uttered with absolutely no sense of humor. He hated Reflash's bullshit puns almost as much as I did. That one had actually been pretty mild, though so I was pretty sure something else had put a bug up his ass. I liked Backdraft, if there was any guy in the club that I would consider myself closest to in any regard, Backdraft was it. I was wondering what was up with him but didn't feel right in asking with everyone here. That, and I knew Backdraft was a big boy and capable of handling shit. If he needed me, he knew where to find me.

I looked him over and raised an eyebrow, an invitation to talk later but he didn't catch on. Instead, he leaned back in his seat and propped his boots on the table, glowering in general. His hazel eyes sparking under his dishwater blonde hair only a couple of shades darker than mine. He was in need of a cut, he just had better not let the guys at his firehouse do it like last time. It'd turned into a half shaved head going out looking all manky to at least one call. Funny as hell and the whole thing posted to YouTube for posterity's sake.

"Hey!" Reflash barked, "Get your fuckin' feet off Skids' table, man! You're in a fuckin' restaurant, not your house. What's the damn matter with you?" Backdraft dropped his feet to the floor immediately and put up his hands, shaking his head and ignored the exchange. Something was definitely up his ass... I really wanted to know what, but couldn't risk losing focus on why I'd called everyone here just now. Chrissy's life sort of may depend on it.

I looked around the table and sighed, and laid it out for them. They listened and Golden let out a low whistle.

"You sure drew the shit end of the stick with this case. I had no idea you'd drawn the Franco thing," he said.

"Look," I said, "I don't know, and I don't care what you guys have heard, or what you think about the whole Maguire shit-show, but I can attest – Chrissy is one of the good ones and she legit doesn't deserve this shit." Silence met what I had to say as the rest of the guys mulled it over.

Leave it to the lawyer to come to the aid of one of his own, "I've come up against Chrissy Franco a few times in court, and Youngblood is right. She *is* one of the good ones, and I was and am sorry as hell what happened to her." Yale looked slowly around the table, his deep brown eyes making contact with every man who looked back, which of course, every single one of us did.

"So what are you asking exactly?" Backdraft asked and some of his moodiness diminished.

"Take it in shifts, post up outside her room when we can, the threats are credible, I can feel it, and I can't be everywhere at once."

"Who's with her now?" Skids asked.

"Jaime," I answered and he nodded. "He's breaking the bad news about the investigation grinding to a halt. I'm supposed to head up there with some decent food when I'm done here and relieve him."

"I'm in," Reflash said, "I'll go fix you something up to take with you. You too, Poe."

"Thanks," Poe said. "I'm in, too, but I'm going to have to get going in a minute, break time's almost over. Just get a text pool going and I'll let you know when I can cover."

"Thanks," I said and nodded.

"Shoot, you know I'm in," Oz said and ran a hand over his bald head. Half black and half Cuban, Oz had been a correctional officer at a maximum security prison originally. He'd signed on with the ICPD and worked the jail, now. He was also a beefy motherfucker. We were on the same basketball team in the spring and played regular matches against the fire guys.

"Thanks, Oz."

One by one the guys knocked knuckles around the table and declared themselves in. I nodded. Yale asked, "Anybody from that firm of hers been up to see her yet?" I shook my head and he snorted, a disgusted noise. "Figures, most of them are a bunch of bottom feeders."

"I know that her friend's family has been up, they tried to see her when she was in ICU but hospital policy is no one but immediate family." I shook my head and said, "At any rate, thanks guys, I fuckin' owe you."

"You don't owe us shit," Skids said and got up. "I gotta get back to the bar, I'll let you boys know when your food's up."

"Thanks, pops!" Poe called after him, green eyes sparkling. Skids flipped him off over his shoulder. Poe ran a hand over the top of his medium-brown hair and grinned hard with a perfect set of teeth only braces could have given him. The lot of us laughed. Skids wasn't any of our daddy, he just liked to act like it sometimes.

"Right, I'll make a schedule – just as soon as you all start texting me your availability, and remember she doesn't know about the threat, so let's try not to spill the beans if you talk to her."

"Get the fuck out of here," Backdraft said with a grimace and I smiled and huffed a bitter laugh.

"Brother, she's been through hell in a handbasket, enough is enough for the time being."

"I don't disagree, but I'm not talking figuratively, I'm talking literally – Skids is waving at you from the bar, so get the fuck out of here!" he grinned at me but it was forced.

"Oh, shit! Thanks." I got up to a masculine laugh track and went for the door, Poe on my heels. "Talk to you soon," I called back and felt loads better. I mean, we couldn't keep it up forever and there would likely be gaps, but something was better than nothing and it was a lot better than it was before – her having no one looking out for her.

I grabbed the food and went out the door and back around to the alley, looking forward to heading up to the hospital and seeing how she was doing.

6

*C*hrissy...

Three long days without Tony. David, Sami's brother, had come to see me, though and had brought their parents' well wishes. He said they had wanted to come, but the funeral arrangements had taken over everything right now and that their mom wasn't doing so well. I understood, and the visit had been entirely too short. That had been my only visitor aside from any official police visits from Tony or his partner. At least the firm I belonged to had sent flowers, though, so I knew I wasn't completely forgotten. It was a beautiful bouquet along with a get well card full of signatures from people around the office. Still, it would have been nice, would have broken up the monotony had someone come to see me.

I honestly didn't know how to feel about it. I mean, I'd been shot, it wasn't like I was having my appendix out. That, and it was painfully obvious, after being here a week or more, that no one from the firm actually cared. When it came to the legal visits, only Tony acted like it wasn't completely about my case when he managed to come, which had me seriously rethinking my life's priorities.

I'd always been one to keep my circle small, even before my parents had died, but having only one friend in Sami Lynn, maybe I'd been keeping it *too* small. I'd made my career everything, but my career, as was obvious now, didn't love me near as much as I'd loved it.

"You sure you're gonna be okay?" Detective McDonnell asked after breaking the news that nothing else could be done, that the man who had killed Sami was in the wind and might have to hurt or kill someone else before he could be found.

I sniffed and nodded, "I just had really hoped, you know?"

"Yeah, I know, kid. I'm really sorry."

"I'm just sorry that something potentially horrible has to happen to someone else before anything can be done."

"Eh, not always... sometimes we get lucky and something like the gun used turns up in a traffic stop or on a banger and the case suddenly has new evidence that we can trace back to the guy. It's a lot of hard work, but in a case like this, worth every bit of shoe leather worn off."

My face scrunched up as I tried to stop myself from crying yet more. Nine times out of ten, when I burst into tears it wasn't for myself and it wasn't now. I still felt so *guilty* about Sami. Sami who still had her parents, and who had been engaged. Sami who had everything life had to offer in front of her and wasn't afraid to go out and live it. She'd been my best friend since the third grade, thick as thieves, we'd even gone to the same college together and now she was *gone* and it was all my fault for not wanting to be alone.

"Aw, kid, I'm so sorry," Detective McDonnell said. He handed me a handkerchief from inside his suit jacket's pocket and I took it. He'd been here a while, the evening news buzzing quietly in the background and he said, "You really shouldn't listen to any of that garbage. They don't know you or what they're talking about."

"What?" I asked, bewildered and he looked up at the screen. I looked up too and saw my picture from the firm's website resting above the reporter's shoulder. I pressed the volume button on the inside of my bedrail, the reporter's voice coming through the speaker beside me a little louder.

"... on this edition of *Word on the Street*."

It cut to a microphone in front of a black man in a pair of grease stained coveralls with one of those industrial, thick canvas, warm construction jackets over it.

"You know, I'm glad she's not dead because I don't wish that on nobody, but if anybody should be up on charges for that other girl's death it should be her. Mm-mm-mm that was a *damn* shame."

Detective McDonnell scoffed, "Yeah, not how the legal system works, buddy."

I stared wide eyed as the image cut to a white police officer in uniform, the reporter off camera and behind the mic saying, "What do you think about the Christina Marie Franco case?"

"I think it's a shame that someone can't do their job without everyone having an opinion."

"You know that Samantha Lynn Hayworth's funeral is tomorrow, right?"

"No, I didn't know that."

"You don't have an opinion about the situation?" the reporter asked.

"Yeah, yeah I do, but I'm going to do the right thing here and keep it to myself."

The image cut to an older woman, Italian by the hair and the dress. She reminded me of my grandmother as she said, "Those poor, poor, girls." She crossed herself. "I pray for them."

Another man, this time in an Indigo City Angler's hat, "I feel sorry for the blonde girl whose picture's been all over the news, that lawyer's the one that deserved to die."

I closed my eyes and again Detective McDonnell made a rude noise, "These people don't know what the hell they're talking about."

"Don't they?" I asked.

"No, they don't." Strong, dispassionate, and angry, Tony's voice rang out from the doorway into my room. I craned my neck around carefully and he came in, handing one bag of takeout to his partner.

"From Skids and Reflash," he said and Detective McDonnell's eyes lit up.

"Alright now! I'll be sure to tell 'em thank you."

Tony nodded and asked me, "You have dinner yet?"

"It was disgusting, I barely ate it," I said honestly and Tony laughed.

"Glad your appetite is coming back."

"Thanks," I murmured as he opened up one of the Styrofoam clamshells on my tray table and fished out a plastic fork for me.

"Hot and fresh from the Ten-Thirteen. Reflash's hospital special," Tony declared and I frowned.

"The Ten-Thirteen? I don't think I've ever heard of it."

"Ever hear of the Cormorant Bar & Grill?" McDonnell asked.

"Oh! Seriously? Why do you call it the Ten-Thirteen?"

Tony smiled, "It's the address, Ten-Thirteen Muller Street."

Detective McDonnell chuckled, "It's also the call sign for officer in need of assistance and some days, the Cormorant is just the kind of assistance we need."

"I feel like I should have known all this double entendre about it."

"Well, you're on the defense side of things, we aren't always inclined to share," Detective McDonnell said but at a sharp look from Tony said, "What? I'm just sayin'."

I laughed a little then and was pleased to realize that it hurt, but not nearly as bad as it had just yesterday or the day before. I was still on pain medicine, but I was trying very hard to be very careful about how much I took. Addiction ran in my family, and though my parents had never had any trouble with drugs, I had uncles and cousins on both sides who did. I didn't want to go down that path if I could help it.

"You alright?" Tony asked.

I nodded, and took another bite of the heavenly mac and cheese in one of the small pockets of the take out's clamshell. It was a hearty meal with a rich potato salad in the other small pocket and what looked like smoked brisket in the main portion. Whoever Reflash was, he knew how to cook. I wanted to ask about the unique name, but didn't feel comfortable with Detective McDonnell here. I mean, I didn't know if he knew about Tony and me from before, and I didn't know if that could or would put Tony into some kind of compromising position with his boss or the department... but at the same time, I really wanted him to stay on my case.

I was almost afraid that if he weren't the one working it that I really would be alone and that I'd be forgotten; fading into obscurity completely until I might as well not exist at all. Well, honestly, I was less afraid for me than I was for Sami and her family... I mean, my name attached to this, I was afraid that it wouldn't go anywhere and my friend and second family would never receive justice. *God, this was all so awful...*

"Hey, you okay?" Tony asked a moment later.

I blinked and looked over at him carefully. Just about every movement I made affected my back and injuries somehow, so every one of those movements had become careful and deliberate.

"I'm fine, sorry. I guess it just takes some extra effort and time to think, all the pain medicine, you know?"

Tony's partner nodded in understanding and took another bite of his food, but not Tony, he stared at me with a penetrating gaze, gently searching my face for the truth. I should have known better than to attempt to lie in the first place. These men were trained detectives with the Indigo City Police Department. They likely took their coffee with extra cynicism in the morning. I don't know what I'd been thinking other than I didn't want to put anything I'd been thinking in the air... I guess I wanted to protect Tony, as silly as that sounds. I mean, he was a grown man and clearly knew how to take care of himself. I just... he was being so nice to me when the rest of the world was being so ugly and I didn't want that to go away. Not yet.

Thankfully, he let it go. He gave me a nod and I resumed eating so I didn't have to talk about anything else, at least for the time being.

The news had ended and I was grateful for that, and I just let the TV carry on with the same channel. Detective McDonnell said, "Las Vegas vacation," and I looked at him.

"What?"

He chuckled, "Those meds really are doing your head in," he said and stabbed his fork at the screen. I looked up at the sparkling green background with its blocks of white, several taken up by letters. Wheel of Fortune, he was playing along with the gameshow that came on after the news.

"I like Jeopardy better," I said without thinking.

Tony barked a surprised laugh and his partner said, "Well you're in luck; it's on next." He shifted in his seat and grumbled, "Jeopardy," before scoffing. Clearly, I had offended his finer gameshow sensibilities.

"Could be worse, she could have said 'The Price is Right.'" Tony came to my defense but I grimaced.

"It was the only option on earlier today... I can't deal with soap operas."

"Ooo," McDonnell cringed in sympathy.

"I'd give anything for my tablet and Netflix," I said. "Or better yet, my Kindle."

"I'll see what I can do to scare those up," Tony said.

"Yeah?"

"Yeah. Going to need some things from your place eventually. I'll go check it out on my way home."

I nodded and said, "Thank you, I really appreciate it. I would usually rely on Sami for things like that."

"Ain't you got any other friends?" McDonnell asked and I colored.

"Dude!" Tony cried and McDonnell cringed, realizing as soon as he'd said it how it sounded and instead of embarrassed or hurt all I could feel was sympathy for the poor man. My dad had been much the same way. Blurting things out and completely not meaning the way they sounded.

"Sorry, I need to think before I speak sometimes," Detective McDonnell muttered.

"It's okay, um... my parents died in a crash when I was in college and Sami and I had been friends since third grade. I made some friends, but with my career, didn't have a lot of time to develop those friendships much past the acquaintance stage of things, you know?"

"Fair enough, and you didn't owe me any kind of explanation, you know."

"It's alright, I guess I'm just a little self-conscious about how it looks."

"Looks ain't everything," he said with a gusty sigh and I nodded. Tony watched our exchange, brow creased, though with worry or displeasure I couldn't quite tell. He'd been quiet, texting back and forth with someone on his phone while McDonnell and I talked.

Still, even with him distracted by the device, it was nice just having people here. We finished our dinner and the men stayed and watched Jeopardy with me before they got up to go.

"I'll swing by your place on the way home and see about getting that stuff for you. You remember where any of it is at?"

"Bedside table, maybe the coffee table. I honestly can't remember."

"It's okay, I'll find it."

"Thank you."

"No problem."

"See you around," McDonnell said and I smiled.

"Thank you for coming and taking the time out of your lives and busy schedule."

"Not a problem," Tony said with a wink and his expression? I believed him.

"Night, Ms. Franco."

"Good night, detectives."

I settled back and flipped through the limited channels until I found something tolerable and sighed, settling in. My nurse for this evening, Pasquale, came in and gave me my meds and pretty soon, I was fast asleep.

7

*T*ony...

"Remind me why we're doing this again?" Oz asked when I met him up the hall from Chrissy's room. I looked him over, taking in his bored and unimpressed look and sighed, trying to put it into a neat little box not that he'd 'get' because Oz wasn't stupid, but more in a way to make him give a fuck about it. That was the thing about Oz, he just didn't give a fuck unless you gave him a reason to. Once you did, though? He was all in.

"Because like it or not, she's one of our own," I said and he raised an eyebrow.

"Okay, how do you figure, man?" He was listening, which was at least something.

I explained about how she may be on the defense side of things but how she was one of the rare ones doing it for all of the right reasons. He just looked at me with that 'what do you take me for?' look and I sighed.

"Let me guess, you think she's an asshole."

"Yup. All lawyers are."

"Until you need one," I said flatly.

"Still assholes then, too."

"Fine, okay," I said nodding, "She's an asshole like I'm an asshole. You may not like me, and think that I'm an asshole, but you put the donation in the hat when it's passed and you stand up and do the right thing anyways because we're all part of the same damn community, the blue one."

He looked me up and down and stuffed his beanie hat for that big bald head of his in the side pocket of his tactical pants. "You're right," he said and I felt my insides go liquid with relief. "I think you're an asshole." I laughed, I couldn't help it. Oz was always good at catching a guy off guard. Through his own grin he said, "But you're right about the other stuff too," and the last vestiges of apprehension left me.

"Thanks, man."

"Just doing what we all do best, the black knight routine."

"Don't you mean white knight?"

"Man, what is it with all you motherfuckers and everything having to be white all the damn time?"

"Hey, you're the one being racist on this one, dude!"

"I ain't racist. Shit, I got a color TV at home."

"What? How? I can't even with you sometimes, man." I couldn't stop laughing.

"Go on, get out of here. I'll be here 'til Poe gets off then he'll take over for the next watch."

"You going in to talk to her?"

"Hell no, man. She's a lawyer didn't you just hear me? They're all assholes. I'll post up *outside* the door."

"Good deal, because I wasn't totally sure how I was going to explain that to her."

"What, she don't know about the threats?" he asked, frowning.

"Man, weren't you listening back at the Ten-Thirteen? No, she doesn't. She needs time to heal without more stress added on."

He shook his head, "I ain't into all that, man. That's all you. You asked for help, I'm here. That's all I give a shit about."

"Tell me about it, and I appreciate that; you have no idea."

"Don't be getting all emotional on me now," Oz said dismissively and I grinned, shaking my head and held up my hand. We knocked fists and I left.

Jaime had taken off ahead of me by a few minutes so it was just me heading back down to the garage. I rode to Chrissy's place first and banged on the super's apartment. He grumbled about it, but gave me the key to Chrissy's new lock and door. I went up to her apartment, the doorway freshly framed; the door giving off the smell of fresh cut lumber under the heavier scent of new paint. I stuck the key in the lock and twisted, giving the door a shove.

"Damn."

I tipped my head back and let out an explosive breath at the ceiling. I knew that crime scenes didn't magically clean themselves up, but this shit had slipped my mind. I guess maybe I'd thought that management or the super might have done something about the worst of it, but apparently not.

The stink wasn't great but it was manageable. I opened up some windows and looked around, heaving a sigh. This was, for the most part, a one man job but the couch needed to go. The blood wasn't coming out and she didn't need to come home to this. I pulled out my phone and dialed and knew I was going to owe and owe big.

"Yeah, it's Youngblood…"

Two HOURS later the couch was lined up to go out the door and there were three trash bags sitting on it, ready to go down to the dumpster in the alley. Backdraft wasn't a happy camper, but he'd gotten here just in time to help me out with the trash haul and hadn't had to deal with the joy that'd been scrubbing blood and dried wine out of the hardwood floor on hands and knees. The stains were still super apparent, but nothing short of pulling up and laying new boards was going to help that.

"You ready?" he demanded.

"Yeah."

"One, two, three; lift!"

We wrestled the damn couch, a real nice silvery microfiber that looked like suede, out to the alley. We set it down by the dumpster. We looked at each other, chests heaving and arms burning and Backdraft asked, "This ain't just about feeling sorry for a victim, is it? You like her, don't you?"

"Be lying if I denied it." I said.

"Didn't you *date* this bitch a few years back?"

"One, she's not a bitch and two, yeah, yeah we dated."

"Well then what happened?"

I shrugged, "It just didn't work out." He gave me a look like *seriously,* and I rolled my eyes. "It wasn't like it was some epic fucking romance or anything. It was three and a half dates and none of them made it past first base."

"Dude, all that tells me is that you seriously suck at sealing the deal." I turned and he followed as we made our way back into the building and up to Chrissy's floor.

"Wasn't like that, either. Chrissy's a classy girl. Not some 'one and done' type deal. At the time I really was hoping we'd reconnect when we were both in a better position."

"You could have had her in multiple positions if you'd tried harder," he cracked and I shook my head.

"You may be all about the Holster Humpers, and Badge Bunnies but that's not my thing."

He frowned and shook his head, "It was fun while it lasted, but I'm pretty much over it, now."

"What's going on with you?" I demanded and he sighed, and leaned back against the brick wall of the building next door to Chrissy's.

"Shit's going sideways with Torrid," he said and didn't sound happy about it. I searched his face and asked, "Sideways how, exactly?"

"Same shit, different day... I work too much, I'm never home. We're always broke, and somehow that's my fault. You know, typical couples crap. What else you need me for?"

It wasn't 'typical couples crap,' we all liked Torrid enough, but she was a high maintenance bitch and Backdraft needed someone decidedly less so. He wasn't suited for an alpha female, being too damn alpha himself. He needed someone decidedly more submissive, but it wasn't my place to tell him something he already knew.

I shook my head and said, "That's it, man."

"Seriously? You called me down here just to move a couch and three bags of trash?"

"Yeah."

"I thought you needed help cleaning up, I thought there was more."

"No, man. I just needed a hand with the couch. Too awkward to get it on my own."

"Shit, I take back every curse I uttered when I hung up the phone," he said. I laughed and he asked skeptically, "You need anything else?"

"No, man. Get out of here." I pushed off the wall of Chrissy's apartment building and opened up my arms. We bear hugged and slapped each other on the backs.

"Sweet, call me anytime if it's going to be like that," he declared and I nodded.

"I'm holding you to that, asshole."

We clasped hands and bumped shoulders, slapping each other on the back in a manly hug one more time.

"See you around, brother."

"Keep the shiny side up, man."

He turned around and I watched the emblem on the back of his cut, our club's colors; fade into the dark. It made me smile every time I saw it. Most people wouldn't get it, but the 'Young' in my road name totally did. We were a real life pack of superheroes when you thought about it, and every time I watched one of my brothers' walk away, I saw that shield and that knight's piece with the rays coming off of it and thought to myself that it was just our team's emblem.

I loved being a cop. I didn't always love what came with it, the suffering, the broken, and the violence, but I loved being a part of the solution to it all. I wouldn't trade that part for the world.

I looked at Chrissy's suddenly empty living room and sighed. Her laptop was on the coffee table along with its charger, plugged in off to the side and fully charged. I think that was our first clue that this whole thing hadn't been a robbery. Well, that, and the fact that there was way too much media attention surrounding Chrissy and coincidences were pretty few and far between when it came to police work. Usually the most obvious answer was the answer. Occam's razor totally applying. That was the philosophic principle that if two options presented themselves, it was usually the simpler of the two that was the answer. The more assumptions you had to make, the less likely that was to be the answer.

Take Chrissy's place, for instance. It was neat and clean, dusted and everything orderly that hadn't been fucked up after the whole having her shit kicked in. Nothing was out of place, simple deduction being that no robbery had occurred and the gunman was legitimately here to kill her. Sami Lynn Hayworth may have been the first one shot, but that was because she'd been in a direct line of sight to the front door, Chrissy's position in the apartment hadn't been.

I could make other, subtler deductions about Chrissy's lifestyle and tastes based on what was present. She didn't have a cable box. That meant one of two things. Either she wasn't much of a TV watcher or she was too busy with work to bother with owning cable. The latter was definitely the simpler answer because of the stack of movies on top of the Blu-ray player and the fact that there was a Netflix emblem on the Blu-ray's remote.

I felt a little like a creeper going through her little one bedroom, but I located her tablet and her kindle and had my curiosity resolved as to why she needed both. The kindle wasn't one of those ones that could double as a tablet. Instead, it was one of those weird ones that looked like a printed page. A pair of reading glasses were perched forlornly on the edge and it struck me.

I was in Chrissy's *home.* Going through her belongings and yeah it was to help her, but this moment deserved so much of my attention and care. This was a total invasion of her privacy which had already been violated on so many levels, first by that asshole, and then by me and CSU. Now, here I was again for a different reason, but *damn*. I needed to do everything here with respect.

I opened closets and looked for a bag to put it all in and I came up with a big beach tote. I wondered then if it was something she liked to do. Judging by the wear on the buttons of her kindle, she liked to read. There was a light dusting of sand in the bottom of the bag and I suddenly had an image of her on a beach somewhere, lounging back in a chair, painted toes digging into the sand. It was a nice image, sun gleaming on her skin, bringing out those Italian roots and kissing it with that olive tone most women dropped serious dough at a tanning salon for.

"Shit, McCormick. You have one hell of an active imagination." I said to myself on a sigh.

As much as I both did and didn't want to, I went through her drawers and found her some of her own things. Underthings, a nice set of pajamas in a silvery satin, top and bottoms. They were one of those sets that looked like – and felt like – expensive shit. I folded them with care and found another set just beneath them in a burgundy. I packed those, too. I skipped the skimpier lacey things and tried to get my mind out of the gutter but it was hard.

Chrissy Franco looked like a younger version of Monica Bellucci. All large dark eyes, high cheekbones and those lips that begged to be kissed. Though I'd never gotten to see under her pencil skirts and satin blouses, the way the material had clung to her figure left all the right things to the imagination but left no doubt that the body under them was straight bangin'. It'd been such a bitch *not* taking her up on the offer of a one-night stand on our last date, and I'd kicked myself for it a lot over the last few years, but still, I stood by what I'd said.

Christina Marie Franco was a woman who deserved way better than that, and I wasn't going to be that guy.

I pulled the shit together that I thought she would need along with the items she'd requested and made sure that everything was good. Satisfied, I took the bag and items out to the living room, made sure the bag was packed tight enough and wound her laptop cord up and stashed both the laptop itself and the cord in the top of the tote and with a last look around, scooped up her purse and her keys and went out the front door, locking it up tight.

I went down to the super's apartment to give him the keys and he scowled at me.

"Those are hers, you're going to see her ain't 'cha?"

"Uh, yeah."

"Then what're you tryin' to hand 'em to me fer?"

He slammed the door in my face and I had to laugh a little. Sometimes the people in this city were, well, they were just something else.

I stashed things between the two hard sided saddlebags on my bike and tried to decide if I wanted to swing by the hospital, or just head home. It'd been a long fucking day, so I went with home over the hospital for now. I mean, I had said I would bring her what she'd asked for tomorrow when I'd seen her, except in about an hour and a half more, it would *be* tomorrow.

I rode across the bay bridge, locked the bike in the garage, and called it good for tonight. I'd gone above and beyond, it was true, but then again, Chrissy wasn't just any vic, either. I needed to quit lying to myself that I would do this for anybody because it straight up wasn't true.

Here was to second chances and all of that.

8

*C*hrissy...

Nearly a week had passed since Tony had brought me some things from my apartment. It'd been a brief visit. He'd caught another case and I had been disappointed. I hadn't seen him much since, but he had called more than a few times to check and see how I was doing.

It was more than I could say for my coworkers at the firm. I hadn't received so much as an email from any of them and when I had called to sort out how much sick leave and vacation I had accrued, to see if it would cover the long road to recovery ahead of me, it had been all business with the woman in HR.

I didn't feel like a valued employee at all, just another number, a statistic... a nobody.

Three light raps fell on the open door to my room and I turned my head carefully. It was getting easier, the motion not pulling as badly, or sending that jolt of agony through my back and out my chest from where I'd been shot.

I was even able to somewhat hobble to the bathroom nearly on my own with the use of a cane, now. Still had to have someone spot me, but it was better than the humiliation of a Foley catheter and bedpans.

I frowned but more in curiosity at who was at my door...

"Mr. Parnell, what are you doing here?"

Damien Parnell was one of the fiercest ADA's Indigo City's District Attorney's office had ever had. He had the highest conviction rates that the city had ever seen and I'd once put a dent in it, so I was surprised to see him here. I mean, he hadn't taken the loss I'd handed him exceptionally well at the time, so...

"Thought I would come to check on you, I have to say, as far as adversaries in the courtroom go, you have to be one of my all-time favorites."

"Oh?" I raised an eyebrow and clasped my hands in my lap after laying my tablet on the top of my tray table. My one arm was still in a sling, and would be for a long time to come, but sometimes supporting that hand gently with the other eased some of the pain.

"I hope these aren't totally unwelcome." He pulled a bouquet of light pink roses out from behind his back and I smiled.

"As long as you aren't hitting on me, I think we'll be fine."

"Can't make any promises," he said with a wink and smiled. I smiled, too and felt my body ease at his gentle teasing.

He took the vase that the bouquet from the firm had come in and stuck it under the sink's faucet, turning the tap. The flowers the firm had sent had died in like three days, despite my day nurse's attention and care. Poor Pasquale had tried everything to make the blossoms last, but for some reason, they just didn't.

The roses that Damian Parnell was unwrapping seemed to be much heartier, and came with a plant food packet that he added to the water.

"They're really beautiful, thank you."

"No problem," he said, pulling up a chair. "Now really, how have you been holding up?"

"I wish I could say I've been doing alright, but it's hard."

"I can't even imagine," he said, his shrewd, dark eyes traveling over my face.

I pressed my lips together and nodded, "Has something else come up? Has the investigation started moving again?" I asked.

He looked solemn and shook his head. "No, I wish I had something else to report on that front, but I don't. I've been... in touch, with the detectives working your case, but there's been no movement yet. Nothing new has come up. Still, I've taken a vested interest."

"Why?" I asked and he gave me a crooked smile.

"Because like it or not, you're one of the good ones Ms. Franco. You give your clients a zealous defense, but not once have I seen you play dirty or underhanded in order to secure the win. There are some of us out here who admire you for that."

"Oh," I murmured, taken aback. I didn't think anyone had anything positive to say about me. Not anymore.

"That and I think it would be remiss of me *not* to take a vested interest in your case. Not when it's suddenly become acceptable to shoot the lawyers when the outcome of a case is less than what was desired. It's anathema to the entire purpose of even having a criminal justice system, don't you think?"

I went to nod and stopped myself just in time, though the motion was growing easier. "I have to entirely agree with that point, counselor."

He smiled and his dark eyes sparkled. "I really do wish you a speedy recovery," he said gently and stood up.

"Thank you," I said, trying not to choke up. It was nice that he'd stopped in, but I found myself sorry that he had to apparently go so soon.

I'd only had a scant few other times that anyone had come to visit me aside from Tony, one of them had been last week. Sami's brother and her parents had come to see me after her funeral. Her mom and dad had apologized to me for not coming sooner and I still couldn't get my head around that. Them. Apologizing. To me. After what I'd done... calling Sami, telling her all about it; not telling her to stay away until things had calmed down.

It was all my fault, and I'd broken down, told them as much, but they wouldn't hear anything of it. They refused to heap anymore blame on me that I hadn't already buried myself under. They'd told me that they had tried to come once before, right away while I'd been in ICU, but that they hadn't been permitted to see me as they weren't family. Tony hadn't been family either, but he had the grace of his badge to open doors for him.

I'd told them I was so sorry that I had been the one to have lived and I had instantly felt bad at the devastation in Janine's bright blue eyes. She had been a second mother to me for a lot of years, and when my mother and father had died, they'd instantly taken me in as one of their own.

Bob and Janine Hayworth had given me a stern lecture after that, and their son, David, Sami's older brother had been the one to stop them. They'd promised to come back and see me and I believed them, but I also knew we all needed some more time.

"I should really get going," Prosecutor Parnell said. "You look really tired."

I nodded and said, "I am, a little but really, thank you for coming. It means a lot."

He nodded, "Get well soon, I'd like to see you back in the courtroom."

"I'll see you there," I said and forced a smile when I honestly just felt like crying again.

"I'm going to hold you to that."

He winked and headed out of my hospital room door, pausing in the doorway and suddenly reaching for the handle.

I heard him ask, "And who might you be?" as he shut the door and heard a shouted, "Hey!" before something out in the hallway crashed.

The crashing sound made me jump slightly which sent pain rattling down my nerve endings. I sat frozen, heartrate elevating, breath crushed from my lungs with fear as I waited, waited, waited.

Finally, the door to my room opened and Pasquale breezed in like nothing had happened out there.

"What was that?" I asked.

"What was what?" he asked smiling.

"That crash, and who was Parnell talking to?"

"Parnell?"

"The man, the visitor who just left my room."

Pasquale shook his head and looked at me as if confused, but I could tell he was lying. He held out a paper cup filled with my midday dose of pain pills and antibiotics and waited for me to take them. I stared at him past the cup and he sighed, shoulders dropping.

"I don't know, and honestly, it's nothing for you to worry your pretty little head about. That fine ass detective that keeps coming around here has had a guard on your door for a while now, all of them wearing the same motorcycle jackets he does. I don't think they're all cops, but I could be wrong."

"What?" I asked, and I could feel the color drain from my face.

"Look, sunshine," Pasquale said, and I stared up at him. "You're fine. That man is totally sprung on you and I could *really* use the eye candy, like that fine specimen of a man that came in here just now, around here. So please, *please* don't chase the parade of beefcake away."

I started to shake my head, the muscle pulling, so I stopped.

"I can't... I mean I won't."

Pasquale looked me over and sighed. He was the best nurse, and dare I say, had become almost a close friend over the time he'd been caring for me. He was sweet, and vibrant, and apparently a drag queen during his off hours, but all that left me, was seriously dying to see his show.

He leaned down and looked me in the eyes, "That's a good girl. Now, I told you the truth, so you have to do a solid for me." He presented the paper cup and smiled, taking the bite out of his next words, "Take the damn pills and relax. You're safe here."

I smiled and some of the tension melted away. I met his warm and caring brown eyes and smile with a slight, much more nervous smile of my own, but did as I was told. I took the damn pills.

I was worried, though... what was Tony keeping from me?

9

T**ony...**

I was headed up the second flight of stairs from the garage when a dude crashed into me and knocked me back onto the first landing. A voice I knew was yelling something, and when I looked up, it was to Yale vaulting the railing, suit and all, to land next to me and take off down the last flight and slam out the door into the garage.

Pursuit training took over, and I pushed off the wall and vaulted the short flight to the cement landing, flying out the door right on Yale's six. He was chasing after some guy in a black coat and hooded sweatshirt. The same black coat and hooded sweatshirt on the surveillance video from the flower shop.

I caught up to Yale who was sweating, chest heaving and overtook him pretty quickly. The dude reached the steel cables cordoning off this level from the next level down and put his hands on the top, leaping and coming down on the other side. We were right behind him but still, by the time I reached the cables there was no sign of him.

Yale caught up to me a half a second later and we listened, but there was nothing to hear except a car fire up.

"Shit, he's coming up," I said and pulled my weapon, ducking out from between the cars parked up against the railing into the garage's lane as a late model gray sedan barreled around the curve, tires squealing. I stood in front and took aim but it was no good, I had to move my ass or get hit, and so I moved my ass, ducking off to the side and rolling, coming up in a crouch, weapon pointed but there was nothing to shoot at, not without potentially hitting either the parking attendant in the shack or someone beyond on the street.

The perp behind at least one known threat on Chrissy's life had blown through the parking barricade's arm, shattering it and didn't even slow down, his tires screaming as he made the turn out onto the street. Horns honked, pedestrians cursed him out but there was no use, he was gone. I holstered my gun and looked over to Yale.

"You get it? Please tell me you got it." I said between heaving breaths.

He stood there, panting, his shoulders dropping and nodded holding up his hand, the plate number from the car hastily scrawled on it. He bent, putting his hands on his knees and struggled to breathe and demanded between deep breaths, "Is it... always... like... that?"

I nodded, and he shook his head, "Look at the bright side," I told him. "At least you're good for cardio for the week."

"Man, fuck you."

I laughed and then he laughed, and we both took our time getting our shit together. The parking attendant was on the phone, likely with dispatch, his eyes wide in his face as he stared at me and Yale. I held up my badge and he hurriedly said something into the phone and I nodded, unable to really say anything else, but I was thinkin', *yeah, you're cool buddy. We're the good guys.*

"I think I'll stick to the DA's office," Yale said a minute later, as we listened to the sirens approach.

"I think you did fine, man... but what happened?"

He filled me in. That he'd gone to visit Chrissy, and was making like he was going to leave, even though he was going to post up outside her room. When he'd come out, the guy was asking what room she was in.

"I asked him who he was and he threw his bouquet, hit me in the face with it."

"That how you got those scratches?" I asked, pointing to his cheekbone, above his trim brown beard. He touched his face and came away with a light smear of blood on his fingertips.

"Damnit, yeah. He had a big bunch of white roses, asked for Christina by name. He took off running the second I asked who he was. I gave chase; he knocked over a nurse's cart in my way and hit the stairs. I don't think he thought I would keep up."

"Yeah, well, surprise!" I waved my hands in the air and Yale laughed.

"Yeah, surprise indeed."

When the uniforms got there, we filled them in and I dropped into the driver's seat of their cruiser and called, "Yale, gimme that tag."

He rattled it off to me and I swore, "Doesn't it fucking figure? Stolen."

"The car or the plates?" he asked.

"Both, car and by default, plates."

"Put out an APB anyways."

"Thanks, Dad. I totally don't know how to do my job. Whatever would I do without you?"

"Alright, alright, Youngblood. No need to turn into a butthurt princess on me."

I shook my head. "Sorry man, this just chaps my ass."

"You and me both."

"You good to give your statement? I want to go up and check on Chrissy."

"Yeah, go ahead, I've got this." He jerked his thumb in the direction of the stairs and returned his hand to his hip to match the other one.

"Cool. Catch you later."

I went up to Chrissy's floor and was pretty much immediately stopped by her murse, that would be man-nurse, Pasquale.

"Oh, I am not *even* covering for you anymore, motherfucker."

"Hey, are you even allowed to talk like that?" I demanded.

He put his hands on his hips, but on Pasquale, it just made him look like some kind of angry housewife. I honestly think I just pissed him off more by my lighthearted attempt to call him out on his language. I'd have told him to calm down, but telling an angry drag queen to calm down worked about as well as baptizing a cat. Typically, you ended up scratched and bleeding either way.

"I do not care, G-man. I happen to like that girl and right now she's in there a thousand times more scared than she should be not knowing what's going on."

"Relax, woman. I'll handle that part, good news is, we're more than likely going to get a real protective detail going after this. Now where's those flowers?"

He dropped his hands off his hips and moved his head in that attitude filled way that queens just had and snapped a perfect turn, halting, and sashaying up the linoleum floor like it was the runway at NYC's fashion week. He stopped at the nurse's station and snapped another perfect turn and held out a hand as if he were Vanna fucking White, and raised one eyebrow.

"Thank you."

"Don't mention it," he said and it dripped with condescension. He walked away and left me with the scattered roses and the switchblade tucked between the stems. Yep. Credible threat indeed... but curious. I waited for someone to come up and keep chain of custody intact, before I went in to see Chrissy.

When I went through her door she whipped her head in my direction and winced.

"Easy, you're cool. Everything's cool."

"I don't think it is." she declared and in the very next breath demanded, "What aren't you telling me?"

I sighed and dropped into the chair beside her bed and told her the truth, "There was a threat, while you were in ICU. We investigated but hit a dead end. With all the crazy surrounding your case, there wasn't enough to it to consider it a credible enough threat to warrant a protection detail, but the guys in my club and I agreed there was something to it. So we mapped out volunteer shifts and they've been here keeping an eye on you."

She didn't look happy with me, but at the same time looked grateful, which was a hell of a thing.

"To be honest with you, though. We probably could have saved ourselves some trouble, at least while that nurse of yours was on duty."

She scrunched down her lips and tried like hell to look disapproving or angry but couldn't at the mention of Pasquale.

"He made me promise not to say anything," she said finally. "He's apparently been enjoying the 'man-candy,' as he put it." I laughed and she smiled but it soon faded.

"Did you catch him?" she asked and my own smile melted away.

"No, but his attempt today gives us something to work with."

"Was one of you out there?" I asked, "When he showed up?"

I smiled then, "No. He was in here, with you."

She frowned and asked, "Damien Parnell is a member of your biker gang?"

"We prefer 'squad' not 'gang' and yeah, Yale is one of us."

She frowned, "Parnell went to Columbia."

"Long story, and how did you know that?"

"Courthouse gossip."

I looked her over and sighed and asked, "Look, legit, are you okay?"

She rolled her lips and nodded carefully. "I think so, I mean, I never saw his face, so I couldn't tell you if it was the same man who shot me or not..."

"That's okay. Much rather when you ID that guy that he's in custody and behind the glass. Preferably in a lineup."

"I won't argue with you there," she said and I smiled.

"Well that's a first."

"What is?"

"A lawyer who doesn't want to argue."

She smiled again and with each smile that I won out of her, became more relaxed.

"I'm glad Parnell was here, and I'm glad you're here now."

"Yeah?"

"Yeah."

Silence for a minute as we just looked at each other, but finally my curiosity got the better of me and I had to ask. "Where'd those come from?"

She looked at the pink roses in the vase by her sink and said, "Parnell brought them."

"Did he now?" I asked, and felt the vaguest stirring of jealousy.

"Yeah, one colleague to another, I guess."

"You lawyers are so fuckin' weird," I said with a laugh to take any sting out of the comment. "No offense."

She bowed her head and smiled some, "None taken. I guess you have to be one of us to get the whole adversarial friendship thing that we do."

"What's the popular word for it? Frenemy?"

She smiled and nodded again, "I guess that's a good word for it."

"I think you might be surprised at just how much I get that one."

"Yeah?"

"Yeah. My Captain and I sometimes have that kind of relationship. I'm his favorite pain in his ass."

She choked on a laugh and winced and I had to believe that her back and shoulder were hurting her some. Likely from being all tense and shit.

"Just take it easy. You're safe now," I said and she looked at me, and I mean really looked at me.

"I know, thank you."

"You bet," I told her, but the words were flippant and didn't carry half the meaning I wished I could convey. For now, though, they had to be good enough. Eyes were about to be back on us and I was pretty painfully aware that I was something like two inches from a rip for insubordination.

Worth it, though.

10

*C*hrissy...

The next day I was discharged from the hospital into the care of a rehabilitation facility. The one I was supposed to go to was here in the hospital complex, but after what had happened, the police agreed that some extra steps to ensure my safety were warranted. So, in short order, I was secretly loaded into an ambulance on a gurney, and taken to a different inpatient rehabilitation facility across the city and checked in under an assumed name.

The media went ape-shit.

Headlines like, 'Where Are They Hiding Christina Marie Franco?' and 'Lawyer Refuses to Speak' were splashed across the newspapers and carried over to the evening news. Word of the incident at the hospital had gotten out and it'd seemingly whipped the situation into yet another froth... as if things hadn't been bad enough already, I felt like a prisoner, even if my cage were a gilded one.

The facility they had moved me to was a nice one, and I spent the next week and a half learning how to reliably stand and walk on my own without any more assistance. That was a lot harder than it sounded. The bullet had gone in through low enough on my back that it could be considered my butt and had lodged in my pelvis, fracturing it badly. I'd been lucky, though. The doctors had told me a little bit higher; it would have destroyed my kidney. More to the left, it would have impacted my spine...

I didn't quite consider myself lucky at all, but I suppose any port in a storm, right? I mean, I had to try and find what silver lining I could in all of this mess. Whenever I thought about it like that, though, I could only come up with one... and he was walking up the hallway now, dressed in his casual attire of black leather and denim.

I watched him go to the front desk and speak to the receptionist, admiring how his black leather chaps framed his extremely nice ass in the jeans he had on. I felt a very definite pang of disappointment that he'd been too much of a gentleman at the time to take my up on my offer of some no-strings-attached fun. Then again, back then, I had been sort of glad for it. It'd meant he'd genuinely liked me and now... well, now who knew?

The receptionist pointed past Tony and I quickly looked down at my kindle so as not to get caught blatantly ogling his behind. I was sitting in the facility's atrium, soaking up some sunshine and making use of one of the park benches they had out here. When I felt his eyes on me through the long line of floor to ceiling windows, I looked up and smiled. He smiled back but it was Mary, the receptionist behind him that caught my eye. She was grinning just a little bit too hard at my expense. She'd seen what I'd been doing and when Tony turned his back on her to look at me, she gave me two thumbs up behind his back and moved them out and in my direction and back in, twice.

I felt myself begin to color but was saved, Tony turned around, presumably to thank her, but Mary's hands were folded on top of the desk, and she was giving him a wide-eyed and innocent look. I laughed and he, asked her for directions. She leaned forward and pointed down the hall and he headed further into the building to come around and access the door to outside.

Mary and I exchanged a look once he'd moved out of both of our sights and both burst out in a fit of giggles. It felt good; nice, normal, and light.

Tony found the door leading out here and trudged across the grass in my direction, but by then Mary and I had both regained our composure.

"Hi," I said, laying my kindle in my lap and he grinned at me, dropping onto the bench beside me.

"Why do I think that I've missed something here?" he asked, looking between me and Mary who was pointedly staring at her computer monitor, fingers clacking against the keys, and away from us.

"I have no idea what you're talking about," I said innocently and Tony laughed.

"You know for a lawyer, you're a bad liar Franco."

"So I've been told."

We each had a light laugh and he looked me over.

"You're looking good."

"Thank you, Pasquale came to visit me the other day and was nice enough to bring me some real clothes. I gave him the key to my apartment, but I think he had other ideas." I looked down at myself, I'd never owned an outfit like it, but he'd come back with two perfectly matched and fashionable jean and light sweater pairings with some fabulous boots in something like six shopping bags. Had dropped my keys into my hand and said, 'Let's go, paper princess, I am not about to dress you any other way.'

"Not your clothes?" Tony asked.

"I'm not even sure that he stopped at my place, to tell you the truth."

"Looks like he spent a small fortune on you. Stuff's nice."

"I thought so, too, but apparently he got them at a clothing swap the LGBTQ community here in the city puts on once a month."

"Nice, look at you, making friends wherever you go."

I nodded and smiled, and tried not to let what he said get to me. I missed Sami Lynn so much, but Tony hadn't meant anything by it, I knew that. It hurt that I couldn't see her family. The press were hounding them for information about me and David had called and said that his parents were going on a sort of vacation to get away from it. That I shouldn't take it personal and that there was no resentment and that they wished very much that they could be here for me. I understood, but it still hurt.

Tony searched my face which must have given it away because he said, "Sorry," and bowed his head. "My fuckin' mouth, sometimes it gets away from me."

"It's okay, I know you didn't mean anything by it."

"I didn't. I mean, I really didn't."

"It's okay," I said again. "Really, can we just change the subject?"

"Sure. So I hear you're gonna be busting out of here, soon."

"A week more," I said softly. "Then I get to go home and deal with outpatient care and physical therapy."

"The fun just doesn't stop, does it?" he asked and I sighed and put on a brave smile.

"Party all the time," I agreed.

He chuckled and leaned back and I shifted. It was hard to get comfortable, my arm still in its sling, trapping it close to my body. It didn't really come out of this position except for the occupational and physical therapy exercises designed to strengthen it, which of course, hurt like hell.

"What'd they say about it?" he asked, gesturing to the arm.

"I'll never regain full range of motion when it comes to the shoulder. It will always be stiff and ache with changes in the weather. It's got a super long way to go, and I'm going to need help with things like brushing my hair and showering for a while still. I'm doing better with getting dressed, but still need help there, too. It's a bitch doing *anything* one-handed."

He nodded and sighed, dropping his head and turning to look at me, searching my face before saying, "Yeah, but if anybody can come back from this stronger and better than ever, I have a feeling it's you."

I smiled, bolstered by his confidence and said, "Trying every day to make this thing my bitch. What about you? Any luck on that other case?" I wish I'd felt the same level of conviction the words held, but I didn't. I was hoping that a change of subject would spare me from having to talk about me and my situation anymore.

I hadn't seen much of Tony lately. He tried to visit regularly, but unlike the hospital, this place had set visiting hours and he wasn't always successful at making it inside the times they allowed. We'd seen each other maybe once a week, but traded phone calls and emails fairly regularly. At least until my phone had started blowing up with interview requests. I'd shut it off after telling the Hayworths and Tony to reach me by email if they wanted to talk. Tony had kept up with me the most, emailing once a day minimum, summing up how the day went. Usually the tone of those emails were polite and superficial, but if you read between the lines, the mutual friendship and comradery of both being cogs and wheels in the criminal justice machine were there.

It was comfortable, and I needed something, anything, that felt that way to cling to so I didn't lose my mind.

"We caught the girl. A sad case for sure, but we got her."

"Isn't every case a sad one when working homicide?" I asked.

"Not always. We don't get to pick the vic, but sometimes we can't feel especially sorry for them. Some of 'em are a real piece of work."

"Isn't it hard not to feel empathy for the killer in those cases, though?"

"Sometimes yeah, sometimes not so much. Depends on the situation."

"Okay, give me an example then."

He looked at the sky and I watched the reflection of the fluffy white clouds against the backdrop of his steel blue irises. It was a striking contrast and one I wished I could capture a picture of. Ah well, some things were better left a memory to cherish. Sitting here having a candid conversation, even if it was a bit macabre, was definitely one of those times I was locking away to replay later as I tried to fall asleep.

"Case I had two years ago, banger gets shot and killed by another banger, pretty common in the south end. Banger one, the victim in this case, was a real piece of work, rap sheet a mile long and was pretty much recruiting kids to run his drugs and guns. Considered himself a real Good Samaritan for it, too. He knew that a kid pinched with that much product or a firearm would be out in less than half the time and would be back to pushin' for him. Bragged that he was doing the neighborhood a favor, that he was helping these kids earn so that when they aged out and their juvie records were sealed they could have some kind of a future."

"A future of crime, maybe."

"Yeah, well you know that, and *I* know that, but it was a hell of a siren's call to these kids who grew up on government cheese sandwiches at school as their only meal a day for sometimes three and four days straight."

"Ugh…" I sighed. "So who killed him, and why?"

"One of the kids who'd grown up playing banger one's little game. Banger one was trying to recruit banger two's little brother. Banger two had gotten himself locked up at seventeen, thinking he was immune to consequences. Was put away on adult charges and as we both know, that shit doesn't disappear. Got stuck, couldn't find decent work; had a record hanging over his head the rest of his life. Didn't want the same for his kid brother."

"I can empathize with that, can't you?"

"Sure, so could the jury, he got out on a reduced sentence and I picked him up last month for killing his little brother. Little brother refused to give him money. Big brother thought the kid somehow owed him for big brother's mistakes."

"That's not exactly what we're talking about here, though. Is it?" I asked, and Tony lifted one leather clad shoulder in a shrug.

"At the end of the day, and this particular case, isn't it? I mean, the first time around people's sympathies and empathies were allowed to cloud their judgment, the man got a reduced sentence because the victim was a piece of shit and the perp had a violin to play."

I raised an eyebrow at his cynical world view but heard him out.

"Second time around, no sympathy, no violin, dude goes directly to jail, but at the same time, that doesn't bring his little brother back."

"The system failed after a fashion, I guess."

He studied my face, "How do you figure that?"

"Well, in order for the system to work correctly, you have to judge a case based on the *facts* presented. It's flawed in that people are inherently emotional creatures, and so divorcing ourselves from those emotions and thinking logically and critically isn't always our strongest suit. It's a flaw in the system, but one we can't always work around. One we have to live with, remain aware of, and work diligently not to let it get in the way of the truth."

"I don't disagree, beautiful." He heaved a big sigh and it was a sentiment I echoed.

"We win and lose every case, sometimes in unexpected ways," I murmured and thought about my own situation.

"Hey."

I looked over and met Tony's very serious and very penetrating gaze as he said, "None of this is your fault. You did your job. These people... hell, *people* nowadays seem to have no real concept of reality. They just don't know when or how to quit. Their actions are in no way any kind of reflection on who you are, or what you did."

I closed my eyes and nodded.

"You know, Miranda really was innocent. I don't get to say that about many of my clients, I know that, but Miranda? She was the real deal. She was genuinely afraid for her life when she did what she did. I have zero guilt or regrets that I won that case and she went free."

I was pointedly staring down along the grass and away from Tony, fixating on a bundle of yellow trout lily growing against a wall. Tony's hand on my knee, giving it a squeeze brought me back around to look at him.

"I kind of figured; I'm sorry you're taking the heat from this."

"Just one more service I offer," I said meekly at an attempt at humor and it worked, he smiled big and chuckled.

"You should have been a cop with a sense of humor like that."

I smiled too, "A little late for a career change, especially now," I said lifting my permanently injured arm out from my body slightly for emphasis. I knew what I could get away with, without hurting.

He nodded and took his hand off my stretch-denim clad knee and gripped the edge of the bench seat.

"Yeah, maybe so," he agreed and it was nice. We sat quietly in the atrium of the rehab facility for a time, neither one of us needing to say anything, just comfortable in each other's presence.

11

*T*ony...

Sitting at the bar in the Ten-Thirteen, a bottle of my favorite beer in front of me, Skids polishing a glass in across from me, and flanked by Yale and Backdraft. It wasn't a bad way to end the evening. It was a quiet Tuesday, the local news on the screen above the bar.

"Hey, turn that up?"

Skids turned around and looked, reaching up to hit the volume on the side of the TV we were all watching.

"The hashtag is trending, 'where's Tina?' The private defense attorney disappeared from Trinity General Hospital in the dead of night..." Backdraft scoffed and I was with him on that one, *"...and no one has seen her since!"*

"Did any of these assholes stop to consider that maybe she doesn't wanna be found?" Skids asked and set down the glass he'd been working behind the bar, picking up another one.

"I don't know, man. You'd think they'd just let it die already," I answered. I looked away from the main station in town and the shitty things people had to say in their nightly edition of 'Word on the Street' but my attention was mercilessly dragged back by Yale elbowing me in the ribs.

I looked up and splashed all over the screen were screen captures off of Facebook, some dude commenting 'This that lawyer ain't it?' with a picture of Chrissy and I sitting in the little garden in living color on the screen.

"Shit."

"Cover's blown, man. Go get her," Backdraft said and Yale was already on the phone.

The screen panned out and showed the fucking reporter standing in front of the care facility that Chrissy was in.

"We're here now, to finally get Ms. Franco's side of the story."

"Fuuuuuck!"

I booked it, pulling my own phone out of the inside pocket of my jacket, my Captain's number on speed dial. He picked up on the fourth ring.

"Yeah?"

"You watching channel nine?" I asked.

"Yep."

"I'm on my way in."

"Got any ideas where to put her that isn't on the city's dime?" he asked.

"Still working on that."

"Well take her home for now. Hopefully it'll be the last place anybody thinks to look. I can authorize the overtime for one of you to stay with her tonight. It'll give us a minute to figure out what else to do, see if she has someplace else to go."

"Copy that, Captain."

I hung up and sat astride the front of my bike. I put my phone away and cursed. I had to get a car out of the motor pool. Chrissy couldn't ride. I switched vehicles in the garage under my precinct and went for one of the unmarked cars with the darkest tint. The whole time going from the Ten-Thirteen to heading to the place she was at, it felt like the last sands were trickling out of some invisible hourglass. Like I was running out of time, the only thing was I didn't know what I was racing against when it came to the clock. I knew she was cool for a minute; that the reporters wouldn't be allowed inside, but still, by the time I got to the facility she was in, it was a total shit show. Uniforms were clashing with media at reception and Mary, the receptionist, was all but standing on her desk to get shit under control.

She made eye contact with me and I slipped past the crowd and headed for Chrissy's room, texting her and the guys. We had to be slick. There was too much of a crowd, too many witnesses with the media all wanting to get their soundbite that we had one thing going for us. Whoever was trying to finish what they'd started when it came to taking her out would have a lot of eyes on them.

Of course, this was presupposing they cared about getting caught or not. You never could tell with these whack-jobs. This could also provide a perfect opportunity for this guy to finish the job. Too many variables, too much shit in the air, and I wasn't the only one who'd broken off and slipped down the hall, either. I saw an orderly coming down the hall in my direction and he called out, "Hey! Hey you! What're you doing? You can't be down here!"

I flashed my badge, clipped to my belt at him and he gave me a chin lift and went right past me, stopping the reporter that'd trailed me down this way. I turned down Chrissy's hall and slipped into her room.

She jumped, startled, and cried, "Oh, god! You scared me."

"Sorry, you have your shit together?" She nodded and pointed to the twin sized hospital bed they had her in and I shook my head, grabbing the bags off of it, the tote I'd brought her and another fancier looking one, likely from Pasquale.

"Looks like you're going to be in your own bed tonight," I told her.

"Really?"

"Yeah, come on. You got anything you can cover up with? Like a jacket or coat?"

"Please don't tell me we have to run the gauntlet of reporters out there…"

My phone rang and I picked it up with an irritated, "Yeah?"

"Cavalry is on its way, Youngblood. Just hang tight."

"Jaime, what've you got, partner?"

"Head for the back entrance, the alley off 51st. Yale's on his way. I got uniforms with me to see about clearing out the problem children out front."

"K. I took a cruiser from the motor pool, have a uni come around back and get the keys."

"Got it, what a clusterfuck."

"Who you tellin'?"

Chrissy stood to the side, transferring her weight from one foot to the other looking downright shattered and like she was going to implode any second from the stress. I went to her and gently grasped her chin, tipping her face to look me in the eye. She looked, breath stilling completely. I could feel her body trembling finely, we were that much into each other's personal space, despite the only contact being my fingers gently gripping her chin.

"You're going to be fine. I've got you." I told her and let that sink in. Her lovely dark eyes widened and I let her go, she didn't move for a long series of heartbeats, her eyes locked with mine. I watched her regain her composure, her slightly parted lips pursing as she pulled it together.

I nodded once and she matched it with one of her own, and I shouldered her bags for her.

"What's the plan?" she asked.

"Back entrance," I held out my hand and she grasped it with her good one. "Stay behind me, keep an eye out behind us as best you can and let me know if we've got anyone coming up on us on our six o'clock. Can you do that?"

"I can do that," she said solemnly.

"I'll try not to go too fast."

"I'll tell you if I can't keep up."

"Atta girl."

I looked out into the hall ahead of us and found it all clear. I slipped out and went for the charting station. The same orderly who'd taken care of the reporter that'd tailed me looked up from behind the desk's wrap and asked, "What's up?"

"Back entrance, alley off 51st, where is it?"

"This way," he came around to lead us and I pulled Chrissy in front of me. She was limping, but making it work, moving along at a good clip. The dude stopped at a fire exit door, one of those 'open it and everyone's gonna know about it' types. He pulled a ring of keys off his belt and went through them to disable the alarm.

"Glad you've got a key," I said and he shook his head.

"Me too, I'm sorry this is happening to you Ms. Fenwick – er, Franco."

"Thanks, T.J. I appreciate it."

He twisted the key in the alarm at the top of the door and depressed the crash bar, I put Chrissy behind me and peeked out.

"All clear."

T.J. and I helped her take the step down and she tucked herself into my side, an SUV turned, pulling down the alley, Yale behind the wheel. I heard a shout at the mouth of the alley, off to one side and I ripped open the door to the back seat. Chrissy needed help, and cried out in pain when it came to getting her one foot high enough to step on the runner board of the cage. Yale reached behind the passenger seat and she took his hand with her good one and with a yelp of pain, hauled herself up into the back.

Shit, it had taxed her royally, she sat down and I shoved her bags onto the floorboard at her feet and swung the door shut. Reporters with cameras, boom mics, and lights were running up the alley and I hauled myself up to ride shotgun and slammed the door. Yale hit the locks and it was mics and hands beating on the side of the car with reporters screaming over one another demanding a statement from poor Chrissy.

"Drive," I said over the chorus of 'Ms. Franco! Ms. Franco!' and Yale put the beastly SUV into motion down the alley.

"You okay?" I demanded, twisting in my seat and Chrissy looked up at me, tears of pain streaming down her face, dripping onto her light gray sweater.

Fuck.

"I'm okay," she said brokenly and wiped at her face. She twisted carefully to look at the reporters back down at the end of the alley staring after the vehicle and brokenly asked, "Why is this happening to me?"

Yale and I exchanged a hard look. Neither one of us had an answer to that except the world was a shitty place full of some really shitty fucking people.

12

*C*hrissy...

I watched the city go by through the dark glass of the SUV's tinted window and felt tears slide down my face. I was one big ball of hurt, my injuries aching and overtaxed by the hustle to get out of there, but I would be lying if I said that was the only reason why I was crying.

Parnell and Tony were both silent in the front seat and their silence was a sober one. Traffic was awful at this hour and every time we stopped, I would turn my face from the glass, afraid someone might be able to see in, might point me out to the other people crowding the corner waiting to cross the street or stop the other people bustling back and forth on the sidewalk.

I was so absorbed with not being seen that I didn't even notice when we pulled up in front of my building. I flinched when Tony opened the back door and he murmured, "Easy, I've got you."

He helped me down carefully after hefting my bags and getting down

107

was far easier than getting up had been. Hitching the totes higher on his shoulder, he kept me in front of him, herding me quickly and efficiently inside, and I blinked, surprised that Parnell was already there, holding the door to the elevator open. We went up to the second floor and hustled to my front door. I pulled the keys out of my purse in the top of my bag while Tony grimaced saying, "Should have had you get those out. My bad."

I unlocked my door, we rushed inside and shut it tightly behind us, and I flipped on the light.

Total destruction.

"Son of a fucking bitch." His voice was somewhere between disbelief and incendiary rage, while I? I felt nothing but pure, unadulterated, defeat.

Fluff from my chair's ripped open cushions littered the room, my couch was just *gone*. Glass littered the floor, crunching under Tony's boots as he un-holstered his big black gun. He checked the bathroom, my bedroom, and all the closets and put it up, once he was satisfied we were alone. I simply stared.

Stupid bitch, was scrawled across my living room wall in black spray paint. Pictures of me were piled in a drift, some torn, others with my eyes burned out with a cigarette. I stood there, feeling hot, feeling cold, feeling empty and feeling so full that all I wanted to do was *scream* and I couldn't do anything... nothing at all. My whole life was just like this room was now. *Utterly destroyed.*

I listened to Tony talk on the phone, his voice a distant buzz in my ears as I surveyed the damage from my fixed point in the room. He ended his call, sticking the phone in his back pocket and I slowly raised my eyes to meet his.

"I have no place else to go..." I said, and the panic and the fear and the *'oh god, what am I going to do now?'* welled up from the center of my being like blood from a cut, spilling out my eyes in a hot rush. Tony's grim expression turned resigned and he shook his head.

"Never mind that now. You got a suitcase?"

"Hall closet," I murmured.

"Good, let's pack your shit."

We went into my bedroom which had a lot of my things ripped from hangars and piled on the floor. The strong smell of urine assaulted my nose and I went to find the things that were still hanging and left in my drawers. My bed had been shredded, the ticking from the mattress welling out of the open wounds and it was a decent visual representation of how I was feeling.

"Take anything that's important to you, anything that's sentimental," he ordered gently.

I handed him things and he carefully put them away. His phone buzzed and he checked the screen and said, "Stay here, I'll be right back."

He went out to the living room and let people into my home. I didn't care... I mean... it wasn't really my home anymore, was it? They'd taken everything from me. My best friend, my sense of safety, my home... just *everything*.

I didn't cry anymore. I didn't feel anything. I just numbly moved through the room and let Tony take the lead. Just gathered every little salvageable remaining bit of precious that I had. The photos I had left of me and my parents. The pictures of me and Sami. The jewelry they'd dropped when they'd been hastily stuffing their pockets. I gripped my mother's locket in my good fist. Somehow they'd dropped it. I pressed that fist to my mouth and tried so very hard not to let the dam break in front of all these people but in the end, it all came rushing up, the bottle I'd kept stuffing all my feelings into broke and I ended up shaking and crying and generally looking like a total mad woman.

But then he was there, shielding me from all of those eyes. Giving me a place to take shelter from the storm, even though the storm raged inside of me. I pressed my forehead to Tony's shoulder and just cried and cried, because what the hell else was I going to do?

ONE OF THE police officers pressed a cup of coffee into my good hand and I automatically took a sip, wincing at the bitterness. There was a crime scene unit dusting every available surface for prints while Tony, his partner, and their captain stood to the side.

They were talking about me, arguing, and I couldn't find it in me to really even care for the time being. I was perched carefully on the edge of my ruined living room chair and couldn't really say how long I'd been sitting here like this.

Tony came over and knelt in front of me and put his hands on my knees. He looked up at me, searching my face, eyes tracking back and forth, catching mine.

"You in there, Chrissy?" he asked, voice low and careful.

"I'm here," I said.

"We're gonna move you to a safe house, outside the city."

"Okay."

"You trust me?"

"Yeah, why?"

He smiled and it wasn't necessarily a pleasant one. More derisive than anything but I could tell it wasn't directed at me, more at himself and maybe the police's inability to *do* anything. He was frustrated, like me, but this was the system we lived with and it wasn't perfect. It never would be, but it was what we had, and despite all of this horror show, I still believed in it.

God, I must be delusional.

"Haven't been doing the best here," he admitted.

"You've done all you could within the confines of your protocols and the law... I get that."

"Okay," he nodded and looked thoughtful. "Okay, baby. Gimme just a few more minutes and we'll get the fuck out of here, okay?"

I nodded and his captain looked me over, calling out, "You're sure about this?"

I looked up at him and swallowed hard, nodding and asking, "Where else am I going to go?"

He took a deep breath and let it out and nodded, his hands on his hips and said, "Okay."

Tony shouldered my bags and let one of the uniforms take my suitcase and motioned for me to follow him out. The uniformed officer fell in behind me and we went for the elevator. Out on the street, it was full dark already, and Tony hustled me into the front seat of a waiting sedan. I got in and he closed the door, going around back and dropping my bags in the trunk. He lifted my suitcase back there and shut the trunk lid and he and the officer traded some words.

The officer disappeared back inside and Tony dropped into the driver's seat behind the wheel. He reached over and took the cup of coffee from my hand, and put it in the cup holder and then helped me to buckle up.

I said nothing as he took us out of the city. If anything, I felt as if a weight lifted from my shoulders. The further across the Bay Bridge we got, the better I started to feel. The rush of pavement beneath the sedan's tires lulling me until I fought to keep my chin off my chest. I was so tired, the crash after all that adrenaline something fierce. Exhaustion crept in and I fought to keep my eyes open, but it was a battle I was destined to lose.

"Chrissy. Chrissy, come on now, wake up for me."

I jolted, opening my eyes and drawing in a deep breath. We were stopped, and I sat up and stretched what little I could carefully in my seat. I looked up to Tony, standing outside the open door to the car. A house was behind him, the front door standing open, a golden rectangle of light spilling out onto the porch, stretching out beyond it onto the gravel walkway and grass.

"Where are we?"

"We're here, we're safe."

I unbuckled myself, reaching across with my right hand to hit the catch on the belt. Tony held down a hand and I put mine into his, letting him help me to my feet.

"Where's here?"

"My place," he said quietly and I blinked.

"Your place? As in your house?"

"Yep."

"I thought we were going to a safe house."

"Ain't no place safer," he said.

"Am I even allowed to be here?"

He chuckled, "You're an adult, the Captain couldn't get it cleared to take you to an ICPD run safe house because of the city's damn budget crisis, and I wasn't about to put you in some crappy hotel. It'll be fine. You'll have your own room here," he swung the car door shut and I jumped, "and the guys will cover for me. We all agree, this shit ain't right."

This was a *huge* personal risk for Tony, and he had to trust me immensely to do it but all he'd asked of me was to trust *him*.

I looked up at him and swallowed hard, choking up with tears again, but this time of gratitude and said, "Thank you."

"Let's get you inside, come on."

I let him lead me into his home and he closed the front door behind us. He tugged gently on my good hand and I drifted along behind him, up the staircase and down the hall. He touched a door and it swung open revealing a slightly outdated but clean bathroom.

"Bathroom for when you need it," he murmured and then led me past two more doors before nudging in a third, "and this'll be your room."

It was a neatly made up guest room. The bed a queen, my suitcase and bags neatly placed beside the dresser. A set of my pajamas had been neatly laid on the bed and he asked, "Need help, still?"

I did but... "Won't that get you in trouble?"

"Just you and me here, you sayin' you'd tell?"

"What? No!"

He chuckled, "Okay then."

I shivered and he asked, "What's wrong?"

"I..."

He waited me out and I took a deep breath and said without looking at him, "Self-conscious about the scars I guess."

"Won't look," he murmured, his blunt fingers already working gently at the straps on my sling. He took it gently from me and laid it aside and then asked, "Okay, how do we do this?"

"Um, I need to get my right arm out, and then the neck over my head and then down off my left. It's sort of easier getting in than out..."

He chuckled and it sounded a bit nervous, "I can see that." His fingertips grazed my skin here and there and I felt it grow heated, an ache starting that had nothing to do with my injuries and everything to do with it had just been too damn long...

He was as good as his word, fixing his gaze on what he was doing, not looking, making what should have been a more than slightly embarrassing process that much more bearable. Of course, I'd had weeks of strangers dressing and undressing me, so this should be simple, right?

Not so much. I was acutely aware that not only was this a man I was attracted to, but also a man I had kissed before. I swallowed and he pulled me closer into the circle of his arms, his eyes fixing on mine as he carefully followed the band of my bra around my back and unhooked it by feel.

He dragged it from my arms, carefully, fingertips barely ghosting along the skin of my arms, raising goosebumps on my flesh as he tossed it behind me on the bed. I took a step back, my good arm across my breasts as he unbuttoned my burgundy pajama top and eased my bad arm down into the sleeve.

The whole process of undressing then dressing me was beyond intimate, and by the time he'd finished easing the last button through its respective button hole, I was just ready to die from the want and desire I had to kiss him. I bit my lips together to keep myself in check and sat on the edge of the bed when he ordered me to.

He took off my boots, and I watched him. He was so careful of me, incredibly respectful and so, so gentle. He had me stand and peeled my jeans down my legs, letting me steady myself with my good hand on his shoulder while I balanced on my bad leg to pull my good one free. I stepped into the satin pajama bottom and he pulled them up for me.

"Tomorrow, you can go through your stuff and figure out what more you need."

"They left quite a bit unscathed, what I have should be fine."

"Me and some of the guys from the Knights will go over to your apartment and clean shit up. I'll see if I can scare up some boxes, but the clothes and shit might end up in trash bags. I'm sorry for that in advance."

"It's alright. I just want out of there now."

"Yeah. I can understand that."

He pulled together the things I'd been wearing and set them on top of my suitcase before he came back to me. He pulled back the blankets on the bed and asked, "Was I supposed to put you back in your sling?"

"No, I just need a pillow to put under this arm."

"Right, be right back."

He left the room and I tucked myself into the bed, he came back and I lifted the bad arm as best I could and he eased a pillow beneath it.

"That good?"

"Yeah."

"Okay, well, uh… Oh, shit, I forgot to ask. Are you allergic to cats?"

"No, why?"

"Uh, you might have a furry visitor at some point, Roscoe, my cat. All gray, short fur, real bruiser looking but a sweet disposition. That going to be okay?"

"Yeah, sure. Thanks for the heads up."

"No problem."

A long silence stretched between us while we just looked at one another. The tension was real, a palpable thing, and it was as if any second the whole world would shatter into a million pieces. He bent and reached up to the lamp which had been on when we'd come in and smiled down at me.

"Good night," he murmured.

"Good night," I whispered back, and he twisted the little black knob. With a click we were plunged into darkness, and I could no longer see his face, backlit as he was from the light out in the hall. He straightened and turned, leaving quietly and closing the door. I closed my eyes and let out a shuddering sigh.

He was something else...

13

*T*ony...

It was hard as hell for me to fall asleep knowing she was just down the hall and hurting like she was. I wanted to fix it, and I couldn't and that drove me next to insane. She was still racked out when I got up the next morning, and I let her sleep, standing in the doorway for a minute watching her chest rise and fall, her face slack and angelic but still tight with pain, a fine line developing between the sweeping arches of her brows.

I went down to make coffee, feed Roscoe, and to make some calls. First thing first, I needed to get her prescriptions that'd been left with the inpatient therapy facility called into the pharmacy closest to my house.

I sighed, because before I could even see to her comfort, I had to call my Captain. He picked up on the second ring, his own voice rough around the edges.

"Hello?"

"It's McCormick."

"Hey," he started and without any preamble went right into it, it was one of the things we liked about each other. "Robbery is running prints and shit out of her place. It's in their hands, that part of things. Still no leads on the murder of her friend, and still nothing on the dude making threats, but there hasn't been one in a minute. Not sure where to go from here."

"Robbery canvas her building?"

"They know how to do their job, Tony. Too bad I can't say the same for you. What the hell were you thinkin' having her gather stuff up and pack it up before robbery and CSU got the chance to do anything?"

"Yeah, sorry. Habit I guess, and the truth on that? Guess I let my heart overrule my head. These cocksuckers have already taken so much from her. Her whole life is down to one suitcase and a couple totes. Completely understand if you wanna give me a rip."

"You taking the day to get her squared away?" he asked, pointedly ignoring the notion of writing me up. I think the guilt at our inability and ineffectiveness up to this point was eating at him, too.

"How'd you guess that's what I was gonna ask?"

"Yeah, well, between you and me, this has got to be one of the biggest pain in the ass cases to ever hit our division."

I made a disgusted noise and agreed with a, "Who you tellin'?"

"Gotta love this social media shit," he griped. "Wish we could go back to the days where you got your news from the newspaper and not the internet."

"I don't think there's even a precedent for what we're seeing." I shook my head as I said it, realized he couldn't see it, and stopped.

"I don't think there is either, I mean, not to this extreme." We were both quiet for a minute and he said, "You've got the day to get her straight."

"Take it out of my vacation if you can?"

"Yeah, yeah, I could do that. Shit, you got more than enough of it."

"Thanks, Captain."

"You bet."

I had close to three hours in which I handled all other business before I looked up and saw her standing in her pajamas, hair tousled in the doorway leading from my kitchen and dining room to the staircase upstairs.

"Who was that?" she asked.

"Your physical therapist. They know to come here and given your circumstances, are willing to make house calls. Your insurance is in the know and still willing to cover. You're good to go."

She blinked and asked a bit incredulously, "You did all that for me?"

"Seems to me it's about time someone out here did something to make your life easier, not harder." She leaned her good shoulder against the doorjamb and I smiled and asked, "Need help with that?" indicating the sling dangling from her fingers. She nodded and I pushed off the stool at my kitchen counter.

I quietly helped her into the sling, carefully avoiding jostling her arm. She adjusted the strap across her chest with her good arm and I wound the one around her waist and threaded it through the metal loop for her. She said, "That's good," when I had it tight enough for her and I stepped back.

"I've got to run into the city and drop the cruiser back at the motor pool. I'll pick up my bike, come back down this way and get your prescriptions on the way. You going to be good for a couple three hours on your own?"

She smiled bravely and said, "As long as you give me the Wi-Fi password."

I grinned and said, "As long as *you* promise to stay off social media."

She sniffed and nodded, her eyes growing glassy and said, "Had to disable all of my accounts while I was still in the hospital. I went to log on and two minutes of it was more than enough for me."

I sighed and shook my head, "Me and my mouth again."

"No, it's fine, really... I know you're just looking out."

"Yeah."

"So, um, yeah."

"Help yourself to whatever's in the kitchen. I'll be back and with food. Coffee is made, there's creamer and shit in the fridge. Can you manage?"

"That's at least one thing I *can* do one-handed," she was smiling again and I nodded.

"Okay."

I slid past her and went upstairs. She'd tried to make the bed, but there was only so much she'd been able to do. I could respect the effort, though. I put her bags up on the bed and opened them for her so she could try and put some things away if she wanted to. I pulled open the dresser's drawers and found them mostly empty. The few odds and ends I dropped into one bottom drawer so they'd be ready for her.

A quick shower and shave, some clean clothes, and I was ready to go. I shrugged into my jacket and cut, and headed out the door after a brief exchange with Chrissy, giving her the Wi-Fi password and making sure she was set for now. Couldn't say I blamed her for not wanting to deal with getting dressed or doing anything today. She looked pretty tired, despite sleeping, and I had to wonder if it was a *good* sleep.

I felt a little lighter when I went out my front door and got in the unmarked. The tension between me and Chrissy was undeniable, as much as it was undefinable. Sexual? Some of it, but a lot of it had to do with the weight of the situation. Shit was dire, nothing was certain for her, in her present state she was wounded, homeless, with the world out to get her. Her future didn't look much brighter and her past was tainted with an appalling sadness. She was alone, cast adrift and everyone was hostile or, even though it wasn't necessarily true in the case of the department, on the surface it looked like everyone was apparently unwilling to help.

I was only one man, and couldn't reverse all of the ills in her life, but fuck if I didn't want to try. I was well aware I couldn't save everyone. I'd been a cop long enough to know that, but I wanted to do everything and then some to save her... because if anyone deserved saving, it was Christina Marie Franco. She was one of the good ones, I wholeheartedly believed that and knew it was the truth, even if none of these other assholes in this city could see it.

I got a text as soon as I pulled up to the booth leading into the precinct's underground garage. I used the key card to lift the gate so I could pull in and checked my phone. It was from my partner.

Finally, a fucking break. You should come in.

I didn't even bother responding, I just went upstairs.

"Holy shit, that's gotta be some kind of a record."

"Guess my ESP was working double-time," I cracked back. "What's up?"

"Neighbor across the hall dimed out some fuckin' teens in Chrissy's building. Apparently the Super has a bad habit of leaving the office unlocked and one of the kids jacked the key to her apartment. Guess one of 'em's a big baseball fan, convinced his buddies it'd be easy and fun times. They knew she wasn't home on account of the fucking vultures that've been this city's news reporters lately. They figured if they fucked some shit up, spray painted her walls, they'd get away with it on account of her address having been posted for everyone and their dog to see. Robbery put out a BOLO to all of the area pawn shops and sure as shit, they got one of 'em trying to pawn the jewelry she had listed with her insurance company."

I dropped into my chair at my desk saying, "Well fuck me sideways, it's about time we got some good news and some kind of break when it comes to this mess."

"Thought you'd like that." Jaime leaned back in his own chair his expression pretty pleased with himself, a grin on his face like the fuckin' cat that'd got the cream.

I raised an eyebrow. "You got something else?"

His face fell and he scowled, "Thought you might actually be happy with that... excuse the fuck out of me."

"Easy partner, I *am* happy about it..." I propped my boots on my desk.

"Let me guess, it's just bugging the shit out of you that we ain't got a shooter."

"Ah, yeah."

"Well, they all fuck up eventually."

I nodded, reclining in my seat and said, "Yeah, well, you got that right." It was just a question on if another body hit the floor, first. I sure as hell hoped not. One was enough.

"So what're you doing here anyways?" he asked, interrupting my dark thoughts.

"Dropping off the cruiser, picking up my bike. You seriously wanted me to come in just for that, though? A bunch of punk kids?"

My partner grinned and I dropped my boots to the floor and leaned in whispering harshly, "Man, *fuck you*. You *do* have something else."

Jaime started laughing at me and said, "Yup."

"Something about *our* case."

"Yup. I got good and bad, what do you want first?"

"You know I like my dessert first."

"Good, because the bad news kind of was a spoiler for the good. They caught our shooter."

"Really?"

"Ballistics just came back on the gun, he got pinched for a liquor store robbery while Chrissy was still in the hospital. CSU was backlogged on weapons testing and they just got around to it. They got as good as it gets for a match on the gun as being the same gun that put holes in our girls."

He tossed a manila file folder onto my desk and I picked it up, flipping it open. "In living color... fancy," I muttered and let my eyes rove the mugshot. The dude wore a dirty red hooded sweatshirt in the picture. Usually, we printed these things out, we kept them in black and white to conserve cost. I could see why my partner had sent it to the color picture, though. I flipped to the next page in the file, the police sketch that'd come from Chrissy's description.

"Damn. She pretty much nailed it."

"Just got to get her in here for a lineup. I already put a request into the jail to have his ass brought in."

"K, but there's more bad news," I said my brain catching up.

"Ah, figured that shit out, did you?" Jaime nodded.

"If our perp was in jail while Chrissy was in the hospital, then the threats, it's not the same guy, is it?"

"Well, our shooter was picked up on the..." he grabbed the file folder out of my hands and looked himself, "21st at around two-thousand hours."

I shook my head. That was after the flowers but before the deal with Yale. So, no, not the same guy. *What the fuck, Christ? When you gonna cut this girl a break? I thought.*

"The thing with Yale was a few days later, so it definitely looks like the shooter and the assclown making threats aren't the same guy."

"Of course not, that would make this shit easy."

"Right, let me know when you've got the guy here. I'll bring Chrissy in for a lineup and then we can see what shakes loose out of the guy."

"Think she'll pick him?" Jaime asked, worried.

I nudged open the file folder and separated the arrest sheet with the dude's mugshot and the artist's sketch from each other, putting them side by side.

"What do you think?"

Jaime sighed. I think I had more faith in our girl than he did when it came to making the ID, but then again, we'd seen it about a hundred times or more. Witnesses got in here for a lineup and the pressure of making a positive ID got to be too much. Next thing you know, they're second guessing themselves and they shake apart right then and there and we get no closer to catching the happy bastards.

"Yeah, well, here's to hoping. Go on and get out of here."

I nodded. I didn't want to be gone long, but we were all more than reasonably certain that nobody knew where we'd hidden her. I mean, it wasn't like house calls were a thing in this day and age, and it was so not even normal protocol for a detective to take a victim home with them like some sort of stray puppy.

I got the hell out of there and rode back across the bridge towards home, stopping at the grocery store and pharmacy on the way. I figured she was probably starving and it'd been a while since I cooked, so I figured why not? I liked to cook, mostly Italian shit, but I was pretty solid on the Irish front, too. It was just typically pointless cooking for one, so I didn't have much by the way of occasion to do it.

I half wondered what I would find when I got there and when I came through the front door I'd found her pretty much exactly as I'd left her, curled up on the end of my couch, her e-reader thing in her good hand, but the screen blank. She looked back at me when I came through the door leading out to the garage and I realized she'd been staring out the front window.

"Hey," I said.

"Hi," she echoed back.

"You doing alright?"

"Yeah, just... thinking."

"Got some news for you."

"Yeah?"

"Yeah, why don't you come on into the kitchen while I fix us something to eat?"

"Okay."

She got up and despite being winged as bad as she was, she managed to make it look graceful. She set her e-reader on the coffee table and padded barefoot into the kitchen behind me. I set the bags on the counter and she managed to get herself up onto one of the bar stools.

I went around and hung my jacket and cut off the back of one of the dining room chairs and pushed back the sleeves on the thermal I'd put on under my tee shirt.

"What's the news?" she asked and I met her solemn gaze and started with the big stuff.

"We caught your shooter."

"What? Are you serious?"

I filled her in on everything and she listened, her attention rapt, and said, "So I suppose a lineup is in order?"

"Yeah, no pressure."

She rolled her eyes and sighed, pinching the bridge of her nose as I unloaded the bags I'd brought in.

"I'll do fine," she said and stared out the gauzy curtains over the back slider out onto the deck. "It's not like I'll *ever* forget that face."

I set down the loaf of bread I'd just pulled out of the bag and leaned my hands on the countertop. "I believe you. Your sketch was spot on."

"So does this mean I'm safe?" she asked and I think my expression said it all because her shoulders dropped.

"Looks like the guy that shot you, and the guy that made a play for you at the hospital aren't the same dude, but to answer your question..." I came around the kitchen island and touched the side of her face. "You're with me, so yeah, you're safe. Nobody, aside from me, the Captain, and Jaime know where you are." Which wasn't *precisely* true. I mean, Yale and the rest of the guys knew, but that honestly wasn't here nor there.

I stood inside her space and just kind of chilled there, hoping it was reassuring and not overbearing. She looked up at me, her breath shallow and her eyes longing, and I understood that. I think what I was feeling was a perfect match to what she had going on inside, at least where we were concerned about each other.

"Kiss me..." she murmured suddenly, and I wasn't about to say no.

I lowered my lips to hers and kissed her carefully, moving slowly. Her lips parted beneath mine, inviting. I took the invitation, slipping my tongue past her lips, chest seizing, heart stuttering inside the cage of my ribs when she let out this low, sultry, desire filled moan that held that perfect edge of relief, that sound that said, *I've waited too long...*

I could have stood there and kissed her for ages, but all things, especially the good ones, must come to an end. Both of our stomachs putting out a loud and grumpy growl put the kibosh on moving things along further and I drew back with a chuckle, pressing a kiss to her forehead before letting her go.

She sat with her eyes closed for a moment, fingertips pressed to her lips as if committing every single last moment of the kiss we'd just shared to memory, like it would never happen again.

Even though it wasn't our first kiss ever, it felt like a first kiss. You know, like *the* first kiss, and I don't know... maybe it was. I knew I wanted more, and I also knew that she was on board with how she was staring across the counter at me now.

"Thank you," she murmured and I smiled crookedly.

"If you think that was any kind of hardship for me, you've got another thing coming..." I growled and she smiled.

"Thank you for that, too."

"You're welcome," I said realizing that I'd done something that even I couldn't fully understand. One of those mysteries of being a woman thing. I also knew that it wasn't a mystery I needed to solve. That whatever it was, it was okay and so I just let it be.

I had a lunch to cook anyhow.

14

*C*hrissy...

The second night in Tony's home was comfortable. He fixed us lunch, did the dishes and just generally wouldn't let me do anything to help saying there would be plenty of time for that when I was more healed. When I got through about half of that first meal, he produced an orange pill bottle out of his pocket and twisted off the top. He took out a single tablet and set it on the edge of my plate.

"Pain pill," he'd said. "I picked up your prescription."

I hated taking them, but I hurt and I needed it. I took it, finished my meal, and he told me to go back in the living room while he cleaned up. He joined me and his cat there and cuddled me on the couch, while I snuggled Roscoe, who was adorable and funny. Tony threw a blanket over the both of us before turning on the TV and I couldn't remember a time in recent memory where I'd been so relaxed. I drifted, falling asleep under the influence of the narcotic painkiller to the sounds of Roscoe purring, revving engines in a chase scene, and the ticking echo of Tony's heart where my head rested on his chest.

He let me, and it was nice. Warm and safe, and lord knows, I needed those things badly lately, finding them to be in short supply.

He'd gone into work the next day and my occupational and physical therapist had come in the afternoon. I'd worked hard, and it hurt, and I'd sweated unbearably. I'd managed to dress myself in workout appropriate clothing, but before either of us knew it, Tony was walking through the door.

"Good, you did good!" Penny, my physical therapist was all smiles, while me? I felt like I'd been through the wringer.

"I like the sound of that," Tony said, shutting the garage door. I stood trembling in the living room where Penny had shoved some things aside to make room for us to do what needed to be done.

"Shoot, I lost track of time. I don't have any time left to help you get a shower. I have to get back to the city, my next client..."

"Its fine, Penny. I'll manage," I said even though I wasn't sure how I would, given all of my hair, there was so much of it and nearly impossible with two hands, forget about one.

"I'll help you load up, save you some time," Tony offered and she smiled.

"That would be great, and I mean it, Chrissy, you did *really* well."

"Thank you," I murmured and blotted my chest with the towel sitting over my shoulders. My left one screamed at me and I stubbornly refused to take any pain medicine for it. Tomorrow was the big day for me, and since I had learned he had been caught, I refused any and all pain medicine save for that one after lunch, realizing a bit belatedly that narcotics in my system could taint the identification. I wanted to make absolutely certain any ID I made was free of any taint because *I* needed to know. I knew it was too late and pretty much a fruitless endeavor from a legal standpoint, however.

I'd done my homework, and to be completely rid of the pain medicine they had me on, I would have to wait four whole days for it not to show on any urinalysis. Believe me, I had asked if we could wait. Then again, were I the defendant's lawyer in this case, whether there were drugs in the eyewitness's system or not; I would have played both sides. Drugs present, the ID was tainted because the witness was impaired by their pain medication. Drugs not present? Well then a witness suffering my injuries was impaired by the pain they suffered. It was a no-win situation, and honestly, eye witnesses made false identifications all of the time, and I was scared that now, when it really mattered, more karma would come calling and I would do the same.

I was a nervous wreck on the inside, more nervous than I had ever been walking into a courtroom, and that was saying something. Still, I didn't show one iota of those nerves on the outside. I couldn't afford to. I'd been sure of myself the previous afternoon, but the more I thought about it, the more time dragged by, the more I started doubting and second-guessing myself. In short, I was a hot mess.

I hugged Penny goodbye which was a little lean in, and a light touch on my good shoulder from her, and Tony grabbed up some of her gear. She picked up her big round inflated rubber ball she'd had me sit on while we'd done the exercises for my arm and Tony followed her out the front door and out to her car. I went into the kitchen and got myself a glass of water from the tap.

Tony came back in from outside and I listened to the heavy tread of his boots cross the hardwood floor. He stopped in the kitchen and I felt his eyes on my back, belatedly realizing that the workout tank I was wearing only covered half of the ugly scars on my shoulder. I immediately pulled my hair out of my ponytail and let it cover, my face burning with... I don't know. I couldn't quite quantify the emotion but I guess if I had to, I would liken it to shame.

I heard Tony's jacket hit the back of the chair he usually hung it on, and those heavy footfalls come my way, his shadow looming over me at the sink. He started to move my hair aside and I turned, whirling on my sneaker and backed up against the counter.

"Don't... please?"

His blue eyes penetrated mine and he nodded carefully, leaning in none the less to kiss me. My eyes fluttered shut as his mouth moved carefully over mine. I kissed him back, and it was just as magical and as beautiful as the kiss the day before. I blindly set my glass aside on the counter and went to reach for him, but dammit, I'd misjudged and it slipped off the counter's edge and shattered on the floor.

The crash of breaking glass made me jump and cry out, and I stuffed my hand against my mouth and squeezed my eyes shut. Cringing from my memories.

"It's okay; it's totally okay..." he murmured soothingly, and smoothed some of my hair out of the way of my face so he could see me. "It's just water and just glass, I've got it... no big deal." He gently moved me the opposite direction of the mess around the kitchen island and said, "Go grab a stool, sit down."

I swallowed hard, on the verge of tears, my heart racing, pulse jumping painfully out of the side of my neck, chest crushed as I struggled to breathe normally, in through my nose hold for a few seconds, and out.

The first panic attack had happened in the hospital, Pasquale had recognized it instantly and had helped me through some exercises. I knew what they were now. *I am in control.* I told myself. Tony went about cleaning up, letting me have some space, and by the time he was done, I felt better. Still rattled, but better.

"You alright?" he asked, and I nodded.

I knew in the front of my mind that it didn't matter, that Tony was the last person who would judge, that any number of medical personnel had seen the scars, but for some irrational reason Tony was *different*. He wasn't someone I wanted to see the ugliness... He just... wasn't.

He came around to me and I twisted on my seat to face him, looking up at him and biting my bottom lip. He looked like he was going to give me a pep talk but the words died on his lips. He searched my face and stepped in close, between my knees and lowered his face to mine. I closed my eyes, and let him kiss me, kissing him back and sighing out with relief. I wanted so badly to feel something *good* and Tony's kiss was like heaven.

His hands smoothed over my hips and up to my ribs and he gathered the hem of my fitted work-out tank with his fingers, slipping his hand underneath and putting it against my skin. My desire for him shot through the roof at the same time my anxiety rose. I broke the kiss and pulled back and said breathlessly, "I can't... my scars."

He growled low and intense and said, "Baby, you're gonna be on your back; no way I'm even going to see your scars."

His words, even more than the intensity behind them, stole my breath. I found some, just enough to say, "Okay." I couldn't believe this; that he wanted me with how broken, and damaged, and well, *soggy* I'd been. I felt like my emotional state held the consistency of wet cardboard and I knew for a fact that that was totally unattractive, yet here we were, and here he was, arms around me, tongue tracing the seam of my lips, begging for access which I gave to him, and gratefully.

His hands went to the outsides of my thighs, rubbing my legs, up and down through the skin tight material. I toed off my sneakers and pressed myself to him, my left arm tucked into the side of my body, protecting it. My free hand was cradling the back of his head, thumb lying along the side of his face, the stubble of his five o'clock shadow rough against it.

He pulled my body tight to his and I could feel him, hot and hard, straining at the zipper of his jeans. I moaned into his mouth, wanting the barrier of clothing between us gone, but still off my game enough, unsure enough, that I didn't know how to ask for it.

He put his arms around me and I held tightly to him with my good arm, my bad one curving around his ribs as he lifted me and took me over to the dining room table. He kicked the chair at the end aside, hooking it with his boot and sweeping it out of the way and set my ass on the edge of the solid, polished wood rectangle.

"Lie back," he ordered and I did, carefully, trailing my fingertips down the front of my body, between my breasts, to rest my hand on my stomach. He watched the movement, his gaze full of heat and pulled at the back of his tee shirt, dragging it off his body, over the top of his head.

Oh god, the body that it revealed... fit and rippling with corded muscle, he looked like someone that belonged on the cover of a magazine in his jockeys. Not standing in front of me, hooking his fingertips into the waistband of my yoga pants and dragging them off my hips. I arched and winced at the pulling pain in my shoulder and lower back on the opposite side, but he had them down far enough that I didn't have to hold the awful posture for very long.

He went for me, curving his arms beneath my body and helping me into a sitting position. I dragged my good arm into the fitted tank top, and he lifted on it carefully, pulling it over my head and slipping my bad arm out of it. I was sitting nude on his dining room table and I couldn't find it in me to be the least bit sorry about it. I wanted this, I needed him, and with every heated rake of his gaze, I loved how I felt beautiful again. Desired. Desirable.

He ordered me to lie back again and I did, body clenching with want and need as his blunt fingers worked the leather tongue of his belt through the buckle. It gave with a little sigh and he cursed, unholstering his gun so it wouldn't fall, setting it on the table up near my head as he bent over my body to kiss the side of my neck and nibble at that sweet spot that made my toes curl. I touched him, ran the fingers of my good hand through his hair; caressed his body with the hand of my bad arm where I could reach him without pain.

He moaned, uttering a breathy, "Oh god, Chrissy," into the side of my neck, his breath warm, his body warmer, skin heated and near scorching against my own. I reveled in the heat and the closeness and found my body wet and ready when I reached between us to tease myself. He took his hands off me just long enough to push his pants and shorts off his hips, the thick length of him bobbing free and slapping him in the stomach. My eyes widened, the head of his cock was resting just below his belly button and he was far larger than I'd ever considered. The man was a dream come true.

He smiled and planted one of his palms flat against the wood next to my shoulder, leaning in, stroking the head of himself up and down my pussy, slapping my labia with it and it was incredibly hot. God, I wanted him and I moaned, whimpering out a breathy, "Please?"

He pressed himself at my opening and pushed inside me slowly, letting my body adjust; not rushing, even though I could tell by the strain and concentration on his face that it cost him dearly and that he hadn't wanted to be patient. He eased his entire length inside me and I arched slightly, moaning, clenching around him, wanting more of him. He bent over me and brushed my hair from my face, smoothing it aside gently, carefully, and I realized that our similarity in height did us one favor, it made it so missionary would put us face to face, incredibly intimate, however, he was slightly lower than that for now, his standing putting him slightly beyond being able to kiss me comfortably.

I couldn't complain, he felt so good, so real, *so alive,* and I needed all of those things just now.

"Please don't make me beg," I whimpered and he smiled, straightening.

"Wouldn't think of it, baby." He drew back and carefully surged forward, moving gently in and out of me, careful of me, and it was both beautiful and frustrating. I wanted more, I wanted deep penetration and a punishing rhythm, but he was right. What I *wanted* and what I *needed* were two different things.

He eased his way in and out of me, steel blue eyes never leaving mine, and was so careful, so gentle, that the roaring inferno of want and desire slowly burned down to embers until just a warm, comfortable glow was left behind. A torturously slow build was beginning between us. He was going to make me come, but on his own terms, in his own time, and all I needed to do was relax and enjoy the ride.

He bent over my body, mouth closing warm and soft over the stiff peak of one nipple, his hand closing warm and firm over my other breast and I let out a throaty moan. *God, yes, oh yes... just like that.*

I couldn't be sure if I spoke the words out loud or not, but it didn't matter. Nothing mattered but his body sheathed in mine, the warmth and the vitality of him pressed against me and surrounding me.

My breath came in deep, luxurious, waves, slow and even with every long, slow thrust of his body into mine and I couldn't ever remember a time a man had made so much of it about *me.* He hunched up to allow me to get my hand between us and growled against my breast, "Touch yourself for me, make it happen."

I pressed my fingers to my clit and rubbed in firm but gentle little circles and it was all I could do to contain myself. The feel of him inside me, on top of me, the warmth of his body, the tender mercies he bestowed upon my breasts... it wasn't long before I shattered over his tabletop much like the glass had shattered on his floor, only when *I* broke? He didn't just sweep me up and discard me. He swept me up, put me back together and made me a stronger whole through his care.

15

*T*ony...

I pulled out, staying in her as she came around my dick had me un-fucking done. Her body shuddered beneath mine as I joined her, coming in a hot spill over one shapely hip. Making a fucking mess, but I didn't care. What I cared about was the pleasure filled scream crawling its way up her throat, spilling between those so-kissable lips to hit the ceiling and drip down my walls.

It was beautiful, so wild it was insane, and I fucking adored that she would *let go* with me. That she would trust me, and let me take her there. That she would trust me to bring her back.

She lay panting on the polished wood of my dining room table, eyes unfocused and body trembling, shivering with fine little aftershocks. I pulled up my pants and tucked everything back in. I would have liked to join her in getting naked, but first things first – I had to get her cleaned up enough to get her upstairs and into a proper shower. I went around to the side of the table and moved another chair out of my way so I could bend down and kiss her.

My hand naturally found the silkiness of her hair, smoothing over it again and again, running my fingers through it keeping it back from her forehead. She slowly came back, focusing on me and I smiled.

"Hey, baby," I whispered.

"Hi…"

She tried to sit up and I stopped her with a quick but gentle, "Not yet, just relax. I'm gonna grab something and clean you up a bit then I'll help you up. You good?"

I knew the answer to the question by the semi-glazed look in her eyes and her languid movements. She nodded faintly, her eyes closing and I was loving that she was feeling good for a change. I had a feeling the pain would be creeping back in on her any minute, so any reprieve I could give her was a good thing.

I kissed her one more time and straightened up, going over to the paper towel rack and ripping some off. I turned on the tap at the sink and let it run warm, dampened some of the towels and went back to her, cleaning up the worst of the mess gently and taking the wad of towels back to the trash.

I helped her sit up carefully and had her wait a minute before trying to get down. She still seemed a bit shaky and that was okay, we weren't in any rush. No hurry at all, as far as I was concerned.

She gripped the edge of the table and bit down on her lower lip as she carefully slipped off the edge and back onto her feet. I stood beside her and helped her and her hair moved aside from the site of her injury in her upper back. I got a good view of her scars, both top and bottom and I have to tell you, I marveled at what modern medicine could do. They weren't that bad. Just slightly dimpled, pink and shiny depressions in her skin. The one on her shoulder blade honestly no bigger than her thumb and the one down low on her opposite hip, just above her ass? Well, it was no bigger than mine. I honestly didn't know what to expect, but it wasn't that. I mean, they were almost dainty for all the damage they'd caused her.

She made to turn and I stopped her and whispered, "They aren't that bad, precious. I mean it." I traced a fingertip around one and pressed my lips to it, then traced around the other before going to my knees and kissing it. "Not that big, not at all," I murmured.

She turned and I let her this time, putting her arms around my shoulders and looking down at me, tucking herself against me as I rested my chin on her stomach and looked up into her lovely dark eyes.

"You mean it?" she asked and I nodded.

"Seen much worse, precious."

I stood up and she drew back just enough to let me before immediately tucking herself back in against my body, curving her arms around my waist. She rested her lips against where my neck met my shoulder and I put my arms around her right back, holding her carefully. She sniffed and rested her forehead against my shoulder and I frowned.

"What's the matter?" I asked her and she sighed out.

"Nothing, I mean... just promise you won't be mad at me."

"*Mad* at you? Why would I be mad at you?" I tipped her chin so she would look at me and she did, a confused storm of emotion going on behind them.

"I should have said something... I haven't exactly been keeping up on my birth control with having been shot and hospitalized and all of that. Normally, I take the pill but..."

"Shit, yeah... say no more. I didn't even think either. It's cool. We'll do the morning after pill just to be sure. It'll be okay."

"Really?" she asked and I harrumphed.

"Takes two to tango, lover. It's your body, not mine. You get to say what you do with it. If that's what you want, I'd be a real asshole not to support your decision. My mamma didn't raise me like that."

"I thought you might be a good Irish boy," she said cuddling closer, voice relieved.

I smiled, "I *am* a good Irish boy, raised right by his momma and all; but I'm just a so-so Catholic. Had to give them something to be disappointed about, otherwise I'd be perfect."

She smiled and giggled a little saying, "I guess we can't have *that.*"

"What about you?"

"I'm a good Italian girl, not the best Roman Catholic, but also, I'm a defense attorney... so I guess I'm *really* not perfect."

I chuckled and said, "Nah, you're just overcompensating. I've heard that about you."

She scoffed and leaned back, mouth dropped open in a perfect 'o' of surprise, brown eyes wide and sparkling. She took one look at my face and the humor on it and stopped smiling like a doughnut and gave me the real deal.

"Oh my god, you jerk!" she cried, and slapped me in the chest lightly with her good hand.

I laughed and said, "Against advice of counsel, I'll plead guilty to that one."

She pushed out her lips in defiance and said, "Well, I don't know who your lawyer is, but after that, *I* would never represent you."

I laughed and said, "Oh, hang me out to dry, would you?"

Her expression toned down to one that was oh so serious and she looked me straight in the eye and said, "Never."

I believed her to my very core, and that kind of fierce loyalty out of her? Fuck. *That was hot.* I bowed my head and kissed her lips, holding her firmly but carefully to me. She returned the kiss, so serious, in a way that said she was willing to seal this deal and I loved that she wasn't afraid to commit. I mean, this was one of those times that you didn't need words. That even though our bodies did the talking, we knew without a single doubt, what the other was thinking and feeling.

When the kiss broke, we stood there between my kitchen and dining areas with our foreheads pressed together, just soaking each other in. It was one of the best moments, if not *the best* moment I had ever shared with a woman, or any other human being.

The cooler ambient temp of the room caught up with her before me, because she shivered lightly in my arms.

"Come on, I'll gladly help you with that shower you missed out on."

"I'd really like that," she murmured and I had to smile. It was a done deal.

I led her up the stairs and into the bathroom, twisting knobs and getting the tap going. When I deemed it warm enough, I pulled up on the thing sticking up out of the bathtub faucet and let the shower spray take over.

"If I help you in to get warm, you steady enough I can go grab towels and leave you for a sec?"

"Absolutely, I should be. I just can't really get this arm high enough for long enough to deal with my hair and my balance isn't strong enough with the leg and hip to bend over far enough to compensate."

"Man, you really gotta relearn how do to *everything* don't you?"

"Just about, I guess I should be grateful he shot me in my non-dominant hand. If he'd hit my dominant side, my occupational therapist said I would even have to relearn how to write or sign my own name."

"Jesus Christ." I couldn't even imagine that one.

I helped her into the bath and made sure she felt steady under the spray, she nodded, and I slid the curtain closed so that I could go grab a few things and finish taking off my clothes. I stepped across the hall into my bedroom and ditched the clothes first, throwing them in the laundry pile of 'needs to be washed' in the corner.

Back out in the hall, I grabbed some of the nice, big towels out of the linen closet before I stepped back into the bathroom. I flipped on the fan and called out "How you doing?" to let her know I was there before pulling back the curtain.

"Good," she said faintly, and her voice was a bit on the dreamy side. She stood under the spray, head tipped back, hair slicked tight to her head, water sluicing down her body in these rivulets that accentuated every plane, angle, and curve, magnifying her skin. The whole effect was alluring and damned if I wasn't starting to get a semi; a semi that wasn't going to stay a semi for long when I stepped into the tub and she turned those lovely dark eyes on me.

"Hi," she said, an edge of nervousness in her voice.

"Hey, precious." I picked up her good hand and brought it to my lips, pressing a kiss to the center of her palm, turning my head to do it, but not taking my eyes off her.

How could I take my eyes off her? She was one of those natural beauties that seemed physically impossible, except she wasn't and she was standing nude and perfect right in front of me, in my shower, and I couldn't tell you how much I loved that... even though I hated with every fiber of my being the *why* of it.

She stared at me, those dark eyes of hers so wide, those kissable lips slightly parted in awe and silent invitation. I couldn't say no to an invite as sweet as that, so I carefully stepped even further into her space, cradling her face gently between my hands while I kissed her. She held onto me. The hand on her bum arm resting on my hip, the other lying alongside my neck, thumb smoothing back and forth over my pulse that leapt for her.

She was everything to want in a woman. Beautiful, smart as a whip, and gave as good as she got. She'd been fierce before and if I had anything to say about it, would be again; she just needed a confidence boost. Someone to stand behind her and remind her that *she's got this*. I could do that for her. I wanted to do that for her. First, I needed to remind her just how much she was worth and I could start pretty simply by washing her hair.

There was something incredibly intimate about washing a woman's hair for her. I'd learned this through some of the trials and errors in the relationships that'd gone before, but this particular pro-tip I'd actually learned from Chrissy herself on our second date. We'd gotten into a discussion about how you could tell the person you were with was worth keeping around and she'd told me that for her it was by how intimate a man was willing to be with her. It'd been an offhand remark, but she'd said, 'It's the difference between a man handing you the bottle of shampoo while you're in the shower together and him taking the time to lather your hair for you.'

It'd stuck with me, all these years, and I'd realized that I'd been that asshole quite a few times in the past. Handing the girl the bottle rather than taking my time with her to do it right. For Chrissy, I wanted to take the time and do it right and honestly, not because she needed me to, but because I *wanted* to.

"All I've got, sorry..." I murmured before emptying a generous amount of my shampoo into my hand. She had a hell of a lot of hair compared to me, so I imagined I'd need a lot more soap... just saying.

Shit. I don't think I'd ever been so nervous to do such a simple task in my life. I mean, what if I didn't do it right? She took a deep breath and turned around giving me her back, her scars, her most vulnerable side and I slicked my hands through her hair, burying my fingers in the clinging strands and working the soap through it.

"Lean against me if you don't feel steady," I murmured and she did, as soon as I'd gathered up all her long, thick hair, she put her back against my chest, her good arm raised, hand curved around the back of my neck, her other arm hanging limp and straight to her side.

I had a perfect view over her shoulder of those perfect goddamn tits of hers and my cock was so not complaining. I wasn't trying to be about that right now, though. I was trying like hell to be what she both wanted and needed in a man because I wanted to believe that when the crisis was over, when it'd been averted, that she'd maybe stick around this time because I knew I wanted to.

If there was going to be a split between us this time, it wasn't going to be a mutual one. I didn't want her to go. I enjoyed our talks. I loved how easy things were with her. I really loved that she *got it*, even though she was technically batting for the other team, she knew what it was to be with a cop and around a bunch of other cops.

I was seriously regretting that we hadn't tried to make it work years earlier. I feel like I'd missed out on so much.

"Turn, careful now, tip your head back and rinse... that's it."

She clung to me, trusting I had her as she tipped her head back, eyes closed so that the warm water from the showerhead could slick through her long tresses and rinse the white lather away. I spent some time washing her body and then quickly did my own despite her protests that she would at least like to do *something* in kind.

I gave her a cheeky grin and told her, "If you wanna, I won't turn down a blowjob later."

She laughed, high and bright and nodded, and the mood wasn't so somber anymore, yet remained comfortably intimate. I pulled her close, kissed her gently and then twisted to turn off the tap. I got out of the tub first so that I could reach out and steady her. The bathmat one of those memory foam things, was one of the best buys I'd ever made for this house when my parents had turned it over to me.

They hadn't died, far from it, they'd retired down to Florida and my brothers, one older, two younger had all gone on to do great things. Well, greater than a cop's salary anyhow. I'd been an apartment dweller for a fair bit and when my parents had decided that the Maryland winters were too much and wanted to move to sunnier climates, they'd let me buy them out and take over payments on my childhood home. It was fuckin' huge for one person, but there wasn't much left owed on it and I could use the boost.

It was as if Chrissy'd read my mind. I wrapped her in a towel and she took a breath as if to ask me something but stopped before she voiced anything. I chuckled and said, "Go on; ask."

"It's rude," she said and I stopped rubbing her down through the towel and sighed.

"So was having our first time together be on my dining room table. I'd like to think we're at a stage with things that what might be considered rude by polite society's standards is just plain straight talk between two people who are comfortable enough with each other to do it on said dining room table."

She smiled and laughed a little and said, "You should have been a lawyer."

"Now *that's* rude," I said. "Now what were you gonna ask me?"

She scoffed and slapped me lightly on the shoulder and said, "What's wrong with being a lawyer!?"

"Nothing, precious, but that wasn't what you were gonna ask me."

"Oh my god! You're incorrigible!"

"I'm aware... now spill."

"I was going to ask... isn't this place a little big for just one person?"

I chuckled and said, "I was just thinking that", and launched into the explanation.

"You mean there's *four* of you? Your poor mother!"

I laughed, hard and loud and pulled her into my arms, kissing her soundly as she giggled against my mouth, too.

"No, baby. There's only one of me. My brothers are a handful all on their own."

"So I imagine."

I told her about my family, led her across the hall into my room and showed her some pictures. I helped her into one of my button down shirts. I know, I know, she had her own stuff here. Probably a few of those lacy, sexy nighties made it into the mix, too... but there was something about a beautiful woman in nothing but your shirt that... mm.

She sat on my bed, her long legs curled under her and stared at the framed photo of my family in my hands. It was an old one. Taken the day I'd graduated the police academy, but it was one of the few I had with all of us in it. I looked over her shoulder while I brushed her hair and told her stories about each of my brothers as she pointed them out. None of them particularly flattering, of course.

It was comfortable, it was nice, and I found I was seriously enjoying brushing her long hair. Mostly for how much it calmed her, her body relaxing. A tension she and I both didn't realize she held all the time just slipping away.

I could do this forever, but unfortunately, we both needed to eat and get some sleep. She was coming into the precinct, into the city with me, tomorrow. It was gonna be a big day for her. Still, when she started to talk, I let her.

"I miss my parents," she said softly. "My mom always knew what to do, you know? She would know just what to say to make things better."

"Yeah?"

"Yeah." She drew in a deep breath and set the photo of my family aside and said, "I don't know what she would say about all of this, though, and it makes me miss her even harder."

"Maybe it's not about what your mom would say this time," I said.

"I don't follow," she murmured.

"Maybe it's about what your dad would say," I suggested. I mean, it stood to reason. Typically, it was the man of the family who traditionally dealt with violent situations.

"He'd honestly probably tell me I never should have taken the case," she said with a bit of a bitter laugh.

"You really think so?"

"Yeah," she said and I could hear a hint of a smile in her voice. "He wouldn't mean it like that, though. My dad was sort of the absent-minded professor. He would say the most socially awkward things sometimes and it totally would be what he meant without actually being what he meant, you know what I mean?"

"What did your dad do?" I asked, I couldn't ever remember if she'd told me.

"Linguistics professor at the university. He was kind of a savant when it came to languages. Spoke seven, but his specialty was Italian. My mother was a housewife and pretty much needed to be to keep him in line or he'd disappear for days poring over old texts and translating them. He was kind of a nerd."

I chuckled, and put my arms around her, hugging her back into my chest and lightly resting my chin over her shoulder. I looked down at my big family, mom, dad, and all four boys and couldn't imagine life without my brothers in it. It must have been pretty lonely for her growing up like that.

"I can't imagine being an only child," I said finally, watching her fingertips caress over my image behind the glass.

"I wasn't, really. Sami was right next door. She moved there in the third grade and we might as well have been sisters."

"Yeah?"

"Mm-hmm. If my mom or her mom found one of our beds empty in the middle of the night, it wasn't anything, they knew where we were. My mom and her mom ended up best friends, too. It was nice. A little dicey through puberty," she laughed, "but we made it through."

"Sounds like one of those one in a million friendships."

"It was."

"You guys doing okay?"

She heaved a big sigh and said faintly, "I think so. I mean, it hurts, but Janine, Sami's mom, made it around to see me a couple of more times since the day of the funeral. David, her brother, too. I don't think Bob, her dad, can handle it. Sami was a daddy's girl. The press was hounding Bob and Janine so bad, they had to leave the city and get away for a while, otherwise I think they would have come around more."

She fell silent and I nodded, asking finally and in a total attempt to change the subject, "What would you like for dinner? I'm pretty good at the whole cooking thing, always liked doing it, but really got into it out of self-defense with my ex."

"Before or after our disastrous attempt at dating?" she asked, laughing.

"Before," I said honestly. "Hasn't really been anyone since you. Another stab at it, here or there, but nothing beyond a couple of weeks or a one-off fling that wasn't gonna go anywhere."

"I tried dating another lawyer," she said. "It was only for a minute and pretty much ended the same way we did except..."

"Except what?" I asked when she fell silent.

"Except without the regret."

I smiled and smoothed my fingers through her long hair, petting it almost, when I realized what I was doing and that it was kind of weird. It kind of tickled me pink that she'd regretted walking away, almost, if not more, than I had.

"Yeah, about the same for me too, you're the one that got away, Franco."

"You mean, *the one*?" she asked.

"Ah, yeah."

"Wow, didn't think I made that strong of an impression."

"Well, you did and you do." I slid off the bed from behind her and stood up, holding down my hand to her. "Come on, let me fix you something to eat, then we can hit the hay. You've got a big fuckin' day tomorrow."

She nodded tiredly and let me help her to her feet.

"That I do," she agreed but I could tell she was thinking. I could tell she was thinking hard. Truth be told? I was, too.

16

hrissy...

"Nervous?" Tony asked me the next morning.

"Yeah." I gave him a nod and he buttoned the last button on my blouse for me, Roscoe looking on from the bed. Tony rested his hands on my shoulders, barely touching the left one and made me look him in the eyes.

"Don't be nervous," he said and it was definitely an order. I laughed lightly. He sounded like because he said it, I simply wouldn't be and surprisingly it worked to some degree. As if his confidence in me was somehow transferable and he transferred some to me.

I smiled small and he asked, "What next?"

"Um, I typically tuck it into my skirt and zip that up, and I guess now we put my arm back in the sling."

He'd already helped me into my pantyhose, which I'd deemed absolutely necessary if only to hide how badly my legs were in need

150

of a waxing. He'd chuckled and asked why I didn't shave and I'd been honest, "Waxing lasts longer and the hair grows back finer."

"Interesting. Maybe we can get that taken care of today, too."

The plan wasn't exceptionally brilliant but necessary. He couldn't take the time off from work to drive me back to his place in the middle of the day and so he'd arranged for me to stay with people he deemed safe and who could look out for me after the lineup was concluded.

"Don't ask me to do your make up," he said when he'd gotten my skirt and shirt smoothed and centered.

"I think I can live without it this time."

"Good, 'cause you'd probably end up looking like a clown."

I laughed and he chuckled with me and I knew he was trying so hard to help hold me together. I slipped into a low set of kitten heel pumps and he helped me to strap into my sling. He'd pulled up half my hair into a pewter barrette that I'd liked that had vaguely Moroccan design origins. The cabochons on it made of hematite, a silvery black stone that sometimes was magnetic. It matched the iron gray satin blouse I wore tucked into a form-fitting black pencil skirt.

I looked professional, but when I turned to look in the mirror I felt like I also looked half done. Usually I had my makeup done and my hair was much more elaborate than simply half up. I looked in the mirror and the sling crossing my body and felt... less. I was somehow less than I'd been before and the man who'd made it that way, made me feel that way, I was about to be face to face with.

My heart did a somersault in my chest but I refused to let it plummet. Instead, I stood up straighter and asked Tony who was tucking a light blue button down shirt into a pair of lighter gray Dockers behind me, "How do I look?"

"You look good," he said, "why?"

"Feeling a little uncertain, I guess."

"Nope, not allowed." I tripped on a laugh at his deadpan delivery and he said, "Oh no, don't laugh, I'm dead serious, precious. You are," and he pulled me gently by the hips into the circle of his arms, "one seriously badass woman. You pretty much single-handedly defended one of the highest-profile cases in the history of Indigo City, and won. You survived internet trolls, two gunshots to the back, more than a few downright terrifying threats, the media, and living with me for three days straight without being up on murder charges of your own." I laughed, and Tony quirked a smile, "My point is, baby, *you've got this.*"

I pressed my lips together and nodded. I mean, he was right. The hardest part about this is maintaining professionalism and by that, I mean, keeping my hands to myself when I was sure to want to take shelter against Tony.

I let out a pent up breath and nodded saying, "You look good, too."

"Aw, thanks."

"Like you better in the leather and denim though."

He chuckled and said, "Me too, now let's get out of here."

He slipped on a pair of professional looking brown loafers and pulled down a blazer and I went out the door before him. Down in the dining room he retrieved his gun and holster and his badge off the table and threaded them onto his belt. He gave his jacket and cut a fond pat, and let out a gusty sigh laden with regret.

"I hate it when I have to get in the monkey suit almost as much as I hate getting back in the bag."

"Back in the bag?" I asked, unfamiliar with the terminology.

"Yeah, it's a cop thing, means back in uniform."

"Ah."

"After your lineup, I have just enough time to get you over to the Ten-Thirteen before I got to be in court."

"Joy."

"Yeah, that's about the size of it. Come on, coffee's on you."

I barked a bit of a laugh and he opened the door to the garage. I plucked my purse down from the coat tree and said, "Oh, shit. I forgot my phone…"

"On it." He ran upstairs for me and brought it down. Every time I looked at it, my heart sank a little more. Voicemail box full, but never any messages that I'd *want* to hear. Never anything personal. It was as if I didn't even exist to the firm anymore and I had just earned them *a lot* of money. I'd received my cut of that money and my bank account was still healthy, even after breaking my lease, so there was that. I'd canceled all my cable and things while I'd been in the hospital, so there'd been very little to do there. I just had to move everything out by the end of this month. Still had plenty of time, but still…

"You're going to be fine, I believe in you," he repeated, misreading my melancholy. I put on a brave front, forced a smile and nodded.

He held the door open to his two car garage and I stepped carefully down the steps, his truck was daunting, parked on the other side of his bike. It was a big Chevy, newer and clean. Didn't look like it'd been driven much, but with the motorcycle, I understood why.

He opened the passenger door for me and pulled a footstool over from the corner, he stood close to spot me and said, "Use your good hand, grab the 'oh shit' handle." I handed him my purse and took his advice, but still, it hurt like a mother getting myself up into the cab. I would be thrilled when I could take a pain pill again. I'd pretty much weaned myself down to two a day, and was pleased that I'd gone as long as I had without completely *needing* to take one. I worried that addiction was a possibility after my injuries, but so far, so good.

Tony handed me my purse and shut the door. He threw the low stool he'd brought out as a stepladder into the bed of the truck and rounded the hood to the driver's side. I swallowed hard, the anxiety over what I was about to do resurfacing. I think he knew, because he laced his fingers between mine and held my hand the entire drive into the city.

It was almost forty-five minutes and I realized that I'd missed the city, but the time away from it had been good. I felt myself tense when he turned into the core's traffic, and I took my hand back reflexively. He let me and said, "Probably a good idea," in a conceding tone of voice.

I gripped my hands together in my lap and took deep and even breaths. By the time he pulled into the garage at his precinct, I felt like I was a dead woman walking. It wasn't a good feeling.

Getting out of the truck was much easier than getting into it had been and Tony was again there to catch me or steady me. We were careful of being too familiar with one another, in fact, we'd talked about it at length over dinner. How it would be unseemly or could get him into trouble if he were perceived to be too close to a victim. I understood it. Anyone and everyone would jump on even a whiff of impropriety and I didn't want that for him. Things were already bad enough.

Nobody knew where I had disappeared to, no one knew where I had gone or when I'd be back or that I was even here. I kept telling myself that with every clack of my heel against the cement on the way to the elevator. When we got on, Tony selected the fourth floor and I swallowed hard.

"Easy, precious. You're not going to see him the second you step off the elevator. We're gonna get you to the room, rack 'em up on the other side of the glass and you're gonna knock him down. Then we're gonna wait until he's all the way back in holding before you even set foot outside of that room. That's how we do things."

"Thank you for telling me, I mean, it's nice to be prepared."

My palms were sweating and my nerves vibrant and alive. I was stiff and hot and while outwardly I appeared calm, my heartrate liked to pretend I was at a rave or something. I walked alongside Tony between twin rows of desks, officers at them filling out reports, through a doorway into a cubical farm. Tony took us right and gave a chin lift to a man in a fishbowl of an office.

The man said something in his phone hastily and set it down in its cradle. He came out of his office and said, "Ms. Franco, I'm Captain Rollins, welcome to the 12th." He reached out to shake my hand and I gave him mine and shook back firmly, hoping he would go easy. Handshakes were interesting anymore, you never really realized just how connected your back was to literally *everything,* until making even the smallest of movements just plain hurt. Handshakes were one of those things that had become a bane of my existence. I couldn't understand why shaking my right hand bothered my left shoulder so much.

"Youngblood, Ms. Franco," I heard behind us and I jumped slightly and turned, it was Jaime, Tony's partner.

"Sorry, I'm just nervous, I guess."

"No need to apologize, right this way, we'll get you settled and get this over with so you can go –"

He stopped himself and had the grace to look embarrassed.

"It's okay, really," I said quickly, before he could apologize for having been about to say 'home.'

An awkward silence descended on our little group until Tony cleared his throat, the Captain stood aside and held an arm out and said, "Right, um, Ms. Franco, if you'll come this way, we'll get you settled and get this done."

"Thank you, Captain Rollins." I stepped up beside him, taking the offered arm which was a sweet, if old fashioned gesture. Tony stayed at my back and Jaime fell into step beside me on my other side. They led me further back and into a hallway with another freight type elevator in it. The Captain opened the door into a small room with a window leading out into the hall. I stepped into the room, and realized that the hall *was* where the lineup took place, that the wall was painted with the stripes across and numbers on it, that would go over even the tallest man's head.

The Captain picked up a radio in a small docking station off a narrow entryway table pushed up against the window, and said, "Captain Rollin's to detainment, go ahead and bring up lot alpha, Charlie, one, three, zero, six."

A voice crackled over the radio, "Detainment to Captain Rollins, that's alpha, Charlie, one, three, zero, six, over?"

The Captain depressed the button on the side of the radio and said, "Confirmed."

He flipped a switch on the wall and the lights went out on this side of the glass, he flipped another, and bright, bright floodlights switched on, on the outside of the room, above the window pointed at the wall. Whoever was standing against it would be blinded. The door opened hurriedly and Parnell stepped in and he shut it firmly behind him.

"Sorry I'm late," he said.

"S'alright," Jaime said. "You're just in time for the main event."

"Doesn't the, ah, accused have a lawyer?" I asked.

"Public defender," Tony grunted.

"Oh."

The elevator door whooshed open from the left and a guard from the jail stepped off. He called out, "Single file, ladies! All the way down, stand under numbers six, five, four..." he called out each number as each man passed him and I swallowed hard. None of them were dressed the way he had been that night, no red hoodies, which I was glad for. I was almost afraid they would all be dressed that way. All of them were white men, with brown hair and light colored eyes but when number three stepped off the elevator, my heart nearly stopped.

"I see him," I blurted out and Mr. Parnell spoke up.

"Just wait for it," he said in a conciliatory tone of voice.

"You're sure?" Tony asked and he sounded a bit anxious himself.

The men all stood profile under their numbers and the jailer ordered them to face forward. They turned and I took an almost involuntary step back, fetching up against Tony, who put a hand on my shoulder lightly to steady me.

"They can't see me, right?" I asked and I knew it was a stupid question, they were all blinking and trying to shade their eyes from the blinding overhead lights, but they couldn't. Their hands were shackled to their waists and they couldn't bring them up high enough to make a difference.

"They can't see you," the Captain said and I shook my head.

"Right, I know that, I guess..."

Parnell interrupted me gently and asked the official question, "Ms. Franco, do you see the man who broke into your apartment and shot both yourself and Ms. Hayworth."

"Number three," I answered immediately. "Number three kicked down my front door and shot my best friend Samantha Lynn

Hayworth, and when I tried to run, he shot me in the back, twice." My heart was thundering in my chest, pulse leaping out of the side of my neck, and my hands shook. Yet my voice barely trembled. It was solid, it was steady, and I knew by the slight squeeze that Tony gave my shoulder that I had, indeed, correctly identified mine and Sami Lynn's assailant.

The Captain depressed the button on the side of the radio and said into it, "Take 'em back down to holding. Keep Alpha-Charlie-one-three-zero-six, on current charges, further charges pending."

"Copy that, Captain."

They led the men back onto the elevator and I heard the mechanisms whisk him away and I breathed out, a pent up sigh of relief. The captain switched out the blinding lights and switched on the muted lighting in here.

"Please tell me I correctly identified him, I just need to hear it," I said and Parnell smiled at me, the smile not an entirely friendly one.

"Oh, you got him," he said. "Best eyewitness ID I've ever had to work with."

"What happens now?" I asked.

"This is a capital murder charge I'm about to bring, even though Maryland did away with the death penalty. I have to convene a grand jury to indict still, though. You going to be up for testifying in front of that grand jury?"

"Absolutely," I said without hesitation. I mean, I knew what happened next, I was a lawyer, but it was like my lawyer brain had short-circuited or something and I just wasn't able to access it. I think these men knew that, though. I think they understood that I wasn't standing here as Christina Marie Franco, Attorney-at-Law. I think they knew better than I did that right now, I was just Chrissy Franco, gunshot victim who had watched her best friend since third grade murdered in cold blood right in front of her eyes.

I closed my eyes and felt tears track down my face and Jaime pressed a handkerchief into my good hand.

"Thank you," I murmured, following it up with, "I'm so sorry, usually I'm tougher than this," and it was true, usually I *was*. Still, this was something incredibly different. Usually when I was on this side of the glass, I was representing someone on the other side. Guilt swirled through my veins and it was an unexpected emotion given everything else I was feeling. I swallowed hard, and tuned in to what Parnell was saying.

"...I'll give you a lift to the courthouse, Youngblood."

"Need to swing by the Ten-Thirteen and drop Chrissy off, first."

"We'd better hurry, then. Court begins session in an hour."

"You ready?" he asked me and I nodded mutely.

I'd come this far, I was ready for anything...

<h1 style="text-align:center">17</h1>

*T*ony...

    She was silent the whole way over to the Ten-Thirteen. Yale parked us in the loading zone and said, "Make it quick, core traffic is going to be a bitch and we only have twenty minutes to get there."

I got out of the car and went around to the driver's side back door and opened it so she could get out on the sidewalk. Gotta love Old Town's one way streets. She stepped out carefully with very little help, Yale's old school Mercedes much easier to get in and out of than my truck. I walked with her to the door and opened it up for her. She went inside and I followed. Skids and Reflash both at the bar, Skids behind it, Reflash, too.

Golden and Angel, a pair of identical twins, twisted around on their stools. Golden was a cop, but Angel had legit earned his name. He was one of the city's medics and had earned his namesake thusly.

"There she is," Golden said cheerfully and I was safe and among just club and would take their ribbing later. Chrissy turned to say something to me and I covered her mouth with mine. She made a surprised noise and stiffened but relaxed into the kiss almost immediately. I pulled back and looked her right in the eyes.

"You did outstanding, precious."

She swallowed hard and nodded, saying, "You'd better go. I heard Judge Spunkmayer's name mentioned. She'll be pissed if you're late and things will go badly for you the rest of the day as a result."

I popped a quick kiss to her forehead and backed off. I shot a look over her shoulder to my brothers who all sat around looking a bit gobsmacked and said, "You guys take care of my girl."

"We've got you," Skids said, but didn't sound exactly happy about it. I wasn't either, not about the fact I considered Chrissy my girl, but about the fact I had to leave her side while she was here, in the city.

I left, got back in the car with Yale and we hit it. We lucked out and hit just about every green light on the way there, it was about the only luck we had, though. The defense was on their game when it came to the case I was testifying for. Another banger on banger scenario. One we thought had been airtight, but the slippery bastard, one from Chrissy's firm no less, managed to poke a big fucking hole in things. One that Jaime and I were gonna have to follow up on.

When I got back to the Ten-Thirteen, it was hopping, and that made me nervous. I caught Skids' eye behind the bar and he pointed up. I nodded and went back out front and to the glass door between the restaurant and bar and the boutique next door.

I used my key to get in and took the stairs two at a time up to the top. The door a few feet down the hall and to the left was Skids, I rapped on it, the universal secret decoder knock that was to announce to the guys on the other side an Indigo Knight was on this side of the door. Angel opened it up and gave me a chin lift.

"Hey, how is she? *Where* is she?"

"Laying down, man, she's okay. Relax."

I pushed past him into Skids' living room, Golden saying, "What's up, man?"

"She okay?"

"Yeah, yeah... she's in the guest room laying down. That shit really took it out of her this morning."

"Yeah, I was there, I know."

"Hey, no need to be a dick to *us* about it," Angel frowned.

"No, you're right, my bad." I sighed and pinched the bridge of my nose. I liked these two, a lot. Golden played on the ICPD's basketball team against his brother. Angel was on the medic and fire side of things. I sometimes wished Angel was a cop, these two on the same team would have wiped the floor with ICFD.

"What happened?" Golden asked.

"She feels like shit, shit went sideways in court, it's just been a red fucking letter day."

"Gotta look at the bright side," Angel said, dropping into a seat across from his brother.

"Yeah," Golden agreed. "Way I hear it, she rocked that ID."

I nodded and joined them at the table, pulling out a chair and dropping into it myself saying, "Yeah, yeah she did."

"So what has you so worried?" Angel asked, taking a drink out of his Mexi-Coke, so called because it was one of them glass bottle ones made with real sugar that was an import from the country. Just because the boys were Hispanic, didn't make Mexico their country of origin, however. They were born and bred American boys. Their grandad had been an immigrant, their daddy American born like them. Their mom, however, had immigrated, and had just two years ago landed her citizenship, just in fucking time, too, at least now with our orange overlord in office.

While Indigo City wasn't a sanctuary city, it'd been an unspoken rule of the department that status didn't matter. We didn't actively go arresting vics on their immigration status, at least not anymore. It's one of those things that'd gotten the department into trouble. Not because it wasn't the right thing to do, but because the unsolved crime rates in the poorer neighborhoods had skyrocketed right along with unreported crimes.

People had been too scared to come forward or were too scared to even call it in on fear that their illegal status would be uncovered and back to their country of origin they'd go.

The city was a fucking PR nightmare at this point when it came to community relations, and cops on the beat had finally wised up and had just stopped asking. It helped, but it wasn't perfect, and the rift just grew bigger with no solution in sight. At least, not for now.

Golden reached back into the fridge and used a bottle opener off his key chain to crack one of the Mexi-Cokes for me, pushing it across the table towards me.

"Looks like you need something stronger, though," he commented dryly and I picked it up, twirling the bottle between my hands to read the label all the way around.

"Got any Jack to put in it?" I asked, and Angel laughed.

"Downstairs."

"Nah, I gotta drive, anyways."

There was silence at the table for a long minute and finally Golden sighed, "She's really a tough chick," he said and I nodded.

"I know that."

"Thanks for the vote of confidence, you guys." Her voice startled all three of us. We turned as one to the hallway leading back into the rest of Skids' place and found Chrissy leaning against the wall, her good shoulder pressed to the green painted surface. No tellin' why Skids had picked an Army green to paint his walls, but he had and surprisingly, it kind of worked.

She was barefoot, her blouse slightly wrinkled, her hair foaming around her face where she'd let it loose from the clip in order to lie down comfortably. She was beautiful, even unkempt. In fact, maybe even more so because of it.

She pushed off the wall and came to me, hugging me to her one-armed, bending and kissing the top of my head. I put my arms around her and pressed my ear to the satin between her breasts, listening to the beat of her heart inside the delicate cage of her ribs. I didn't care about sharing this intimate moment in front of my club brothers. I don't think she did either. We'd spent the entire day apart and after so many tumultuous emotions both for her and for me, we needed this. A closeness, a contact that grounded and centered us both.

I was so going to take her home and make love to her tonight, but first...

"Feel like staying for dinner downstairs?"

"Sounds really good," she murmured softly.

"You boys joining us?" I asked.

"Yeah," they echoed in unison, and both of them were all smiles.

"Thanks for not making a thing out of this," Chrissy said softly and they both shook their head.

"That's your business," Golden said.

Angel, the easier going of the two, said, "You guys look pretty good together."

And they both left it at that.

I followed Chrissy back to the guest room where she'd left her things and took up her hair clip off the side table where it rested by her purse. She slipped into her low heels and I gathered up her hair into a loose ponytail. I didn't have a brush, or a comb to do anything else, but the clip was burly enough for a loose pony and so that's what I did. Just something enough to hold all that long, sable soft hair back from her beautiful face.

She turned and looked at me and we both just sort of gravitated into each other's arms, lips meeting as if by magnetic pull. We kissed and it was something real, with none of the stiffness or unease of anyone watching. We couldn't keep our hands off each other, but we were going to have to downstairs. There was public, and maybe cops from the 12th down there and you never could tell with people. Someone construes something as inappropriate, they'd dime you out... as much as it was anathema to a cop to dime another cop out, it happened and we didn't need her case turning into a shit show for yet another reason and they'd pull her case files out of my cold, dead hands...

"Gotta be on our best behavior downstairs," I murmured, giving her the heads up.

"Oh, right, cop bar."

I chuckled, "Yeah, and public. Should be alright, though. We'll grab some dinner and then grab a cab or an Uber back to the station to get my truck and I'll take you home."

She smiled and it wasn't entirely without mischief when she asked, mock-innocently, "Will we have to behave there, too?"

"Don't think so, but then again, Jesus might be watching so…"

She burst out in a light laugh and shook her head saying once more, "You're incorrigible."

"Yeah, and you love it."

"Starting to," she whispered, voice husky, and to that I only had one response and that was to kiss her again.

"Mm," she moaned against my mouth, a short, small thing but the sound traveled straight to my cock which perked up and definitely paid attention.

Down boy, I silently admonished and broke apart from her with some serious effort.

Dinner felt like it took forever, and even though the place had cleared out some, it was still plenty full. We tucked ourselves back into a corner booth, but still there were some lookie-loo's that were craning their necks and who followed us with their open staring as we walked through to take a seat. All of their eyes were on Chrissy.

I let her into the booth first, and slid in beside her, Angel and Golden sliding in across from us. It was a six person booth, all of them on this side were, but there was no tellin' if one of the other guys would show up or not to join us so it was always good to grab a spot with a little extra room.

Dinner conversation was pretty polite and bland, mostly trading a few war stories and pointedly avoiding the couple of elephants in the room. The big one being the threats on Chrissy and things being a bit dicey where her being out in public was concerned. The other, smaller one being what it could do to her case if it were found out that she and the lead detective were bumping uglies. That part was a hell of a lot easier to keep under wraps, though by making sure we were nothing but stiff, cordial, and polite with one another where there was a potential for a camera to catch us.

I made sure to keep my hands on the table where they could be seen, and Chrissy pretty much did the same. She wasn't a dope, it's part of why I liked her, and I figured if we were careful we'd get through this and out the other side and once the case was closed, go from there. Enough time passes by and it goes from 'oh my god, how could they' to 'oh my god, how sweet.'

I wasn't the first detective in history to get involved with a victim or witness, the trick was to not be caught out doing it during an active investigation and jammed up for it.

As always, the food out of Reflash's kitchen was top-notch, but the place was starting to get packed again with the dinner rush, and there were a few people I'd caught pointing cameras in our direction. I threw more than enough money down on the table to cover mine and Chrissy's tab and told Angel, "Make sure the wait staff gets the rest, man. We gotta bounce."

"Cabs out there?" Golden, who was sitting on the outside, looked back around the booth and out the front windows. I was already on my phone, pulling up the app to get an Uber enroute.

"Already on it," I said, and with a good ETA, too. Three minutes or less. I texted the driver to text us as soon as he pulled up in the loading zone out front and sat back.

"Everything okay?" Chrissy murmured and I detected a hint of nerves.

"Yeah, everything's good. It's just starting to pick up in here and that means it's time to go."

"Yeah, I was wondering about that..." she murmured and I smiled.

"Gonna be fine, precious, you'll see."

She nodded and forced a smile when she too caught a camera in her direction, although, it was kind of hard to miss. The chick snapping the photo used her fucking flash.

"Did I seriously just see a flash go off?" Golden demanded.

"Ah, yeah," I answered.

"Aw hell no. Where is he? Who did it?" he asked.

"The blonde chick at table seven, out on the floor," I answered and he twisted around and looked.

"The one in the hooker heels?" he asked, and Chrissy laughed a little, hiding it behind her hand.

"I'm sorry, that wasn't right laughing, it was terribly judgmental," she said and Angel smiled at her like she'd done something cute, which she had.

Golden got up and stretched saying, "Naw, fuck that. She went there first, takin' pictures and shit like you ain't got a right to privacy or to eat a fuckin' meal without everybody all up in your shit."

Chrissy's expression sobered and she nodded. I looked up at Golden and told him, "Stay inside the lines, brother."

Golden winked and said, "Check me out, this holster humper doesn't know what's gonna hit her in a minute."

Chrissy looked up at him aghast, and asked, "You'd honestly go there?"

He winked at her and said, "No way José, and that's *exactly* the point I'm gonna make."

Angel started laughing as Golden walked away with a certain amount of swagger in his step and it was all Chrissy could do not to explode with laughter herself. The blonde was looking our way, and I schooled my face into good cop face while Chrissy did a fucking admirable job of looking dubious.

The blonde's attention diverted to Golden who pulled a vacant chair from a nearby table and turned it around, straddling it and talking to the blonde and her friend at the two seater table they occupied. Angel shook his head.

"He can be such an asshole," he said.

"Yeah," I agreed. "But in this case, he's using the power for good."

"Oh, I hope it doesn't sting too much," Chrissy said and with a sigh added, "It looks like he's quite the charmer."

"That's Golden," Angel said with a nod. "He learned it from me."

We shared a bit of a laugh and my phone went off with a text from the Uber driver.

"Okay," I said standing. "That's us." I stood aside so Chrissy could get out of the booth and Angel gave us a little salute.

"Night, Youngblood, night Ms. Franco."

"Good night, Angel. Thank you for everything, and its Chrissy, if you please."

"Anytime, and okay."

I took her around and out the front door, giving our Golden boy and his new pet project a wide berth. I stepped out of the entryway and onto the street first, giving the Uber driver a nod and looking both ways up the sidewalk which was relatively clear. I opened up the back door to the car and waved Chrissy out. She kept her head down and hustled into the back seat and I closed the door, getting in up front myself.

"How you folks doing?" the driver asked and I took stock of the inside of the car. It was nice, clean, and the dash cam was a good personal safety touch for the guy. I approved with half the crazy shit that went on in this city.

"Doing good; how about yourself?" I asked.

"Doing fine."

He signaled and pulled out into traffic smoothly and we rode in silence a ways. He looked into the rearview and asked, "Hey, I know you, miss? You seem awfully familiar."

"Um, no, I don't think so," Chrissy murmured and he frowned and I knew he was trying to place where he'd seen her.

"Do us a favor, man." I said gently and he glanced my way. "Just leave it alone."

When we pulled up to the station it clicked and he said, "Oh, man, wait! You're that lawyer! The one who got shot. Man, I'm sorry what they did to you, Tina. That just ain't right."

She looked up suddenly, her expression darkening.

"What did you call me?" she asked.

"Sorry, uh, Tina... like the hashtag, you know? Hashtag where's Tina?"

"My name is Christina, not Tina, and thank you for the ride."

I got out quickly and she did too, before I could come around and get her door. I called out, "Thanks man," and went to the garage surface entrance, putting my badge up against the RFID reader so that my access card in the holder behind it could be read. The door buzzed, the red light on the pad switching to green and I dragged the door open. Chrissy rushed inside and I ducked in right behind her as the Uber driver looked on.

The door shut behind us and she let out a breath saying, "God, can't I go anywhere in this city without someone looking at me funny?"

I shook my head and said, "Come on, let's get you home."

"Yes, please; let's," she agreed.

I went to my truck and pulled the stool out of the back for her. She was so upset, but on the angry side, that she hauled herself up this time without so much as wincing. I threw the stool back in the bed with a clatter and shut her door, going around to my side.

The drive across the bay seemed to help. Her shoulders were losing some of the tension that rode them, her expression calming into one that was almost meditative as she looked out over the water.

We stopped in at the pharmacy, one, so she could get her morning after pill, and two, so I could grab some condoms until she could get an alternate form of birth control online and working for her.

Still, even with the stop, by the time we got back to my place, and I pulled into the garage, she was downright placid. She took a deep breath and let it out in a long sigh once the garage door had finished closing.

"Feel better?" I asked.

"I'll feel much better when we're upstairs and in bed."

I smiled, "Ain't gotta tell me twice."

I got out of the truck and went around to help her down, taking her hand gently and towing her up the stairs and to my room.

I took off my coat, hanging it in the closet and kicked off my shoes into the bottom of it. The belt came next, the gun going on the dresser in its holster, before I thought about it and changed my mind, setting it within reach of the bed on the nightstand.

Chrissy stilled, she'd laid her purse aside, and had unclipped her hair and was working her blouse out of the waistband of her skirt when I'd made the change.

"Just being overly cautious, don't worry about it."

She nodded and stepped out of her cute black pumps and I went to her, the sound of tearing Velcro loud in the room as I peeled the strips back from each other to get her sling off of her.

She lowered her injured arm carefully, wincing, and I asked her, "When was the last time you had a pain pill?"

"A while," she admitted, "but its fine for now."

I took her at her word on that, I mean, only she really knew her own body and what was going on with it, but it didn't sit well with me, and I worried. I turned her back to my front and drew her to me until we were pressed together, my fingers finding the top button of her blouse. I undid it, letting my fingers drift down from the next, to the next; to the next. I let the tips of my fingers trail against her silky skin between buttons, unfastening them carefully as I went, bumping over the lace and wire of her bra between her breasts her breath catching, her arms hanging limp to her sides as I supported her body with mine.

When I reached the last button and let the material fall away from my hands, I put my hands gently on her hips and took a half step back, dragging the shimmering material off her shoulders and down her arms, letting it fall to the floor. It landed with a hushed whisper on my bedroom's area rug and I let my hands drift up her back, pleased at the sweep of goosebumps following them. I rested them lightly on her shoulders and dug lightly with my thumbs in that sweet spot that always seemed to be tight on me.

Her breath spilled from her lips, carrying a groan of pleasure as I worked away the tightness in her muscles, easing the tension in her upper back and neck with careful, even pressure. The sounds she made causing my dick to rise to attention, I wanted so badly to turn her around and kiss her. To start working us the rest of the way out of our clothes and get us both into the bed that waited for us.

I kneaded between her shoulders, carefully along her spine and along the supple curve of her neck to either side until she was nearly asleep on her feet and as relaxed as I could get her. Only then did I take back my hands, and start in on my own shirt, quickly, before she could come back to herself.

18

$\mathcal{C}$**hrissy...**

I rolled my head on my neck and just stood there for a moment, basking in the Zen that Tony had created, wanting to give some back. I smiled to myself, knowing just the thing and turned around slowly.

"That was nice, thank you," I murmured, sinking down to sit on the edge of his bed. *Just perfect*, I thought to myself. He let his dress shirt join mine on the floor and hauled the white tee shirt he had on beneath it over his head in that way that guys did that just drove me crazy.

He smiled, a twinkle in those bright blue eyes of his when I crooked a finger at him, motioning for him to come closer while saying; "You're going to have to undo those pants for me."

"Yeah?"

"Mm-hm."

He reached for his pants, slipping the button free of its loop tortuously slow, and drawing the zipper down tooth by tiny tooth. I smiled up at him and had to laugh, biting my lower lip.

He slid the pants and his boxers down his hips and let them fall the rest of the way, smoothly stepping out of them and dragging each foot across the area carpet to rid himself of the socks. I laughed and asked him, "What, were you a stripper in a former life?"

"Ah, think I could have been?" he asked.

"Maybe," I murmured, taking his cock softly into my good hand, wrapping sure fingers around him and stroking up and down his length.

His eyes closed and he let out a moan, "Oh, that's nice..."

I leaned forward and he took a half step towards me and I kissed the tip, sliding him past my lips and along my tongue. I worked him in slowly. He was long, and I didn't want to choke, because how unsexy would that be?

I took him deeper with each stroke, teasing the underside of him with my tongue, compensating with my hand when I reached my limit and couldn't take any more of him. I was so careful with my teeth, and I sucked his cock until my jaw just *ached*, and then I sucked him some more. I was completely enamored with the soft sounds he made, the gasps, the little 'oh's' when I managed to do something he found particularly nice.

He clenched his fists at his sides for the most part, but finally touched my head. Sweeping my hair back so he could look down the length of his body and watch me.

He sucked in a breath between his teeth when I looked up at him and shook his head, drawing back and letting it out the rest of the way explosively.

"I need you," he said, the emotion naked and raw in his voice.

I stood up and went to him, our mouths crashing together in a frenzy of need as his hands scrambled to the zipper on the back of my skirt. I felt it rush down my legs and he got the panties and hose started down them, breaking his mouth from mine to order, "Sit."

I sat on the edge of the bed and he peeled the offending clothing down my legs and let them drop. He reached for the box of condoms he'd tossed on the dresser when we'd come in and ripped it open, tearing one off swiftly before raising it to his mouth and tearing it open with his teeth. He grabbed the slippery rubber disc and set it over the head of his cock, pinching the tip and rolling it all the way to his root.

I backed up carefully and centered myself on the bed and he climbed up to be with me, settling between my thighs, touching me gently with his fingers and finding me more than aroused, more than wet and ready for him.

He put his fingers in his mouth and sucked them and I felt myself take a sharp inhalation of breath. He smiled that reckless grin of his down at me and lined himself up with me, entering me much more quickly, thrusting with a little more force than he had the day before. Not out of any kind of roughness or inconsideration, but more from just a sheer need to be one with me.

How did I know? I could see it in his eyes, and when he bent over me to put his mouth against mine, I could taste it in his kiss.

He moved deliberately, carefully, with surety and control. He wanted me to feel good, he wanted to feel good and though I was usually a major full on participant during sex, my injuries made it hard to do what I wanted, and what I liked. Still, Tony appeared to understand that, too.

"Mm-mm, precious, not this time. You just lay back and enjoy the ride... let me do all the work," he murmured. I closed my eyes and relished the sound of his voice, loved the even strokes and the warmth of his body against and inside mine.

He pushed himself up on his knees and kept a slow and easy pace, his hands smoothing over my skin, taking his time, building himself, as well as me, up. Taking us high and higher until I was breathless with wanting, needing that little bit more.

I gasped and touched him wherever I could, tracing every contour I could reach with gentle fingertips. I met his eyes and he met mine and we both smiled, he slid his thumb between us at the top of my sex and teased me, bending to kiss me as I tightened up that much more inside, the weight and feel of him everything, just *everything*; the totality of existence. I clung to him when that existence exploded into light and feeling. Euphoria spilling through every nerve ending and vein in an effervescent rush, in wave after wave after wave.

He collapsed over me, burying his nose in my hair, pressing his lips against the side of my throat, gently teasing the sensitive place just near my ear and I shuddered again beneath him. Both of us were winded, neither of us willing to move, to separate ourselves from one another, and truthfully, I almost wished that we could stay like this forever.

Eventually the panting gave way to languorously slow and deep breaths, which led to him pushing up off of me just enough to look at me. He smoothed my hair back from my face and smiled down at me, letting his gaze travel my features even as I let mine travel his. His lips found mine and we kissed for a long time.

I felt him soften, and the longer we kissed, the more he began to grow hard again, but he stopped first. Reaching between us he held the condom on himself and pulled out. I shivered with how good it felt before immediately mourning the loss of him inside me.

I moaned and groaned and admittedly whined about it and he smiled and laughed, kissing down my chest and stomach before promising, "I'll be right back."

He got up and threw the used condom away, before grabbing the pile of them off the dresser and transferring them onto the night table. He came back to me then, pulling me against his body, kissing me as if he needed to, as if he were poisoned and I were the only cure.

"God I can't get enough of you," he whispered and I smiled against his lips.

"Put another one on," I whispered back and he pulled his head back and asked, "Yeah?"

"Mm, yeah. I want on top."

"You sure?" he asked, but he was already rolling one on.

"I want to try," I said, suddenly a bit more shy than I'd been the moment before and he nodded.

"You can do whatever you want with me, baby."

He got the condom on and laid back, putting his hands behind his head. I tucked my bad arm close to my side and got up on my knees, he brought his hands back to help me straddle him, and to help position himself, and I swear to god, I nearly came all over again just sliding down his length.

He bit his lower lip and looked me over shaking his head in that way that said that he didn't just like, he absolutely *loved* what he saw. I rolled my hips, lifting off him a touch and let gravity bring me back down. I wasn't going to be able to do this long, my hip already twinging, my lower back tightening to damn near cramping, but the position was so good and the way he smoothed his hands over my hips, up my body... oh god, I knew it was doing it for him, too.

Still, he stopped me, holding me down onto him, making eye contact and telling me in no uncertain terms, "Don't worry about me, you just take care of you. Do what feels good, baby. I'll get my own."

I nodded, and stopped trying to do such long and deep strokes, instead, grinding on him in the way that usually did all of the things for the woman, but not so much for the guy. Let me say this, *it did all of the things* for me.

I tipped my head way back, my hair tickling my lower back and likely the tops of his thighs and shoved being self-conscious and just *let go*.

Tony laughed and teased my nipples, taking joy in mine and I loved that he cared for me so much, that he was alright with my not being able to give as much as I was taking.

I was so close, so very close to coming and I wanted that last little push. This, right here, was probably the closest I had ever been to coming just by virtue of having a man inside me. The heavy weight of orgasm taking root, growing, filling me with that beautiful light that wasn't really a thing but felt like it was.

I bowed my head, and I knew it was as if I were listening to music only I could hear, but it was true to an extent. I listened to Tony's voice, low and sexy, encouraging me, telling me how beautiful I was. I listened and it touched me, taking me the rest of the way. I felt my body contract around him, then expand, and then I was falling. Tumbling over and over and over, cascading out of the sky like rain or falling stars, all without my body moving from where Tony now held me against his chest, his hands buried in my hair, holding it away from my face as he took over, thrusting up inside me.

He kept the orgasm rolling through me. As soon as one ended, another built and spilled overtaking its place until I was a quivering, sweating mess in his arms. Body twitching, boneless as he was as good as his word, taking his own pleasure from me. I let him love me into a blissed out coma and it was by far, the best sex, of my life.

19

*T*ony...

    I loved her hard. It was worth it, too, but I still worried. I left her panting, lying on her stomach in my bed. I was careful moving out from underneath her, and immediately went to her purse, looking through it for that familiar orange bottle. I found it, read the contents to make sure, and shook a round tablet onto my palm.

I went across the hall to the bathroom and drew some cold water from the tap and came back to her.

"Mm?"

"Pain pill, some water. Take them for me, please?"

She pushed herself up on her good arm and got her legs under her and once she was steady, held out her palm for the pill. I dropped it in, and she popped it into her mouth, taking the water with a face and swallowing the tablet down.

I winced in sympathy, those fucking things were nasty, always melting on contact. She drained the glass and I set it aside and joined her in the bed. She immediately cuddled against me, head on my shoulder; bum arm resting across me. No more need for a pillow when I would do. The thought made me chuckle and she asked in a dreamy, far off voice, "What's so funny?"

I told her and she giggled, and cuddled closer. I kind of adored her when she was like this. Girlish and giggling, sweet and relaxed.

"Thank you for this," she murmured sleepily.

"For what?" I asked.

"All of this. Taking care of me, taking me in, standing by me when no one else has... just all of it."

I gave her a squeeze and kissed the top of her head and asked, "You like this?"

She craned her neck way, way, back and looked at me and said, "What are you asking?"

"Just if you like this... being here, with me like this."

She swallowed hard, and my heart was thundering against the inside of my ribs. She searched my face, her own grown very serious and she said, "I really like this... being here with you. I don't think that 'like' is really a strong enough word for it."

"Oh yeah?"

"Yeah."

"What is a good word?" I asked. Hoping; wishing that she'd pick another one that started with 'l' and ended with 'e'.

She smiled and I could see the fear in her eyes. So much had changed in such a short amount of time for her. This was a change, a complication, I should have seen that before I'd started us down this path, this conversation... *too soon, too soon, too soon...*

"You don't have to answer that," I said, holding her close. "Not yet, not ever if you don't want."

"Tony, it's not like that... I'm just... it's just..."

"Complicated?" I supplied.

"No!" She cried, thought about it and closed her eyes and spilled her truth... "Scary. I mean, what if the novelty of it wears off? I'm going to be like this for months. I'm afraid. What if you get sick of me, what if it's not fun anymore after I'm well? What if –"

I kissed her to shut her up. I put my hand on the side of her face and dragged it up to look at me and slid right down and put my mouth on hers and kissed her. I wasn't polite about it, either. I shoved my tongue past her teeth and hauled her body tight to mine and poured every ounce of passion, respect, and desire I had for her into it. I couldn't tell her, I just had to go for broke and make her *see*.

When we broke the kiss, we were both panting. She stared at me, her large, dark eyes impossibly wide and stunned.

I said, "I like this. I like you, and I like having you here with me. No rush, baby. I want to follow through and stay the course and see what happens is all."

She stared at me and swallowed hard, tears brimming, collecting in her long dark lashes like stars. I eased my thumb along her cheek, smoothing it over her light, olive skin, and smiled. She was so goddamn beautiful.

"I... I want to do that, too," she said and I felt my insides turn liquid with relief.

Disaster averted.

"I don't want to do anything to screw this up, precious. As fucked up as this road has been, I feel like we've both been on it in kind. A partnership of sorts, and I like that. It's been real comfortable."

"It has," she agreed.

"Good. If it's ever not, I need you to tell me. Promise me?" She swallowed hard and nodded and I begged her, "Say it."

"I promise." She pulled herself carefully with her bad arm up so she could kiss me, I guess something on my face causing *her* to worry. I didn't want that. I didn't want that at all. We lay in the dim light of my bedside table and kissed like sunrise, or my having to go to work the next day wasn't a thing, and I was okay with that.

I was a homicide detective. I'd run on less sleep.

WE FELL into an easy routine while we waited on the gears of the criminal justice system to finish grinding along. The assclown that'd shot Chrissy had been, predictably, denied bond and that meant that the prosecutor's office was taking a few extra days to convene the grand jury.

Originally, the death penalty only applied to first degree capital murder cases, and if any case fucking qualified, it would be the Hayworth case, but, back in 2013; our esteemed governor O'Malley signed a bill abolishing the death penalty. I know, dick move, right? At any rate, we still needed to dot all our I's and cross all our T's if we were going to make shit happen and put both of these fuckwits away for life, where neither of them could pull this shit on anyone else.

So that's what we were working on doing. Putting them away forever, and by them, I meant both Kevin Cohan *and* our shooter, Michael Silver. I looked over my shoulder at Chrissy who was sitting at the dining room table, her laptop open, looking pinched and a bit drawn. Physical therapy had whooped her ass today, and it showed.

I was cooking dinner in the kitchen when she let out a pent up breath that sounded wholly frustrated.

"What's the matter?" I asked.

"It's nothing," she lied and closed her laptop lid.

"As a buddy of mine likes to say, 'you can't bullshit a bullshitter,' so spill, what's up?"

She smiled a bit wanly and her shoulders dropped, she turned to me and said, "I need to find a new job."

"What?" I demanded, squinting at her. "The firm being douchey about you still taking time off?"

She looked disturbed and scowled, shaking her head, "Not exactly," she said.

"So what brought this on?"

"I don't know, crisis of faith, maybe?" she said.

I came over, a plate in each hand and she pushed her laptop aside. I set one of the plates in front of her and mine in front of me and took a seat at the table at a right angle to her.

She picked up her fork off her plate and let out an explosive breath, stabbing irritably at her food. I leaned back and considered her and finally said, "I think it's less a crisis of faith and more you're starting to go more than a little stir crazy."

She looked at me apologetically and said, "Kind of hard not to when I feel like I'm on house arrest."

"I hear that, precious... I hear that."

She wasn't safe anywhere yet. It'd been nearly a week since she'd been in the city and pictures had cropped up on social media marked #IFoundTina like mushrooms after a fuckin' rain. She was a viral sensation all over again, except not a goddamn fucking one of them wanted to acknowledge that the virus was destroying her life.

The local news had interviewed our fucking Uber driver for Christ's sakes, and there was even a viral mix video set to music called the Where's Tina Bitch Mix of her coldly telling the Uber driver that her name wasn't Tina, it was Christina... of course the video clip stopped there and didn't show her thanking him for the ride.

Everyone thought it was fucking hilarious but her, and I and the guys... oh, and Pasquale. He went on an epic fucking rant about it in full drag at one of his shows. It'd been put up on YouTube and he'd reached out to let us know it was there. *That* had been pretty hilarious. Had made Chrissy smile, which wasn't as rare as all that. I made her smile, too, but this one had been an important one. A much needed one.

The worst part was, we knew the guy that'd been lobbing threats was still out there and that our time here was growing short. Social media was busting their ass trying to figure out who I was since I was in just about every photograph with her, and it was only a matter of time before it got out and the news vans made their way here. It was a good thing that my folks' names were still on the deed. I'd taken over payments but my credit was kind of shit so we hadn't fully transferred the deed just yet. We had every intention of doing it before they passed to avoid estate taxes and shit, but for now, we were safe.

Until the jig was up, Chrissy and me were living in a little bubble under my roof, and that was something we were both okay with. At least until the rabid horde of the internet chewed through that insulating barrier, too.

"I don't want to leave," she said, voice hollow and cold. She'd stopped eating her food and was looking at me now, and I realized pretty quick, she'd been thinking along the same lines I had been.

"You're not going to have to," I promised her and reached out, taking her hand that was resting on the table beside her plate. She was out of her sling, which she shouldn't be, but I couldn't blame her for that, either.

"Someone out there –"

"Hasn't threatened you in a minute, doesn't know where you are, and isn't going to find you." I said, raising an eyebrow. She was silent, and I could see how much she wanted to believe me, but she knew as well as I did, that shit didn't mean anything.

"That's not exactly true," she murmured and I frowned. She drew in a deep breath and blew it out, opening up her laptop and turning it around to face me.

It was an email from her boss. White lilies had been showing up at the firm with threatening messages, her boss wasn't pleased with it and the email consisted of a sternly worded message telling someone that all further deliveries should be denied.

"How many?" I asked her.

"I guess three... that I know of at least." She was hesitant and I couldn't quite gauge if she was being coy about the number, so I persisted.

"Why didn't you tell me sooner? Ah, ah, ah! Not a dig on you, baby, I'm just legit asking – not pissed. How many?"

"I told you, three. I stopped looking at my email before I even got to the rehab facility. I guess when I left the hospital and disappeared they started showing up at the firm. Once a week, like clockwork. Today was the first day I checked it, I mean, they have my phone number..." she trailed off and shifted uncomfortably.

"I'll look into it," I said to her and gave her hand a squeeze. She simply nodded, looking miserable.

"How about a movie tonight?" I asked a little while later.

"Romance?" she asked and then started laughing, probably because it looked like I was trying to swallow the bite I'd just taken sideways.

"If you want to watch a chick flick, I'll suck it up and do it, but only if I get another one of those *outstanding* blowjobs later."

She sobered and cocked her head to the side, "Outstanding? I've blown you twice now and haven't gotten you to come yet."

I smiled at her and shook my head, "I never come from foreplay like that."

"Really?"

"Not all guys come from a blowjob, my hand to god." I raised my hand as I swore on it.

"You're serious." She sounded incredulous.

"As a heart attack."

She'd started her period yesterday which was part of her shifting mood, but the other part was that she just needed a night out. There wasn't any place out there safer than the Ten-Thirteen so I thought about it, worked on hatching a plan and in the meantime, tried to distract her for just tonight. I had the next couple of days off and I was looking forward to spending them here, with her, and seeing what kind of trouble we could get into. Of course, and unfortunately, of the non-sexual variety.

She sighed again, looking at the screen and I reached over and closed the lid. She looked over at me and smiled wryly.

"Point well taken."

"Mm, how's the food?" I asked, trying to direct her back to it.

"It's good, it's good! Sorry, I guess I'm just not very hungry." Still, she made a more concentrated effort in finishing what was on her plate.

Dinner done, I got up to clear the table and went into the kitchen. I turned my back to rinse the plates at the sink and put them in the dishwasher when her arms carefully went around my waist. I jumped, the contact unexpected, but when she hugged herself tight to my back and trembled, I realized she was really at the end of her emotional rope with the shit raining down on her and the added hormones raging. I put my hands over hers and twisted in her grasp, pulling her tight against me and holding her.

"I'm sorry," her voice came, muffled against my shoulder.

"Don't be. You just keep doing what you're doing and be tough. Work on getting well, and when you can't be tough anymore, just let me handle things for a little while. It's okay. We've got this, precious. We've got this."

Her despair was palpable and I hated it, but there wasn't anything I could honestly do about it, at least not right now. About the only thing any of us could do was hurry up and wait. I was kind of pissed that her firm had sent a bunch of bullshit emails rather than calling us, the police, about the threats; but then I realized, what else hadn't they told her about?

Shit. I had the sinking fucking feeling that Jaime and I had missed something. That we'd missed something big, and we needed to go back to Chrissy's big firm and do some more digging.

20

*C*hrissy...

Tony was amazingly patient with me. After my little meltdown at dinner, he'd dried my tears, brought out some blankets and had made a nest for us on the couch. We'd surfed through the available movies on his cable, argued about it back and forth on what we would watch, and had ended up making out. He'd won by default after that.

We'd watched some more action movies, and not just any action movies, horrible 80's action movies starting with the classic oldie but goodie, Road House. Before we'd turned it on, he'd popped popcorn, and before the second movie, he dished me up some ice cream. The entire time, Roscoe slept in my lap, his little paws twitching as he chased mice in his little kitty dreams. I would stroke my fingers through his misty gray, sable soft fur and he would stretch, yawn, and look at me with his golden yellow eyes like *how dare you disturb my slumber, puny human,* before he would close them and go back to sleep.

Tony would just shake his head at the both of us saying, "Aw, boy... I think he's adopted you as one of his own."

I smiled back and said, "He is quickly becoming my little kitty overlord." Tony smiled and reached over, scratching behind Roscoe's ear.

"That is what they do."

It was a perfect evening in, just the three of us, but it still hadn't quite tamed my stir-crazy. Apparently Tony had a plan for that, though.

When I woke up the next morning, he was gone, Roscoe stretched out on Tony's side of the bed, purring. I hated when Tony did this. When he didn't wake me up when he got up. I got out of bed and carefully pulled on his robe, belting it around my waist, and went in search of him. Roscoe leaping down with a thud and trotting after me.

I found Tony downstairs in one of the spare rooms, lifting weights. I leaned against the door, and watched him, and it definitely did something to ease my boredom for just a minute, I mean a girl could only read so many mysteries and watch so many episodes of Lost Girl on Netflix before she went crazy.

Tony caught me watching him, looking back over his shoulder and saying, "Hey," while out of breath, and I smiled.

"Hey, yourself."

He stood up and turned around completely, wiping off his chest with a hand towel and I was *definitely* not bored for the moment. I was, however, thoroughly regretting that it was the march of the red menace, but I could not claim to be bored. He grinned with absolutely no shame at my abjectly checking him out, like I hadn't caught him doing it to me like a thousand times before.

I smiled to myself and laughed, feeling much better than I had the day before. Especially after those damn emails.

"So I was thinkin'."

"Uh oh."

"Funny. Seriously though, you need to get out of this house, and it might not be the most charming date ever, especially for a classy broad like you..." I scoffed and he winked at me, "but I was thinkin' about catching the fights at the Ten-Thirteen tonight and there ain't no safer place for you than in the middle of that many cops. What do you say? Watch the fight, play some darts, maybe have a drink or two?"

I twisted my lips, holding out, but it actually sounded *amazing*. He could tell, though, that he had me on the line. He grinned and said, "I'll be your designated driver."

"Sounds lovely."

"Alright! Now you're talking."

I laughed and it just slipped out when I shot back, "You know, I must really love you if I'm willing to do action movies one night and bars and fights the next."

I don't think I've ever seen a smile so big. He pulled me into him and I shrieked, laughing and tried to push away because let's face it, he was extremely sweaty and it was gross. I ceased all effort when his lips found mine.

He kissed me with such joy, such wild and enthusiastic abandon, I couldn't deny him and I really didn't want to.

"Take a shower with me, then I'll make us breakfast," he growled against my lips and I nodded.

We took a long, hot, and luxurious shower together. We dressed in jeans and he put on a tee, while I went with one of my nicer sweaters. Next week was going to be the week from hell. We had to move the rest of the crap out of my apartment. I knew there was still things there worth saving, and that a bunch of the guys he worked with would be there, but I still dreaded going back. So for now, I put it from my mind and helped him in the kitchen, slicing strawberries he'd bought to put on the pancakes he made along with some whipped cream.

"I'm gonna make a call," he said after breakfast and kissed me before going to the sink.

"Okay, would you like me to stay down here, while you take it upstairs?" I asked.

"If you wouldn't mind. Not trying to hide anything from you, I just don't want to ruin your good mood. It's about those threats that your firm's got. I wanted to fill Jaime in."

"No, it's fine! Thank you for telling me because you're right... I would have wondered."

"I kind of figured."

He went up, and I curled up on the couch with my kindle to read the latest Amber Eckart mystery. I was surprised to find it easier than I had expected to become engrossed in it. He came back down and asked, "You got any laundry you want to do? I'm about to do some of my own."

"Um, yeah."

We ended up being quite the domestic duo the rest of the day, leading up until it was time to leave that evening. My shoulder and back were beginning to hurt, seeing as I'd pushed them pretty far during clean up, and so I put it back in its sling so I wouldn't be tempted to use it.

Physical therapy hurt like hell, but I'd been doing well, they said, so I guess there was that. The progress felt agonizingly slow to me, but I figured that slow progress was better than no progress.

I was pleased that it wasn't as difficult to get into Tony's truck as it had been before, and I hadn't even taken a pain pill that day. I was hoping to avoid it so I could actually have a drink and relax a little tonight.

My nerves jangled as we crossed the bridge and I realized we would have to stay on our best behavior again, but still, it would be worth it. The closer to the city we drew, the more my nerves hummed and rattled and I realized belatedly that I was having a mild panic attack. My heart racing, my breath harder to draw. I swallowed hard and Tony took up my hand and gave it a reassuring squeeze.

I got a little angry then, and the anger helped to ground and center me. I refused to be scared. To have whoever it was run me out my city. The place where I was born, the place that I swore to be a part of the system to protect it... I'd gone to law school intent on becoming the best lawyer I could be with no designs on which side I would choose when I graduated. However, I had been involved on a case, aiding the Innocence Project with research and paralegal work as part of my work study requirement and my eyes had been opened to just how easily the system could be manipulated.

That, combined with the fact that the money in the private sector was better and my student loans were easily enough to drown in, convinced me that it was in my best interest to become a defense attorney. The payout from successfully defending Miranda Maguire had been enough to pay off almost half my student loan debt completely and have a decent savings left over. Living in my modest little apartment and working as hard as I had, well that had taken care of at least a quarter more of it, and I was now in the position of I didn't know what I was going to do.

I was feeling the dilemma and didn't want to give up my job at Reardon, Colfax & Price, and I didn't have to. I mean, I wasn't fired or anything. I was just on sabbatical until a time I felt fit enough to return to work but... *but did I want to?* I mean, honestly, all I'd done was defend a legitimately innocent woman and look what I'd gotten for my trouble. There wasn't any amount of money in the world worth the suffering, the loss...

I was glad that Miranda Maguire was far, far, away from here and safe. I wouldn't and couldn't fault her for leaving as soon as it was possible for her. I wanted to say I would too if I were her, but Tony... I couldn't deny my burgeoning feelings for the man, and I knew that those feelings were enough to make me stay, as crazy as that might sound.

The thought *love makes us do crazy things...* echoed in the back of my mind, and I don't think I could blame myself for that, either. Falling in love with him. *Being* in love with him. I just really hoped that he felt similar and I was honestly too afraid to ask.

The city traffic was typical for a Saturday night, and I stared out the window, watching people and cars go by. I felt a little better about being in Tony's truck. It sat higher than most of the cars and SUV's that we passed and gave the illusion that no one was looking at me, and to be honest, I don't think they were.

Tony pulled down the alley beside The Cormorant and parked his truck in a place that was clearly marked 'No Parking' and shut it off. I raised my eyebrows amused and asked, "Perks of the job?"

"A small one, yeah," he said, opening up his door. "I'm coming around to get you, hang tight for me."

I smiled to myself and sighed a happy sigh. It was nice having a man who was so gentlemanly. One who genuinely cared; I liked that. I also wanted to figure out how I could repay all of his kindness. I wanted to do for him what he did for me. I didn't want this to be one-sided, but rather a partnership, and I wasn't entirely sure how to do that. I would figure it out, though.

He opened up my door, and I handed him his leather vest that went over his coat. He always took it off before he got into a car and I wondered why. I just hadn't been brave enough to ask. He swung it on and stepped back, shielding me down the alleyway with his body as I hopped down. He stepped back enough so I could close the truck door and he chirped the alarm once it was shut. I followed him around to the door leading inside the bar and was acutely aware of how much I wanted to hold his hand but also, of how much I didn't dare.

Inside the bar was packed and noisy, but as soon as we walked through the door, someone yelled out, "Youngblood!"

We looked towards the back to see a bunch of guys waving us towards them and I started threading my way through the tables, self-conscious, but still holding my head high at the startled looks patrons were giving me as I passed by.

If this was what it felt like to be a celebrity, why then no thank you... I thought to myself. Angel hopped down off his stool and gave me a light hug. The guys had taken up two tall six top tables that were side by side with stools for seating. Three dart boards were on the wall, an area kept clear for people to throw in front of them and on the other side of the tables. Beyond the darts were two pool tables topped in a rich burgundy felt as opposed to the classic green. Racks of cues and chalk against the wall, three small tables on the other side of them that seated two each.

Past all of this was a switch backed wheelchair accessible ramp, leading up and back to the private room reserved for large parties. There were TV's along the ceilings above the dart boards and pool tables, and a big screen taking up the majority of the wall inside the glass fishbowl of a room. All of them turned to the same thing as the three above the bar... the sports channel dedicated to the UFC fights, the octagon mat already smeared here and there with blood, one of the lower end fights in progress leading up to the main event.

One of the guys patted a stool and said, "Hop up here, baby," and I looked back at Tony for an introduction.

"Blaze, Chrissy. Chrissy, Blaze."

"Nice to meet you," I said and shook his hand, relieved that it wasn't nearly as annoying as it had been, realizing that I was healing, which was good. He grinned, and it made him very handsome, as if his looks weren't striking enough. He had glossy black hair and fair skin, his eyes a silvery gray color I'd never encountered before.

He shook my hand and winked one of those remarkable eyes at me, asking around the sucker stick in his mouth, "Want some candy, little girl?"

I laughed and was slightly creeped out but didn't want to be impolite, but it was Golden to the rescue getting on Blaze's case saying, "Man, that's some fucked up shit! Why you gonna talk to her like that?"

"Oh shut the fuck up," he said back to Golden, producing one of the sweets out of his inside jacket pocket and holding it out to me. "I didn't mean anything by it." I took the sucker so he wouldn't be holding it out awkwardly forever and he grinned at me around the white stick hanging out of the side of his mouth and asked, "You know I didn't mean anything by it, right?"

"Um..." I couldn't come up with anything to say and Tony started laughing at his friend.

"Man, she just dimed your ass out, hell yeah you came across fuckin' creepy now sit down and order up some fuckin' food. Sober up some." He had come around the table and gripped Blaze by the shoulders, shaking him back and forth a little.

"Why on earth do you even *have* these?" I asked the drunk man, put at ease that the guys around him were willing to give him a hard time and put him in his place, and also being slightly forgiving about his drunken status. Guys thought they were so smooth when they were drunk but sometimes all they managed was painfully awkward, as was the case right now.

"Tryin' to quit smoking," he mumbled and did as Tony suggested, sat down and picked up a menu, hiding behind it and blushing kind of hard. I felt bad that *he* felt bad, but the best I could do was ignore it, much like I was ignoring the cellphones coming out and pointing in my direction, some subtly, some more blatantly.

God, it was like there was blood in the water and the sharks were circling at a table full of people off to our left. Heads were going together and they were blatantly talking about all of us, but then something unexpected happened.

A waiter appeared and dropped a check at their table. One of the guys perked up and said, "But we aren't done eating..."

I heard the waiter say to them, "My boss, the owner, says you are making other patrons uncomfortable. Please pay your check and leave."

"Man, fuck you and your boss!" another man, the one sitting in the middle, said loudly, drawing attention from two other nearby tables.

Golden and another member of Tony's club, Poe, by the name sewn onto his vest, exchanged a look and started over, digging their wallets out of their pockets as they went to the table.

"Problem over here?" Poe asked quietly, and the guy started getting mouthy. Both Poe and Golden exchanged a look and flipped open their wallets, likely showing the man their badges. Golden leaned on the table and exchanged a few words with the man who produced a credit card and wordlessly handed it over to the waiter.

"You want a box?" Poe asked and more words, too low to hear over the general chatter and televisions were exchanged.

Golden went to the bar and came back with a few of the Styrofoam clamshells and the girls at the table boxed up everyone's meals. The waiter returned and the man angrily signed off on the slip and didn't leave a tip, for which I felt bad for the waiter, I mean, it wasn't *his* fault.

We all sat and stood around our table waiting quietly for the five of them, two girls and three guys, to get up and put on their coats. A hush had sort of fallen over the rest of the bar as they went to file out and the guy raised his phone blatantly in my direction. I turned my face hiding behind my hair as the flash went off and I heard Golden grate out, "Come on; let's go, asswipe."

The five of them were escorted out of the restaurant, and it was as if the volume went back up, the atmosphere lightening some with their departure. After that there weren't any more blatant photos but there wasn't anything that could be done about the staring.

The bar was just starting to completely settle down when the red and blue lights pulled up to the curb out front. The conversation lulled again and people turned, but with the tables between us and the Cormorant's front windows, we couldn't really see what was going on.

"Golden says the guy just kept arguing and being a dick, so he and Poe called in the cavalry," Angel said, looking at his phone.

"Well, looks like someone's taking a ride and going up on 'disturbing the peace,'" Backdraft said, bringing a bottle of Killian's to his lips.

I opened my mouth to say something but the world erupted in chaos. Pops went off and the front window of the Cormorant shattered. I was knocked off my stool in a whirlwind of activity and shouting. People were screaming, all I could see was a kaleidoscope of colors as the ground rushed up to meet me, someone on top of me shoving me to the floor.

I screamed but not in fear, in pain, as whoever had swept me off my stool landed on me with their full weight. My shoulder was on fire, like a red hot poker had been jammed through my back and was lancing all the way through me and out of my chest. I closed my eyes and tried to push up but a voice in my ear cried "No, down! Stay down!"

I lifted my head and saw boots, running away, the front door of the bar crashed open, shouting, yelling, sirens kicking up in the near distance, no more than a block or two away. I shuddered under whoever held me down and cried, half in pain and half because *this was all my fault.*

"Easy, okay, I'm gonna let you up. Move slow, I need to check you out."

The weight lifted off of me and I pushed myself up, I wasn't thinking. Shaking and shocked, I tried to push myself up with both arms and my back, my left shoulder blade, *screamed.* I cried out and an arm crossed under me, pressing against my chest and eased me into a sitting position. Stools were yanked aside and my back was pressed against one of the solid steel supports of the table we'd been at.

Angel's face materialized out of the haze of pain and he started checking me over with expert hands, asking questions in rapid fire succession that my terrified and confused mind couldn't comprehend readily.

"Tony, where's Tony?" I demanded and Angel grabbed my face between his hands and made me look at him.

"He's *okay*, Chrissy. Sounds like everyone is okay. He went out front, took off after the shooter. It's what they do. It's what just about *all of them* are trained to do."

"Right, except us," Blaze said but he was on one knee a ways away, talking over his shoulder, his back to us. I startled and realized that another man Tony had told me about before, Backdraft, was in the same position on the other side and Parnell, I mean Yale, was right in front of us. All of them had themselves held at the ready, but for what, I didn't know.

I tried to get up. I didn't want anyone else hurt on my account, but Angel pressed on my shoulders insistently and my left one ground out in aching agony. I dropped back down onto my butt in the midst of spilled beer and Angel admonished, "Stay down!"

I stared helplessly at the alternating red and blue lights flashing against the ceiling and felt tears leak hot down my face and sent up a silent plea, *Please don't let anyone else get hurt...*

21

*T*ony...

"How is she?" I demanded harshly and then bit the inside of my cheek. I didn't need to be a fucking ass to Angel, of all people.

"I think she's okay, a little shocky, definitely triggered, but okay. I'm worried about that shoulder, though. It'd be nice to get an x-ray just to be on the safe side, but I think I may have hurt it sweeping her down to the ground like that. I didn't mean to land on her so hard but..."

"It's cool, you protected her, that's all I can ask."

I looked up the alley beside the Ten-Thirteen at the back of the ambulance. Chrissy was sitting on the back deck wrapped in one of those rough blankets, her arm in a blood pressure cuff as the medic on scene took her pressure for like the millionth time.

Her wide, dark eyes were fixed on me and I ached to go to her and comfort her, but I wasn't finished giving my statement.

We had nothing solid, but the drive by had come just minutes after the douchebag had posted Chrissy's picture to social media. Like everything else that'd happened to her, we couldn't be sure if this was connected or not to the regular threats, but I had a gut feeling it was.

"I'll take her to Trinity Gen myself as soon as we're done here," I told Angel and he nodded. I looked him over and said, "And thanks, man."

"That part was nothing. We got you, brother."

We pulled each other in for a hug, the investigators in charge of this case came over, and I gave my full statement. When I managed to look back down the alley again, the passenger door to my truck was open and Skids was standing at it, Chrissy's jeans clad legs dangling out of the open door.

I went up to hear what was being talked about and heard Skids say, "Don't you worry about none of that. Windows can be replaced, people can't. I'm just glad nobody got hurt, most of all you."

"Thank you," she murmured, but her voice was dull with none of its usual sparkle. I put a hand on Skids' shoulder and he stepped aside and let me through.

"Take her home, Youngblood, Reflash and I are gonna board up these windows; rein in some of the guys to help."

"Let me know if there's anything we can do," I said.

Chrissy echoed the sentiment softly with, "I'll gladly pay for the windows... I mean, this *is* my fault."

Skids and I snorted in unison. "The hell it is," the retired cop grated. "Business has been booming, sweetheart, it's not the end all of be all's, plus, that's what insurance is for."

"Thanks, Skids."

"No problem, Youngblood, now get you gone before the horde down there makes it down *here.*"

I looked back at where Skids jutted his chin at the teeming media on the other side of the yellow tape.

"Aw, fuck. Tuck your legs in, precious; we've gotta roll."

She did what I asked quickly and I shut the door, just as camera flashes started to go off in our direction. We went to Trinity Gen first, got her looked at and some x-rays taken. Everything checked out okay and they gave her some pain meds. She was out of it the whole way across the bridge and I practically had to carry her upstairs to bed.

She was sitting glassy eyed on the edge of my bed staring at me as I took off her boots when she said out of nowhere, "I'm so sorry..." before she finally really broke down and started sobbing.

She'd held it together so well, at the Ten-Thirteen, in the truck on the way to the hospital, all through being looked at while at Trinity Gen. Even all the way home, she'd been rock solid, and to tell you the truth, it'd worried me. Except now, now that she was breaking, all I worried about was whether or not I'd be able to put her back together this time.

"Why is this *happening?*" she asked, her voice mournful and heartrending, her breath warm against my shoulder.

"I don't know, precious, I honestly don't know..."

"I don't understand, what did I *do,* Tony?"

"Nothing, baby, you didn't do anything..."

I held her while she cried it out and wracked my brain on how to fucking *fix* this, and all I could come up with was one solution. A single goddamn solution and I didn't like it one fucking bit.
I lay awake, Chrissy cuddled close into my side, head on my chest, knocked the fuck out. Between the pain medications they'd doped

her up on at Trinity Gen combined with just her sheer emotional exhaustion over the whole fucking mess, I wasn't surprised. I wished I could join her, but I couldn't. Not knowing that it wasn't going to stop. None of it. I think she knew it too, and I didn't want to lose her. I didn't want to have to choose between the city I loved and the woman I was pretty fucking sure I wanted to spend the rest of my life with.

I wasn't going to, either. Instead, I was working on a plan. One that involved several key players. Key players I texted from my phone while Chrissy breathed heavy, deep, and even against my chest, Roscoe curled up and racked out with her on her hip. Pretty sure he knew her pain. Was also pretty sure, in his little kitty brain, he wanted to ease that pain as much as I did.

Every single one of the people I texted hit me back almost immediately, and every single one of them were in. I guess I wasn't the only one who was having a rough night sleeping over this.

We'd been lucky. The shots into the Ten-Thirteen hadn't hit anybody. The worst injury that'd occurred had been to poor Chrissy, with her need to go to the hospital and get checked out. The rest of the people that'd been there had walked away with nothing worse than some superficial scratches from flying safety glass.

It was kind of a miracle, actually, which is how the media was portraying it, based on some of the texts I was getting. Of course, there were also the notifications from my own social media accounts that were telling me that very same press was vilifying Chrissy. Blaming her lack of cooperation with them on keeping her case sensationalized and in the spotlight. I'd seen some pretty sick shit, but that certainly took the fucking cake right there. It also made me want to talk to those reporters, see if they were behind cooking up a more sensationalized story. *In fact...*

I shot a message to one of the guys I knew handling the drive-by. The

Ten-Thirteen wasn't my precinct, so I didn't have a say, but we cops weren't always as territorial nor were we always as glory-hound as films and TV would have the civilian world believe. Every once in a while you had an asshole be *that guy* but it wasn't as often as all of that.

I fell into an uneasy sleep and was up with dawn's early light, so I got maybe four hours roughly. It wasn't my finest hour, but the guys were coming in for breakfast and a round-table in my kitchen.

I slipped out of the bed and pulled on my jeans. I didn't bother with a shirt or even socks, opting to get my ass downstairs and breakfast started. The guys were likely going to show up hungry and Chrissy was going to need to eat.

First things first, I got the necessities out of the way, and by that, I mean I made the biggest pot of blackest coffee I could manage, *then* I went and used the bathroom. I had my priorities straight, and it was a good thing, too. By the time I came out of the bathroom downstairs, hands dripping and going for the linen closet cursing my dumb ass for never having a towel on the rack down here, I heard bikes out front rolling to a stop in my driveway.

I grabbed the hand towel and went to the front door, opening it up and seeing Skids and Reflash in my driveway, I just left it open and walked away. I put the towel on the rack in the bathroom to Reflash calling out, "Yo, yo, yo! Youngblood, where you at?"

"Right here, you dumb ox. Keep it down, Chrissy's still sleeping."

"Heh, not sure how she can after all that," he commented dryly and I sighed.

"Drugs, lots and lots of drugs. Come on in and have a seat; coffee's brewing."

I shook Skids hand then Reflash's and they went into my dining room and took a seat around the eight-person table. I started pulling shit out of the pantry and the cupboards to make pancakes, bacon, and eggs. I had everything required, just needed the time to put it together.

I hadn't bothered closing the front door. It was a nice enough day, and the other brothers would be getting here soon, trickling in by ones and twos. The next to show up were Yale and Backdraft, followed by Golden and Angel, then Poe, then Oz, Blaze, and finally Driller and Narcos.

The last two had been conspicuously absent due to their role in the department hierarchy. Narcos was just that, an undercover on the narcotics squad. He was the rougher of the two of them in appearance, long hair spilling over a wide swath of bandana across his forehead. He had on big, black wraparound sunglasses hiding what I knew to be shrewd green eyes. His long hair a light brown where it brushed his shoulders, his beard just about as long, now, touching the middle of his chest. Driller was his partner and handler, a little more clean-cut but not by much. His dark hair was nearly black but still a somewhat regulation cut. It was long enough on top to maintain a somewhat greasy appearance to fit the part of hardened outlaw criminal. Both of them were covered in tattoos, and fit, they had to be at the top of their game for what they did.

They made a badass team, but it also meant they weren't always present for these little get-togethers and for the shit going down with their *true* club. It just was what it was.

"Well look what the cat dragged in," Blaze said and went up to them to show them some love. They clasped hands and pulled each other in for a hug. Meanwhile, Reflash came over and started poking into my business in the kitchen, which, truthfully, that shit was only a matter of time. Reflash was like that.

"Woah, shit! We got a full house," Narcos said.

"Y'all gonna bust out the kiddie tables?" Driller asked and Backdraft went over and hugged him.

"Yeah, and you two fuckers are sittin' at 'em," he said.

I went in for my own greetings, the damn dining room and kitchen awfully fuckin' small with a dozen grown ass men in it.

"Kiddie tables are out in the garage," I told them. "Let's get this shit started."

Skids got up from the head of the table and pulled out the chair for me, I frowned and he said, "Your house *and* your party, Youngblood." I didn't argue. When the president of your club offered up that kind of respect, you took it.

"Before you go, where's your plates?" Reflash asked, manning the skillet of flapjacks I had going and peeking in the oven at the bacon I had going and grinning. "My man!" he crowed with pride.

"You don't think I listen to you, DC?" I used our term of endearment for the club's vice president. We didn't follow the typical outlaw hierarchy, instead choosing to stick with our more comfortable and familiar policing hierarchy instead. To us, Skids was our chief, and Reflash our deputy chief, hence DC for short. It was our world inside the club and we believed wholeheartedly in that. We had a few major tenets. Our world, our rules. Be good men, protect and serve, and above all, *always do right by our fellow man.*

"I know you listen," he said, giving me a playful sock in my shoulder. I'd bitched once upon a time that I could never get my bacon to turn out like his, chewy but crispy at the same time. He asked if I fried it and when I'd said yeah, how the fuck else were you supposed to do it he'd said to me, "Man, you fucking barbarian, you fucking *bake* it."

Now I did as I'd been told. Cookie sheet, parchment paper, baked it at four hundred and twenty-five degrees for fifteen to seventeen minutes and that shit came out perfect just about every damn time.

"Yeah you ever lose out on being a cop, you can become Reflash's head kitchen bitch," Oz teased, setting up one of two card tables out of the garage and everyone laughed.

"Man, fuck you," I was laughing too, though. That'd been a good one.

I got Reflash reacquainted with my kitchen and when I turned around, Chrissy was standing mutely against the archway leading into the dining room from the stairway. She was in one of my button down shirts and had managed to get into her sling, more or less. Her long legs were a sight for sore eyes, and I longed to have them wrapped around my hips.

She looked at me somberly and the rest of the guys hadn't seen her yet, but they did the second she said, "I thought I heard voices."

Total silence, several of the guys jumped and turned and more than a few of them looked gobsmacked. Had to admit, that shit made me smile, knowing they were jealous and she was mine. I couldn't and wouldn't deny it. I wasn't prone to possessive streaks usually, but I had a bad one where she was concerned. I'd given her up once, it'd been a mistake and it wasn't a mistake that bore repeating.

"Hey, precious. Sorry did we wake you up?"

"Mm-mm. Roscoe did."

I smiled, "Fuzzy little dipshit."

She smiled too, but it was wan and fragile. Yale got up out of the chair at the dining room table closest to her, opposite where I was to sit and held it out for her. She went and carefully sat down, smoothing down my shirt, behind her, likely the only thing she could manage getting into, and I wondered what happened to my damn robe.

I ducked sideways into the living room and snatched one of the throw blankets off the couch and returned to her, draping it over her legs, not just for modesty, but for warmth. The front door was still open and someone had slid open the back slider to get some fresh air through the place, but the spring air out there still had a chilly edge to it.

She looked up at me and murmured, "Thank you," and I bent and brushed her lips with mine. I quickly made introductions between Chrissy and the guys she didn't know and Reflash put the first round of food up on the breakfast bar, letting the guys help themselves. I fixed Chrissy a plate first and asked if she wanted coffee or orange juice.

"Both, please?" she asked meekly, clearly out of her element with all of the guys here and I nodded. Before I could even turn to go to the fridge, a glass and a cup were being passed down the line my way. I set them down for her and went through the line and fixed up my own plate.

We all got food and settled in for the long talk ahead. Just because I was at the head of the table, didn't mean I was in charge, though. It was just my house. Skids started off at my right hand with, "Okay, boys. Let's start with what we know."

"I'm sorry," Chrissy said, voice soft but far from timid, "But what exactly is this?"

"Youngblood?"

I finished the bite of pancake in my mouth and washed it down with some coffee and said, "This is us, trying to figure out how to get your life back, precious."

She thought about it for a minute and said her truth, "I'm beginning to think that's an impossibility," which wasn't that just fucking heartbreaking?

"Nope. Not going to let you give up, not when we haven't exhausted every possibility."

"Youngblood's right," Reflash said from my left, "we're just getting started." He looked at Skids and then me and said, "Right, so what do we know?"

"Youngblood," Skids intoned and I leaned back in my seat.

It was a good question, *what did we know?* It was best to start at the beginning when it came to piecing everything together, and so I did.

"Kevin Cohan, screen name 'homerun hero,' in a fit of moral outrage at the Miranda Maguire verdict, published Chrissy's address on a public forum with the marching orders that someone needed to quote, unquote, 'take care of the bitch.' A one Michael Silver, screen name 'silver surfer' a person completely unrelated to Cohan, except for the fact they frequented the same forum, for reasons unknown to the rest of us, but likely due to the fact he was hopped up on methamphetamine, took those words to heart and took *himself* over to Chrissy's." I took a deep breath. "Where he kicked in her front door, whereby he shot Samantha Lynn Hayworth once in the head, and Chrissy twice in the back."

"Jesus Christ, you want my job?" Yale cracked and there was some laughter around the tables. My eyes were fixed on Chrissy's somber gaze as she sat stolid and listened to the facts of her case laid bare in cold, clinical, semi-legalese.

"Then what?" she asked, like she hadn't thought about this in much the same way a thousand and more times over. I knew she had. She was a lawyer, how could she not?

"While admitted to the hospital and recovering, a third individual began sending threatening messages, and even made another attempt on Chrissy's life."

"Why?" Narcos asked, and I shook my head, my eyes never leaving Chrissy's; proud as hell of her when she sat up a little straighter.

"We don't know," she answered. "Best guess is the same reason everyone else has tried to kill me, but I have to admit, this feels... different."

I had to agree on that one and I said so, "That's because it's one thing for someone hooked on meth to go kicking in doors, and it's another when they start making calculated moves like this new asshole. His MO is completely different from these other..." I groped for the right set of words.

"Morally outraged keyboard warriors?" Yale supplied and I shrugged.

"Yeah, sure, we'll go with that."

"I thought about that," Chrissy murmured.

Golden, who was spinning a coin on my tabletop said, "Of course you have. You've thought this whole damn thing to death. How could you not?" He gave her a reassuring smile to let her know he didn't mean anything by the brooding comment and she nodded in agreement.

"So who could this unsub be?" Backdraft asked from the kiddie table and Driller shoved him in the back of the head while he and Narcos had a laugh.

"What, you going all *Criminal Minds* on us?" Narcos asked.

"You jokers got a better name for him?" Reflash demanded.

"Yeah," Driller responded, "How about douchebag."

"Cocksucker?" Narcos suggested.

"Does it really matter what we call him?" Angel asked, looking at Chrissy who was staring pointedly at the ceiling, eyes glassy as Driller and Narcos blew off steam.

"They aren't making fun of you, baby. They're just a couple of dumbassed pricks," Blaze said and she sniffed and nodded.
"Ouch, that hurts..." Narcos said, a hand on his chest.

"Enough," Skids ordered sternly and the both of them shut up and exchanged a look. Backdraft elbowed Narcos and thrust a chin at Chrissy who was being strong, but was riding that razor's edge on whether or not she was going to fall apart.

She caught my eye and I tried valiantly to telegraph strength down the line, the connection we shared, the bond that was growing stronger every day.

"Yeah, either fucking shut up and help us figure this shit out, or get the fuck out. I love you guys, but in case you haven't figured it out? I'm in love with this woman, and if we *don't* figure this shit out, our only option is gonna be to relocate."

That sobered them up and cut their shit real damn fast, Blaze looked down the table in my direction and said, "Just what are you saying, bro?"

"I think it's pretty fuckin' clear what he just said," Reflash snapped, his famous temper starting to ignite. "If you assholes didn't have enough to figure this shit out and come up with a plan just based on the fact this woman needs our help, how about the fact we don't lose Youngblood as a brother? Huh? That enough for you fuckers to fall in line?" he demanded and a weighted silence descended on everyone around the table.

"I... I would never ask you to do that," Chrissy murmured.

"You didn't have to."

"A man will do some real crazy shit for the love of a good woman," Skids said and sounded like he'd been there, which he had.

Chrissy's eyes brimmed with new, but entirely different tears. She sniffed but they spilled over anyways. Yale handed her a paper towel.

"Thanks," she said her voice broken in only that way that crying made it do.

"No problem," Yale said.

"Okay, so how do we know that this asshole making threats and attempting to kill Ms. Franco here, is the same dude that took pot shots at the Ten-Thirteen last night?" Poe asked, leaning forward.

"We don't, but it fits," I said.

"Chrissy, please..." she corrected Poe dully.

"Okay, so we're stalled out on an ID for this dude, right?" Blaze asked.

Yale spoke up, "I got a good look at him, but he could literally be any Joe in the city."

"We looked at victimology yet?" Skids asked softly and Chrissy met his sympathetic look.

"No, and I honestly don't know who it could be, I mean, I didn't think I had any enemies... not until all of this."

"Doesn't your firm keep a file of every threatening message you receive? I know the prosecutor's office does," Yale said.

"I never even knew I got any threats at all until I checked my email and saw the pictures of the flowers..." she said.

Yale scoffed a bit and said, "I don't know a single damn lawyer whose done their job right, either criminal or civil who *hasn't* been threatened."

"I don't think Jaime and I have ever had a case dealing with one of you guys before, I feel like we may have missed something here."

Yale adjusted himself in his seat, "Yeah, a lot, you might have a rabbit hole to follow there."

"That still doesn't explain how we're going to stop him, or catch him..." Chrissy murmured and I could see the wheels in her head finally had started turning again.

"What 'cha thinkin' princess?" Reflash asked.

"I'm thinking that if my firm had this information but no one bothered to disclose it, or offer it up, I *really* need a new job."

I set down my phone, having texted Jaime that we needed to look into it pronto and said, "She's right, fact remains that she's still a target until we can snap him up. She can't go anywhere thanks to the media and that fucking hashtag."

"So use it," Skids said, and Yale was nodding slowly. I was too, thinking along the same lines.

"Wait, how? You're not suggesting I grant an interview or something are you? Because I really don't want to do that." Chrissy looked uncomfortable and said, "I'd rather be bait."

"Over my dead fuckin' body," I said.

"Maybe you're both right," Driller said with a devious grin.

"Spill, what you got?" I asked.

"Yale gets on the news, tells the world that Chrissy's testifying on such and such date for the grand jury, right? Says she'll be put up courtesy of Indigo City taxpayer funds at the Regency Hyatt as a material witness."

Yale frowned, "We don't use the Hyatt for that."

"Well duh," Narcos said. "That's the point. We don't actually want to give the world the location of the hotel we *do* use."

"Exactly," Driller said. "And the Hyatt is suitably expensive to rile up anybody who pays taxes, but not so out of pocket the city won't spring for one night in it."

"Guys, we aren't using Chrissy as bait," I said.

"I'll do it," Chrissy murmured and Driller shook his head.

Oz grinned and said, "Now hold on now, y'all just stay in the truck. Driller, what you thinkin' man?"

"Good ol' fashioned sting. Get a female undercover officer from Vice to pose as Ms. Franco. A wig, a floppy hat, put her arm in a sling, some big fuckin' sunglasses... it's doable." I was nodding now, catching on.

"You'll have to be there, Tony. You're almost as big news as she is anymore. Everybody wants to know who her great white knight is," Narcos said.

"I can do that."

"Meanwhile, we can keep Chrissy at the hotel we *do* keep witnesses at under full guard," Yale said and Driller pointed his index and middle finger at Yale and dropped his thumb like the hammer of a gun.

I nodded, "This could totally work."

"I can call my contacts in Vice, I know of a couple detectives that would fit the bill," Driller said.

Chrissy looked pale but hopeful, her eyes met mine and I saw worry there.

"It's a good plan," I told her and she nodded.

"Only hitch would be if dude is underworld, any seasoned criminal would see right through this, wouldn't they?" Golden asked.

"You'd be surprised," Driller said. Narcos nodded in agreement.

Okay, we had a solid foundation here.

"You good with this?" I asked Chrissy and she nodded gravely.

"I have to be," she said. "I can't live like this anymore."

I don't think anyone could blame her there.

22

*C*hrissy...

The last of the men of the Indigo Knights left, and I found myself leaning in the doorway to the living room, watching them go. I turned around and eyed Tony who was cleaning up his kitchen, loading the dishwasher with his mismatched dishes.

"They all come here like that often?" I asked, and he barked a bit of a laugh and shook his head.

"Only on special occasions."

"Am I a special occasion?" I asked, and I really think I just needed to hear it again. He set down the dish he had in his hands and rinsed off his hands in the water pouring from the tap before he shut off the sink.

"I'd like to think you already have the answer to that."

I nodded mutely, and cursed myself for letting my feeling so damn *shitty* get to me like that. Turning me into one of those girls who resorted to fishing for compliments. It wasn't attractive and was manipulative, and just plain wrong and I opened my mouth to apologize but he'd reached me by then, hands smoothing over his shirt, over my hips and effectively short-circuited my brain.

"You were gonna say," he said with that charming, little boy smile, the one with *all* the dimples. I closed my eyes and swallowed and told him the truth.

"You know I can't think straight when you smile at me like that?"

"That was sort of the idea," he said with a deep chuckle, before he put his mouth on mine. I sank into the kiss gratefully, my fingers finding the softness of the back of his hair as I held him back, pressing myself into the length of his body, mine coming awake with every bit of contact.

He pulled back minutely and asked me, "Your body done doing its thing?"

I smiled at how simply he put it and was happy to report, "Yes, it's done 'doing its thing.'" I couldn't help but laugh at how he put it and he chuckled too. It wasn't unusual for me to have short periods that only lasted three days at the most, so I wasn't worried. If anything, I was grateful right now, even if the cramps were killer for me every month.

All of that was forgotten, though, the minute he pulled me near, his hand on my ass, giving it a squeeze. He drew me around the back of the couch until we stood in front of it and pulled a condom out of his jeans pocket, before losing them completely.

"Keeping them handy?" I whispered and again with that devilish grin that would have melted my panties if I had been wearing any.

"Uh huh."

"Good."

He tore it open while I watched and rolled it on before dropping onto the couch and waving at me to straddle him. I did, carefully, bracing myself on the back of the sofa with my good arm while he lined himself up for me and slid right in.

I moaned, bowing my head, pressing my forehead to his and despite how the back of my shoulder screamed about it, cupped the side of his face. He looked up for me so that I could kiss him, hands roaming under his shirt, along the outside of my thigh, kneading my ass, smoothing over my lower back as he encouraged me to move and to grind on him.

It was the only solace I got with the insanity my life had turned into, these moments alone with Tony as the world fell away and we were two bodies coming together as one being. Soul-touched, I carefully worked him, sliding up and down along the length of him while his cock went impossibly deep. I arched back, and let him hold me while I gave myself over to the feeling, letting my body go and do its thing. My mind finally shutting off and going *quiet* for half a damn minute.

Peace and a quicksilver euphoria flooded out from my center and I gasped, rotating my hips, not even caring that my lower back twinged and shot pain down my right leg from the motion. I adjusted and did it again only not quite as extreme and Oh. My. God.

It was like a time lapse of watching a flower burst into life, except this was no flower, it was *me*. Electrical impulses firing, traveling down every nerve, like light down a fiber optic line. I was the vessel, the conduit for the joy he sparked in the center of my being to fill me up and send me trembling into some unknown plane of existence.

It was a slow build, but a rush none the less, the pleasure rising warm and heavy, filling my senses until I couldn't tell where I left off and he began. His breath harsh, his teeth setting gently into the side of my neck, the vibration of his pent up groan thrilling down my spine, I begged whatever gods that may silently to let me come, to let us come together, because I could tell he was close, so very, dangerously close.

One or two more rolling thrusts of my hips down on top of him, our mouths crushed together; bodies pressed so tight I couldn't reach between us to give that last little nudge, but damn if I didn't need to. The orgasm zinged through me out of nowhere, my cry muffled by Tony's intensive kiss, swallowed by him, as I felt like I poured right out of the confines of my being, swirling in a lighted rush around the room before being returned to the fragile shell of my body, trembling and spent, my arms trapped at my sides by Tony's shirt, fingers digging into his arms, above his elbows, as I held onto him for dear life, panting.

I couldn't even be sure when he'd unbuttoned the shirt, but it was quickly apparent he hadn't when, shaking, I drew the two sides together to fasten them and found no buttons with which to do it. Good thing I could sew, that was, if we found all of the scattered buttons.

"Don't worry about it," he said drawing me close and nuzzling the side of my neck.

"I don't even remember you doing it," I replied, gasping.

He chuckled darkly and held me close, his shoulders rising and falling, his chest pressed tight against my stomach. I wrapped my arms around his head and held him close, tightly and he sighed out content and listened to my heart for several long moments.

"I needed that." I spoke softly, the dim hush of the living room adding to the intimacy of the moment. He smiled and looked up at me, placing his chin on my chest, between my breasts. I liked this view. I looked down into his eyes and he smiled up at me.

"Me, too." His smile dropped and he closed his eyes and breathed out slowly.

"What now?" I asked, somber, and he smiled again.

"Now, we work on what's going to happen next, we catch the bad guys, you testify in front of the grand jury, and the good guys win the day."

I closed my eyes and smiled at the surety his voice held. I liked the sound of that. The part about the good guys winning the day, but after everything that'd happened to me, I was beginning to seriously question if I was one of the good guys anymore. I mean, I always thought I'd been, and that my intentions were pure, but as a firm believer in Karma, I was seriously beginning to wonder... I mean, if I believed so wholeheartedly in Karma, and that everything a person did came full circle back to them... With this, and I do mean all of this, I had to ask myself, *what did I do?*

"Hey, what's that look for?" he asked and I opened my eyes.

"Do you believe in Karma?" I asked.

"I do, but I believe in God first, baby," he answered. "Which in that vein, I also believe that God never hands us more than we can handle."

"I believe in Karma, even though I don't necessarily subscribe to the whole religious concept. I mean, seems like a legitimate line of thinking, doesn't it? That whatever we put out in the world comes back to visit us, full circle."

"You're wondering what you did to deserve all of this?"

"Yeah."

"Nothing. You didn't deserve it, you didn't do anything to deserve it... Like I said, I believe in God, baby, but there can't be light without the darkness and in the dark resides the devil. How do you know that what's happening to you isn't his work?"

"I thought the devil didn't exist," I said with a small smile.

"That was the crafty bastard's greatest con of all, wasn't it? Convincing man he didn't exist."

I sighed and nodded, he had me there. I bowed my forehead to his and just relished the contact with him, and he murmured, "There you go making me look like the good Catholic."

I laughed, "I told you I wasn't very good at it, didn't I?"

"Apparently not, believing in things like Karma." He winked at me.

I scoffed, "You said you believed in it, too!"

"I did," he agreed. "So if you think Karma's whooping your ass with everything that's happened, let me ask you, how do I fit into things?" I stilled and drew back even more so I could search his face.

"You're one of the best things that's ever happened to me," I said unequivocally.

"There you go then, how do you know *that* isn't your Karma in action?"

I tilted my head to the side and considered what he was saying and finally offered up, "Maybe its best I leave the philosophy lessons to the philosophers."

He laughed, and smoothed his hands up and down my body. I shivered and his smile changed to something private, something dark but deliciously so. It was the kind of smile a man gave when he was admiring something beautiful, something he'd coveted for a long time and finally owned, or had taken for himself and I felt this deep throb in the middle of my being.

It was a sensation unlike any other I had ever experienced before that moment, but the paramount emotion I would attach to it was *relief*. I didn't know how long I had yearned for a man to look at me that way, but not just any man, the *right* man. I don't know how I knew, but I did, I just knew with all of my being with that one look, with the feeling I'd just had like the whole world just snapped into place, that the right man was right in front of me, still inside me, and I felt a rush of almost tears with just how awesome that felt, with the relief and the joy, with the happiness and peace that brought to me...

"Hey, you okay?" he asked me, thumbing away one of the surprise tears. I smiled and leaned down, kissing him. He held my face between his hands and kissed me back, kissed me true and I sighed against his lips in utter contentment.

He drew back carefully and asked, "What was that?" but I was almost too embarrassed to tell him, what with how corny it would sound.

That was me, falling in love with you...

So I just smiled instead and didn't lie and say it was nothing because what'd just happened wasn't nothing. Instead, I said, "I'll tell you when you're older."

He grinned at me and laughed, and I kissed him again, and this time it led to a whole new round of lovemaking, only this time we moved it to his living room floor. Let's hear it for variety.

23

———

*T*ony...

It was hard leaving her the next morning but Jaime and I had a date with a representing attorney at Reardon, Colfax & Price. Not one of the big men themselves, obviously we didn't warrant any of *their* time, but still, we wanted everything of a threatening nature that'd been logged against poor Chrissy to see if we could get a lead on our guy between now and her grand jury testimony.

"You have a warrant for that, I'm sure..." the gentleman was saying and I swear I heard a record needle scratching harshly across some vinyl. Jaime and I exchanged a look and apparently I wasn't crazy and my partner had heard it too.

"Excuse me?" Jaime asked.

"A warrant for those files," the lawyer repeated and I blinked.

"Seriously?" I asked. "You don't want to help Chrissy out and just cooperate?"

"It is Reardon, Colfax & Price's policy when it comes to police matters that we do not release any files concerning any employee without a proper warrant."

"You're serious," Jaime said and sounded incredulous. I was already on it, phone pressed to my ear, waiting for it to ring through.

"Parnell," Yale answered on the second ring.

"You're not going to believe this," I said.

"Try me, I bet you I will," he shot back.

"I need a warrant for Reardon, Colfax & Price to collect evidence in the Franco case."

"Yeah, see, I told you. I'm not surprised. Give me the specifications and I'll see what I can do. Judge Holcomb hates that they do this and will generally sign just about anything just to be a pain in their ass right back for wasting the court's time."

"You got a fax number or email address for this?" I asked, and was hoping they'd at least cough that up to save me and Jaime from having to go all the way down to the courthouse and come back. Like I would leave, as it was, I couldn't be sure they wouldn't destroy evidence in our absence, these fuckers were acting hella shady.

The lawyer they'd sent to deal with us, Mr. Darnell Pritchard, plucked a business card off the reception desk and handed it to me.

"Yeah, Yale, you still there?"

"I'm here, almost done typing this bad boy up."

"The personal touch, I like it. Anyways, you can email the finished product to Reardon, Colfax & Price directly to reception at R C and, and is spelled out, not the symbol then P dot com." He read the email back to me and I confirmed.

"Okay, gotta run if I'm going to catch Judge Holcomb."

"Copy that, thank you." I ended the call.

"You are more than welcome to wait, detectives, however, typically warrants do take some time." Mr. Pritchard smiled and it wasn't terribly friendly. I shook my head and couldn't help myself.

I asked, "Doesn't this place give a... care about *any* of its employees? I mean, one of your attorney's *was shot*, don't you want to help her any way you can?"

"Yes, Detective McCormick, *I* do, but it's the firm's policy that all records and files, employees or otherwise must be obtained through the proper legal channels."

Interesting, he was the firm's mouthpiece on this one, but he didn't like or agree with them or their policy on this.

"No worries, son," Jaime told the lawyer. "You'll get your warrant."

I was kind of speechless to be honest. I'd never seen a law firm be so reluctant to help one of their own before, policy or not.

It was a record, even for us on how fast that warrant came through. Less than thirty minutes and the receptionist looked up and said, surprised, "It's here," and the printer behind her started spitting out pages. Gotta love modern tech for some things.

She handed the pages to Mr. Pritchard who smiled and said, "I'll have those boxes to you in just a few moments, if you'll please have a seat."

Boxes? Jaime mouthed at me and my heart kind of sank. Boxes meant plural, which meant a whole lot of threats because that was the scope of the warrant, any and all messages of a threatening nature addressed towards one Christina Marie Franco. Of course, that was unless Yale had snuck anything else in there.

Maybe ten or fifteen minutes later here came Pritchard with some paralegals dogging his steps. The two paralegals held three loaded Banker's file boxes between them and held them out to me and Jaime.

"There you are detectives," Pritchard said, hands in his pockets. I took two while Jaime took the one.

"Much obliged," Jaime said sarcastically.

"Best of luck, Chrissy is one of the good ones," Pritchard said and he came forward and lifted the top box off of my stack of two. "In fact, let me help you to your car with this. It looks heavy."

"That would be much appreciated," I told him. In the elevator, he came clean with what he really wanted to say.

"Look, I meant what I said about Chrissy being one of the good ones. She really is one of the best. However, she is no longer considered an asset to the firm after what's happened to her. Reardon, Colfax & Price have a very precise set of criteria you must live up to. Chrissy, injured like she is? She can no longer fulfill that criteria and so they've already replaced her with someone who can. It's the way a firm like this works. You're only as valuable as how much you add to their bottom line."

"You have got to be fucking kidding me," Jaime said shaking his head.

"This firm doesn't believe in people, Detective. Only money. She deserves better than what they've given her. She needs well clear of this place."

"How could she not know about all of this?" Jaime asked holding up his box for emphasis.

"The firm has minimum wage lackeys open all the mail and only put through what they consider pertinent to a specific lawyer's current cases. They don't believe in telling their lawyers when things like this come through believing it cuts productivity. Believe me, I was as shocked as you are when we found out."

"What about you?" I asked.

"Looking for a new job somewhere else, myself. A lot of the lawyers who have put any kind of time in here are after some of the things we've heard and seen since Chrissy was attacked."

"Sounds like Reardon, Colfax & Price has a mutiny on its hands."

The elevator made its final descent and hit the floor we were parked on, bumping gently to a stop.

"You're not far off, Detective. Good luck, I mean that."

The doors of the elevator hushed open and he put the box he carried back on top of mine. Jaime and I went to our cruiser and put the boxes in the back seat.

"I'm stopping for coffee on the way back in," he said.

"Yeah, anything but that swill back at the station. This looks like it's gonna take us all night."

"No sense in replacing one bad taste with another," he said, adding, "hopefully something shakes loose."

"Hopefully," I agreed.

We spent the next eleven hours poring over everything in the boxes and wasn't that an epic shit show? There were so many threats ranging from rape, to dismemberment, to death there was no telling how long this had been going on. I set down the last one and pressed fingers into my eye sockets, thoroughly disturbed and disgusted with mankind.

I heard Jaime lean back in his seat and let out a gusty sigh, "There's a few *years* of this shit here," he complained.

"I realize that, man."

"How did she not know this was going on?"

"I honestly don't know but I'm pretty sure if she *did* know she'd have taken some kind of security measures a long time ago." I shook my head incredulous.

Jaime huffed a sort of 'huh,' and leaned forward bracing his elbows on the edge of his desk and looking at me over his clasped hands, one over the other. "What're you gonna tell her?" he asked staring at me with a piercing gaze.

I shook my head, "The only thing I *can* tell her; the truth."

"I don't envy you, partner. Here's to hoping she's not the kind to shoot the messenger."

I shook my head, "Not Chrissy."

"Sound mighty sure of that."

"Ah, yeah. Yeah I do."

Jaime's bushy eyebrows shot up into his hairline and his mouth turned down. He shook his head and pushed back from his desk.

"Well, this was a waste of fuckin' time."

"Hey, you never know until you try," I said picking up one of the cards that'd come with the most recent flowers sent to her job. Same handwriting as the card from the hospital, so same guy. We had a few samples of earlier threats set aside, the handwriting eerily similar, but until we could get any kind of analysis done, there was no confirmation that it was the same guy. Still, one letter in particular had caught my eye and I knew in my gut it was the same bozo.

"I'm headed home, partner. I suggest you do the same," Jaime said getting up and stretching.

"Yeah. Yeah, I will," but I didn't move right away. There was a lot of unresolved shit spilled across our desks and I didn't like it. I went over the letter again, the dude bitching about how Chrissy had ruined his life and how payback was going to be a bitch. That if he couldn't keep his job, his wife, and his kids, Chrissy wasn't going to keep her job either, and how he'd see to it she never got the chance to have any of the rest.

The tone of the letter was *pissed* and I wondered what the hell my girl could have done to earn someone's just sheer, unadulterated *hatred*. I mean, I couldn't reconcile any of her actions as garnering this kind of reaction, but in this case, clearly *something* had happened.

I took my time picking up and took these new threats with me, figuring maybe she could shed some more light on this particular nutbag. Maybe something would spark in her memory, or shake loose. We were still going to go through with the sting. In fact, Yale had made his pretty speech to the news just in time for the six o'clock airing. I might be able to catch the replay on the eleven o'clock news if I hustled.

I changed and went down to my bike. The ride home was a cleansing one, even though I dreaded talking about this shit with Chrissy. Not because I didn't think she could handle it or that she'd be angry with me for bringing it up, but more because I was getting real sick of watching her hurt.

I went in through the garage, but when I emerged through the side door into the living room, it was to the soft wavering blue glow of the television and little else. Chrissy was on the couch, arm in her sling, one leg curled under her and one of the throw pillows in her lap. Roscoe looked up lazily from said pillow as Chrissy absently petted him, her attention rapt on the news.

Yale was standing front and center at the podium used for press briefings at the DA's office, flashbulbs going off in his face as reporters shouted questions.

"Ms. Franco will be under police protection the entire time, she will be relocated from the location she is in to the Regency Hyatt where she will enjoy an evening courtesy of Indigo City taxpayer dollars in the company of the finest police protection Indigo City has to offer. She will be safe, and as yet has not agreed to, nor is willing to give members of the media an interview, so please, don't bother."

"God, I sound like such a bitch when he puts it that way."

"Eh, he's just doing his job, precious. You won't be there. You'll be safe at the real hotel used by witnesses."

"I know, still, you *will* be there, so I'll worry just the same, thanks." She dragged her eyes off of Yale and looked up at me. "Something happened with your new case?" she asked.

"Something happened with yours, actually. Jaime and I followed a hunch, went by the firm you work for to collect those cards that came with the flowers you showed us.

"Ah, and?"

"Baby, I don't know how to tell you this, but they had *three boxes* of threats against you dating back something like four years."

"What?" She stopped petting Roscoe, mid-stroke. He rolled on his back and attacked her hand playfully and she snapped back to reality and jerked her hand to safety. Put out, my fuzzy little man jumped down.

"Whoever sent those emails was looking out for you, babe, because I don't think they were supposed to. We talked to a lawyer with the firm, Darnell Pritchard…"

"I know Darnell," she said faintly.

"He says that just about every lawyer receives threats, but the firm doesn't say anything about it. Something about cutting into productivity or some shit."

"I had no idea..." she said and I could see the horror of the implications seeping into her dark eyes the more she ran through scenarios in her head. I'd already thought about everything she was thinking and then some, except I had a better idea of just how fucked up people could be to each other.

"Tony... what did you find?"

I dropped onto the couch beside her and pulled the notes and the letter out of the inside pocket of my jacket and smoothed them out through their evidence bags.

"These are the notes that came with the flowers. This, I think is the first one. Does it bring anything up? Spark a memory or something?"

She took them with trembling fingers and said, "Turn on a light for me?"

I got up and obliged her, switching on the corner lamp, turning the halogen up until it was bright enough to see by, turning it up slowly so our eyes could adjust. She pored over the letter in her hands and turned it over to look at the envelope it'd come in, conveniently with no return address. She wasn't looking for one, though. She was looking at the postal mark.

She got up abruptly and tossed the pillow in her lap aside, going toward the kitchen. I followed her, getting my hopes up. She was like a dog on the scent and I was hoping whatever had her going would pan out into *something, anything,* to catch this son of a bitch.

Come on, baby. Give us a name, give us a face; let's do this. I thought at her.

She booted up her laptop, and while that was trying to get to where she could do something she picked up her phone and scrolled through her calendar.

"I was wrapping up the Sunderland case back then, my client, Robert Sunderland was accused of killing a thirteen-year-old girl. A hit and run, the police thought he was drunk."

"Wasn't one of mine," I mused dropping into a chair near her. She shook her head and said, "No it wasn't intentional, he was up on vehicular manslaughter charges, it was a DUI so it went through the traffic division, I think. Their case was pretty good." Her laptop finished booting and she let her fingers walk across the keys one handed, chicken pecking in her password with her first three fingers.

She messed around with her mouse and clicked through screens and said, "I won the case, I'm just looking for the name."

"How'd you win? Sounds like it was pretty cut and dried."

"I played reasonable doubt. Gave the jury an alternate chain of events to follow."

"Shit, you painted one guy up one side and down the other, made him look good for it."

She sat back in her seat heavily and said, "Yeah..."

"Who?" I demanded and she looked at me.

"Please don't hate me..." she said and I shook my head.

I got up and bent, kissing her forehead and said against it, "Never, but I need to know who, precious."

"His name was Curtis Wetmore, and he was a friend of my client's. He was at the same bar, and in the car... I presented that there was no proof which of them was driving at the time of the accident, it was Wetmore's car. Oh my god... Tony, what did I do?"

"You did your job, honey."

"But did I really wreck this man's life over this?"

"No babe, he did. He and his buddy both did when they got into that car drunk."

She covered her face with her hand and I held her tight, "I've got you."

"Maybe this is Karma," she said and I let her go so I could grab my phone out of my pocket and call it in.

"I don't think so, not even Karma is this big of a bitch. I think you might want to start looking for a civil attorney, though. Your firm has got some balls..."

"Do you think they're criminally negligent?" she asked.

"Ask Yale, that's more his department," I said shortly as someone picked up on the other end of the line. "Yeah, hey this is Detective Tony McCormick out of the 12th, I need an APB put out on a Curtis Wetmore, white male, approximately five foot nine, slender build, favors a gray hoodie under a black jacket. Do what you can to get me his last known address, I'm going to call the DA's office, see what I can do about getting a warrant. Text it to me as soon as you can?"

"Right away Detective," the dispatcher on the other end of the line said.

"That's what I love about you, Three-Five-One. You're always so helpful."

"Aw, thanks!" She replied and I ended the call. We didn't know dispatchers by name, just number. It was department policy.

"What happens now?" Chrissy asked.

"Now, we wait for the info to come through, we head to his last known and start kicking over rocks."

She nodded, and swallowed hard, still working on coming to grips with maybe having some answers. We wouldn't know for sure unless we got the guy.

"Yale," I said when he picked up. "I need a warrant."

"What for?" he demanded sleepily and I laid it out for him.

"APB is good enough," he said with a yawn. "I hate to break it to you, Tony but the sting is going to be our best shot at this guy and actually being able to put him away for any sort of decent amount of time."

"Shit," I muttered, knowing he was right.

"It's just a couple more days. If your APB gets him, fine, but if it doesn't and he makes a move..."

"Yeah, you're right," I conceded.

"Look, I know you want her safe, we all do. She's had a rough row to hoe, and I'm glad you guys may have figured it out at this point, but right now, all we can put this guy up on is the attempt at the hospital which is circumstantial at best, he could argue his way out of it, even with my ID. If you want him dead to rights –"

"You've made your point, counselor." I knew my tone was unfriendly, but all I could do was stare at Chrissy who was staring at her laptop screen blankly. Her eyes not really seeing what was in front of her. She was way too far inside her own head and I hated that. I hated that we knew, but that we couldn't do a damn thing about it.

"Hold your woman, make her feel safe and I'll get with you in the morning," he said softly.

"Thanks for not taking it personal," I said.

"Seen the way you look at each other, bro... it's as personal as it gets, I just know you've got no beef with me."

"Listen to you trying to talk all hood."

"Man, fuck you."

"Night," I said and couldn't help but laugh a little.

"Night, asshole."

He ended the call on me and I knelt down by Chrissy.

"We follow the plan?" she asked and a grim determination steeling across her features.

"We follow the plan."

I called back into dispatch to modify the instructions to go along with the APB to tail but not to engage, then I did what Yale said. I took my woman to bed, I held her, and I made her forget that there was an angry man out there hell bent on revenge... but I didn't. I couldn't, and I wouldn't be taking it easy until I had him locked up in my pen.

24

*C***hrissy...**

"Man, I'm fucking starving!" I turned, not quite capable of looking over my shoulder, to eye Narcos, the one who'd spoken. Driller sat at the small, two person table with him, cards scattered over its surface as they played something or other.

"What about you, girly? Hungry?"

"No, but I should probably eat something anyways."

"Pizza?" Driller asked and Narcos made a noise like the mere suggestion of it had him dying.

"Man, why don't you call down to the Ten-Thirteen, have one of the guys run us up some food?" he asked.

"Solid," Driller said and brought out his phone.

After a minute he said, "Yeah, Skids. Help us out man, if it weren't bad enough they got us dying of fucking boredom up here, they're starving us to death. It's either pizza or room service." He paused as

237

Skids said something that couldn't be heard on the other end of the line. "Yeah, yeah, yeah. Sounds good, man. Naw, I trust Reflash to hook us up. Yep, still the same place. Alright, alright, cool." He ended the call and said, "Get a call from the lobby and your dumb ass can go down and pick it up," he told Narcos.

"Sweet," Narcos declared and I went back to my sightless staring out the gauzy curtains at the city street below. We were less than seven blocks from the courthouse, in a dumpy old Radisson that was about a decade late for any kind of upgrade. The decor still mostly out of the eighties. It was clean, however, and the bed seemed like it would be comfortable enough from when I sat on it.

We were in a suite, so there was a small living room area in addition to the bedroom, giving me a modicum of privacy from the rough cut undercover detectives if I so wished it. They'd apparently volunteered for this detail, although I had to believe that it was more that Tony had asked it of them.

"You're bugging the shit out of me, princess. Come sit down," Narcos called out and I turned around again.

"Leave her alone, Narc. She's having a rough day, or can't you tell?"

"Eh, Youngblood's gonna be fine, it ain't his first rodeo. Now seriously, c'mere and sit down, play a round of cards, try and take your mind off it."

I sighed and went over. I'd left my high heels by the window and instead padded across the tired but still serviceable carpet in my stocking feet.

"Atta girl," Narcos said dryly.

"You always such a condescending ass?" I asked and Driller choked on the sip of Coke he'd taken out of the red and silver can.

Narcos laughed, "Usually."

"Well knock it off, it's annoying and thoroughly unwelcoming and unattractive."

"Well shit, howdy! Listen to you!"

"She's right, man. Reel it in," Driller said.

I sighed and closed my eyes and apologized, "Sorry."

"Nah, you do you, sweetheart," Driller said.

"What're you playing, anyways?"

"Game called Spite and Malice. It's a two player or I'd deal you in."

"How does it work?" I asked.

The guys exchanged a look and Narcos gave a nod and said, "Okay, alright, so each player gets a stack of twenty cards each, these are your play off piles. Then you get five cards to your hand and..." he explained while I tried valiantly to follow along, my nerves slowly blackening and curling, frying to a crisp with every tick of the second hand on the clock above us.

By the time he was done explaining the rules of the game and the two of them showed me by example how to play, Driller's phone decided to vibrate nearly off the table. The sudden sound had me nearly jumping out of my skin and he picked it up, looking over the screen.

"Food, go grab it," he ordered and Narcos got up, saluting Driller and going to the room's door. We sat in silence for half a heartbeat and Driller said, "You're gonna have to forgive my partner. He's been under for so long that every time he comes back up for air like this, it's like he doesn't know how to come back from it all the way..."

"Isn't that a sign that he should probably quit?" I asked.

Driller nodded slowly and said, "Yeah. Yeah it probably is, but if you knew how much time and effort we had wrapped up in this investigation, you probably wouldn't be so quick to judge on that."

"Probably not," I agreed and pushed to my feet. I wandered back over to the window and looked down to the street, watching the roofs of cars pass by, eyeing the crowns of people's heads, all of them oblivious that anyone was up here watching.

What I wouldn't give to be anonymous like any one of them again...

"Should stop worrying, it's not going to help them catch the bad guy any faster," he said and scraped up the cards, stacking the two decks they were using together in a big pile and setting it aside.

We stared at each other for what must have been several minutes, neither speaking, neither breaking our gaze first. The door opened and Narcos ducked in with a couple of takeout bags with three Styrofoam takeout clamshells in them each.

"A lot of food for three people," I observed and the two of them exchanged a look and started laughing.

"You've never seen us eat," Narcos said and set them down at the table, "Now will you *please* get away from that window. You're making me jumpy."

"Why?"

"Undercover narcotics, remember?"

I frowned, "I don't follow."

"Snipers," Driller explained, untying the top of one bag. I turned back to the window startled and backed away from it.

"Doubt we have to worry about 'em in your case," Narcos said, "But better safe than sorry."

I frowned and still restless, went back to the table to eat. The men went through the bags and found some of the thick paper plates and packs of napkins and cutlery in the bottom of one. They dished up and I waited, seeing as I wasn't really hungry in the first place.

When they began to eat, I helped myself, Narcos stabbing his fork in the direction of one of the containers, "Grab a crab bomb while they're still warm."

"Do it," Driller said around a mouthful of greens, "Reflash makes some of the best damn crab cakes in Maryland."

I took one as instructed and tried it. It really was the best I'd ever tasted, and weirdly, just like that, it was as if peace had been made... I didn't understand it, and I honestly didn't want to. I just wanted the time to pass by and for Tony to call and for everything to be okay, again... except I knew it wouldn't. Things would never, ever, really be totally okay again but it had the potential to come close.

"You know it ain't his first rodeo, right?" Driller asked.

"What? Oh, I know," I said when I'd fully caught up to what he'd said.

"Ain't gonna be his last, either, chick. Best get used to this feeling."

I nodded and sucked it up, because I had to. They were right, this wouldn't be the last time I was stuck somewhere worrying about him, but this would be the worst time. Why would this be the worst? Because I was the reason he was out there and in some kind of danger. That's what made this somehow worse.

"You try hooking in to the hotel Wi-Fi?" Driller asked and I shook my head.

"It's pretty good."

"I figured you wouldn't want me using electronics."

"Not to post to social media and shit where you are, but you got Netflix or some shit on your phone, right?" Narcos said.

"Yes, I mean I have it on my tablet."

"Good deal, fire it up, see if there's something the three of us can deal with. It'll help kill time."

"Okay."

So that's what we ended up doing, huddling around the table watching episodes of Penny Dreadful on my too-small screen in order to while away the hours, until my constant worry wouldn't have me sit still anymore, at which point I locked myself into the bathroom and took a long, hot shower. I blow dried my hair when I got out, which always took forever, but gave me something to at least do.

When I stepped out, the guys laughed at something on the screen and I said, "I'm going to try and go to bed."

"Probably a good idea," Driller agreed. "You've got a big day tomorrow."

"Yeah," I nodded.

"Yeah," Narcos nodded, looking me over in one of Tony's shirts. I don't know why I'd selected it over any of my actual pajamas, but I had, and now I felt a bit exposed.

"Night," Driller grunted.

"Want the tablet back?" Narcos asked.

"No, you guys keep watching."

"Thanks."

"Welcome," and with that I went and crawled into the king sized bed to stare at the ceiling wondering, *why hadn't he called?*

25

*T*ony...

"Our guy is in the lobby," came over the earpiece jammed in my ear.

"Don't move until he does, prosecutor's office wants this air tight," I said into the cuff of my blazer's sleeve. I was lead on this, for better or worse, and I was nervous.

"You're doing fine," Yvonne said, patting my arm in the enclosed space of the back of the SUV. We were pulling up to the hotel and she pulled her floppy hat down a little further over her eyes. Her dark wig spilling down her back and the big sunglasses obscuring things even more. With the trench coat she had on, she looked like Carmen San Diego but still, I had to agree with Driller. A little make up to make her pale skin tone a little more olive and she was just about the spitting image of my Chrissy.

"Okay, we're pulling up to the curb now, be ready," I ordered.

Our driver, another detective from the 12th, pulled up smoothly in

243

the roundabout drive to the hotel. The media was already pressing in at all sides with uniforms holding them back, and I popped open the back door of the SUV in front of the twin sliding glass doors leading into the hotel.

I got out first, back to the camera flashes, a pair of aviator sunglasses on my face to deal with the bright lights. Yvonne slid out awkwardly behind me, her arm in a sling, and I helped her down. She huddled convincingly, shying away from the shouting reporters and I heard her say, "God, how does she put up with it?" just loud enough for me to hear.

"I don't know," I answered, and hustled her into the atrium, past the first set of doors; a couple of uniforms closing ranks behind us, to keep the reporters at bay.

We marched purposefully through the next set of doors and that's basically when the shit hit the fan. When violence erupts, everyone thinks that things slow down, and that it feels like you have all the time in the world to respond, but that's bullshit. We heard the shout, saw him come in from our left and he was just suddenly there, gun pointed at Yvonne.

My gun was out, there was a metric ton of shouting, and just about every plain clothes officer and Yvonne had one pointed at the dude. Sure enough, he'd made a play, and I was looking at the same guy we'd chased in the hospital, gray hoodie under black leather jacket, he stared at us wild eyed, way too much white showing around them, gun shaking like a leaf in his hands, as Yvonne and I moved as a practiced unit turning, him falling right into play, so that his back was to the front desk and ours was at the base of the broad staircase.

We had ballistic vests on, the reporters crowding the entryway outside the glass doors didn't. We hadn't thought the guy would make a play right there in the lobby, in front of so many witnesses, but then again, we hadn't gambled on how frustrated and angry Chrissy's eluding him up to this point had made him.

Where did he get the fucking piece!?

That was my first thought, even though my mouth was following procedure screaming "ICPD! Down! Put the weapon down!"

"She's gotta die!" he screamed back, "You don't understand!"

At which point Yvonne whipped the hat and the wig off of her head and the guy froze.

"No, no, no, no, NO!" he screamed, spittle flying from his lips, wild eyes gone even wilder. "You can't take this from me!"

Now the world slowed, he raised his gun with purpose and a surge of adrenaline hit me, "No!" I screamed but it was drowned out by a cacophony of gunfire, my own weapon belching smoke and flame as I pulled the trigger to save not just myself, but Yvonne next to me, but I didn't want to do it. I don't think any of us did, still... talk about clear and present danger.

Dude's chest erupted in arcs of rich, dark, red and he lifted clean off his feet, up and arched back before he slammed to the white tiled floor. I went forward automatically, Yvonne moving with me on his opposite side.

I kicked the Ruger out and away from his body, and it went skittering across the tile where it was stopped precisely under another officer's boot. I didn't pay attention much beyond knowing the weapon was secure, dropping to my knee beside the guy. I checked for a pulse and he still had it.

"Why, you dumb motherfucker?" I demanded angrily and he turned his head, choking, Yvonne screaming to call a bus, another voice, indistinguishable from the ringing in my ears, but clear enough to know it was on the radio, barking orders.

The fucker on the ground bleeding out said, "Made you do it... nothing left anyways."

Shit.

"You have got to be kidding me," Yvonne muttered and sat back on her heels.

Shit, shit, shit, shit, shit.

"Get a bus! Somebody get that bus right now!"

"Start, CPR," she stripped off the coat and pressed it to his chest and we started giving CPR the best we could, but it was futile. Angel was one of the responding paramedics and took over, shining a light in the guy's eyes while his partner set up the new machine that did compressions for you.

"No good," Angel said. "Get him up on the gurney anyways. As far as those reporters know this guy still has a heartbeat and he doesn't need to die on the evening news."

They hustled smoothly, just as if the guy was still breathing, not even missing a beat and I grunted, "Thanks. He has a family, somewhere..." remembering what the first letter had said.

"No problem, Youngblood."

They hustled him out and took off with him, the siren wailing off into the distance. I'd stood up and stared at all that blood on the floor.

Wasn't the first dead body I'd seen. Just the first one I'd made that way.

"Investigators are on the way," Yvonne said and I nodded.

"Anyone wants their PBA reps, that's their right, but this was a clean shoot," I called. Still, I knew I was calling mine. It was time for all of us to cover our asses.

It was going to be a long night full of paperwork for all of us.

I RAPPED out the code knock on the door to the room that held my woman for real something like way too many hours later. She only had about three hours left before her court appearance and I wasn't about to let her go that alone. I could maybe catch an hour or so with her before we had to get up and ready for the day… still, after Narcos and Driller let me in, and I caught sight of her through the open bedroom door, my body had other ideas about things than sleeping.

"You alright?" Driller asked.

"Yeah," I muttered, eyes glued to her shape beneath the covers just about twelve feet away or so.

Narcos huffed a sardonic laugh, "I did the same thing after I killed my first guy."

That tore my gaze away from her, and I looked up at him frowning, "What?" I demanded.

"Fucked. Found the nearest bitch willing to put out and kept her under me for a day or two."

"Charming," Driller said smiling, "but also, a natural reaction. Just do us a favor and close the door."

I scowled at the both of them but Narcos stopped me with a hand on my shoulder, "Neither of us are making light of the fact you just had to kill a man, brother. I'm just a dick and don't know how to put things… All I'm saying is doing something life-affirming afterwards is a normal thing."

He gave me a little shake back and forth and pushed me toward Chrissy. Driller said, "She doesn't know, we didn't tell her. We didn't want her to worry any more than she was, but don't get it twisted, bro... she's worried. Didn't think you'd call but still, figured the not knowing was better than telling her you'd traded bullets with the perp.

I shook my head, "He didn't get a shot off, but there was no question. Investigation is still ongoing but we all know better. It'll be declared good. There's plenty of video footage of it. Media was right outside rolling on the whole thing."

"Good, that's good," Driller nodded.

"Yeah, at least they were good for something," Narcos agreed darkly.

"You sure *you're* okay, brother?" Driller asked and I nodded.

"I'll be okay, man. Already have my appointment booked with the department shrink."

"Yeah, the modified desk duty is a bitch," Narcos complained. "Leaves you too much time to think about it."

I nodded. That was honestly my biggest fear at this point, that I wouldn't be able to stop thinking about it.

"Thanks guys," I said one more time and the hand fell away from my shoulder. I went into the room with Chrissy and closed the door behind me. I stood at the foot of the bed for a long time, just looking at her.

She was on her back, left arm lying across her stomach, on the blankets which had been pulled to her chest. Her long dark hair fanned out behind her head along the pillow. Her face was turned towards the window and the bluish light from the cityscape outside fell across her features turning her already angelic features, slack with sleep, into something downright ethereal.

She was beautiful in that way that made my chest squeeze down tight, and after the ugly that'd gone down at the Hyatt, her beauty damn near brought tears to my eyes. I couldn't deny that I was in love with her. Not to myself, and I didn't want to. I just wanted to figure out a way to cement her as a permanent piece of my life.

I carefully and quietly stripped down and pulled the blankets away from her, climbing into the bed. She startled awake, drawing a deep and even breath as her dark eyes flew open and she turned, adjusting her body so that I could more easily access her, she reached for me and I nudged her knees apart with my own. She parted her thighs willingly and drew me down to her.

"I was so worried," she breathed and kissed me and I didn't want to speak. I didn't want to tell her what I'd done, just yet.

She wrapped her legs around my hips and my cock nestled against her bare sex. She moaned into my mouth, a light breathy sound and writhed slightly, sliding her body up and down against mine.

We kissed and dry humped like a couple of teenagers in the back seat of the car for who knows how long. All I can say is it was an amazing feeling, and there wasn't anything dry about her when I went to slip inside of her.

I broke the kiss and made sure she was looking at me when I did it, telling her exactly how I felt, telling her, "I love you," as I sank into her slowly.

She held to me tightly, her hands drifting to my face, holding me there so she could look back, searching for something, what I didn't know, but I could see the flood of her own emotions filling her dark eyes as she raised up to kiss me, before drawing back and murmuring, "I love you, too."

I drew back and thrust forward, a little more intense than I'd ever taken her before, but she didn't seem to mind. Instead, she drew me down on top of her, nipping my shoulder lightly, her thighs tightening around my hips, her hand drifting down my body and gripping my ass, pulling me deeper.

I let the fog of love, lust, and pleasure take over as I set a strong and steady rhythm to my strokes and we just stayed like that, working each other's bodies, trying to stay considerate and quiet for the guys outside. Her moans soft, her gasps rich and like music to my ears. I worked her up, taking her higher and higher with me until finally I reared up and seating myself deep, played her clit with the pad of my thumb.

She couldn't keep entirely quiet when she came, but that was okay. I didn't need her to, and it was kind of nice letting the guys outside know that she was mine.

There wasn't anything else I prized more at this point than my ability to make her make sounds like that and it so moved me, I wasn't far behind her, pushing my shirt she had on out of the way, pulling from her body, and coming in jet after hot, white jet over her flat and toned stomach with it's adorable, slight little pouch, right over the top of her pubic bone.

God, she was beautiful, and I knew it'd only been a few weeks, but I hoped she would be able to score another morning after pill, because while I wanted children at some point, with this woman, if she didn't, I would be okay with that, too. It was her body, and I just loved that she gave me the honor and privilege to play with it, and her, like she did.

I bowed over the top of her, pressing our bodies together, sticky with my come, and didn't care. I kissed her mouth, her chin, the side of her neck and growled beside her ear, "I want to grow old with you."

She gasped lightly and drew my face up to look at her, "I'd like that," she murmured, but she was frowning and I could see it was with concern. Then she asked, "Tony, what's wrong?"

I swallowed hard, chickened out, and tried to deflect, asking "Why do you ask?"

She traced gentle fingertips along my cheek and came away with moisture, showing me and whispered oh so quietly, "You're crying…"

I jerked back and swiped a hand over my face and sure enough. I bowed my head and laughed a bit brokenly and took a deep breath and let it out.

"Tony, what happened?" She asked gently. "What's wrong, you're starting to scare me."

I shook my head and let myself be true with her, scared of the consequences, but I should have known I shouldn't be… "Curtis Wetmore is dead," I told her. "I had to shoot him. I didn't want to, but when he realized it wasn't you, he'd pulled on us and he was going to shoot. They're calling it suicide by cop… I killed him, Chrissy."

"Oh my god," she breathed and pulled me down to her. She held me, not just with her arms but wrapping her legs around me too. "Oh my god, I'm so sorry…" she breathed and I just buried my face in her hair by her shoulder, pressed my lips against the soft skin where her shoulder met her neck and let her take care of me… because I know guys are supposed to be strong all the time, but we sometimes needed these moments, too.

Chrissy delivered in the way only she could. Holding me close, making soothing sounds, and just being *her*. Warm, beautiful, understanding, and nurturing. She held me and loved me despite the terrible thing I'd just done and it was precisely what I needed.

26

*C*hrissy...

It wasn't Tony's fault, what he'd been forced to do, and somehow that realization touched off the same for myself, even though he'd been saying it all of this time, it had still felt like somehow, *this was all my fault...* but it wasn't. I could only take responsibility for my own actions, not the actions of crazed sports fans, or even a man who had drunkenly handed the keys to his equally drunken friend.

It wasn't Tony's fault that he'd had to shoot Curtis Wetmore, and it wasn't my fault that Curtis Wetmore had come after me... it was Curtis Wetmore's fault and it was sad that it had come to this, but I couldn't take responsibility for it any more than Tony could.

I had held him for a long time, until we had nearly dried and stuck together, and the alarm had gone off, startling us both. We'd showered and dressed together, and he looked so tired. However, before we'd opened the door to the rest of the suite, he'd stood straight, pulled his shoulders back, and took a deep breath, and aside from the dark circles and slightly red rims to his eyes, you'd have never guessed just how exhausted he was.

I picked my own head up, squared my shoulders and we exchanged a look, smiled, and went out into the world as a team. I liked that, and I think, right now, we both needed that so much.

"Ready to roll, little lady?" Driller asked, shrugging into a blazer of his own. I nodded, and Narcos opened up the door into the hall.

"Good luck, y'all," he said.

"You aren't coming with us?" I asked.

"Undercover, honey. You're the biggest thing since sliced bread – we can't risk having him seen anywhere near you, it'd raise far too many questions," Driller said.

"And what about you?" I asked.

"You won't be seen with me either, I got a different kind of date at the courthouse. Come on now, the imminent threat is over and your chariot awaits."

It all made sense, and I felt more than slightly foolish for having even suggested their visible involvement. I'd lost count of how many times they'd said they were both undercover officers, the protection detail at the hotel, locked in a room with me, had been as low profile as you could honestly get. They'd already been in place, here in the hotel when I'd arrived and we'd not once been seen by anyone else together, other than more police officers.

We took the elevator to the lobby and scurried around to the next one down to the garage. Driller took off first, on one of the upper floors, closer to the surface, while Tony and I continued down, down and further down to one of the bottom floors. The elevator pinged and the doors whooshed open. We stepped out into the glass fishbowl that contained the bank of elevators to a dark SUV waiting, doors open, just outside the milky glass, stained with runoff from the damp concrete walls.

I adjusted my arm in its sling, and nodded towards Tony's partner, Jaime, who held the door for me.

"Morning," he said and I smiled.

"Good morning," I greeted, before I grabbed the 'oh shit' handle with my good arm and stepped on the runner. I helped myself into the back of the SUV and carefully slid along the leather seat to the other side so Tony could get in behind me.

"Good morning," I greeted the driver in kind and he looked in the rearview, eyes sparkling with a sudden and surprised smile.

"Morning, ma'am," he answered. Tony got in beside me and closed the door, Jaime got in up front and passed back a coffee to his partner, then one to me.

I waived it off, "No thank you, my nerves are buzzing hard as it is," I told him.

"You're gonna be fine," he said.

"Oh, I know," I replied with surety, "I just hate court days..."

Both Jaime and Tony turned to look at me in unison and I laughed. The driver put the SUV into gear and said, "How does a lawyer not like court?" he asked.

"It's nerve-wracking as hell, but it's like anything I guess, part of the job." I shrugged a shoulder and the conversation stayed true. Questions being asked, laughter being exchanged, and even Tony was smiling again, even if it held an edge of tired.

"So how do you handle it?" he asked and I looked at him.

"I never really thought about it in depth," I said, "But if I had to have an answer, I suppose I just always come at it from the angle of treating it almost like a performance. I mean, I *am* in front of all these people. Lawyers, court clerks, judges, bailiff's, the jury, even the gallery and they're all there, all eyes on me, and so I... I don't know, I just sort of fake it until I make it, you know? Like the worst improvisation you've ever had to do, but my client is there and they deserve the best defense I can give them, so I've got a reason to do my best, and so I do."

I laughed uneasily and sighed, "That is probably the worst explanation known to man, but it's all I've got," I said.

"Naw, it actually makes sense when you put it that way," the driver said and I sort of felt bad that I hadn't gotten his name yet. He pulled in to drive down into the courthouse's garage and swiped his badge against the reader. The gate lifted and we pulled smoothly into the dim, subterranean complex.

"Thanks, Jules," Tony said and I asked, "Is that your name, then?"

He laughed and said, "Naw, it's actually Jordan Verne, but the guys started calling me Jules, as in the old school author."

"Ah, well thank you, Detective Verne," I said and he laughed.

"No problem."

Tony held out a hand to me and helped me down out of the car. My nerves fizzed like soda pop, threatening to overflow but I patiently waited them out, moving as if nothing were amiss, continuing to mimic the bravery and surety that Tony had put on that morning.

"Okay, let's do it," Jaime declared and opened the door into yet another fishbowl, surrounding the elevators, these ones familiar. I went through the door, Tony at my back and pressed the button to go up.

"You're gonna be okay, precious," he murmured under his breath and I smiled to myself.

"Of course I am, I've got you," I murmured back.

"Heh, knock it off you two," Jaime said under his breath and the elevator doors opened and I stepped on.

OVER TWO HOURS LATER, I was in the proverbial hot seat as Parnell asked me to tell the grand jury what had happened to me. I realized belatedly, that this wasn't a grand jury to indict the man who had shot me, but rather one convened to see if more serious charged could be brought against the man, Kevin Cohan, that had started the entire sordid mess by publishing my address online.

"I was in my kitchen, in my apartment with my best friend, Sami... that would be Samantha Lynn Hayworth. We were discussing the fact that someone unknown to me at that time had published my address on a public forum along with threats against my personal safety."

Parnell stopped me for a moment and handed me several sheets of paper with highlighted passages and asked, "Were these some of those threats?"

I read over them and took a deep breath, "Yes, I believe so." I knew what he was going to ask me to do next and I didn't want to. I really didn't, but Tony had inspired me, and even though grand jury proceedings were secret, and he couldn't be in here, I knew he was just outside in the hall and I drew on his strength none the less.

"Pardon my language," I said, "but it reads, and I quote: 'Fuck that lawyer bitch, no one should have ever given her bitch ass a law degree in the first place. Women belong barefoot and pregnant in the kitchen, not doing a man's job. Someone needs to remind that hooker what her place is, and that's on her knees with my dick in her mouth.'" I put the paper to the back of the sheaf of them in my hands and sniffed, trying not to let the words get to me, but still... this was an emotional thing.

"And the next one please?" Parnell asked quietly, giving me an apologetic look. I stared him in his dark brown eyes and cleared my throat.

"After several responses from other people in the online forum's thread, he says, 'Seriously, someone needs to go over to that broad's place, kick in her front door, and shank that pink ass, I'd bet she'd love it. In fact, here's her address: two-two-one-six, east fifty-third; apartment two-oh-six. Whoever puts that cunt in her place, you'd be a real American hero.'"

I set the papers down and bit my lips together, taking deep and even breaths in through my nose and out through my mouth to keep from doing two things. One, crying; and two, to keep from being sick.

"And what happened on the night of April 11th, Ms. Franco?"

"A man kicked in my front door, shot my best friend in the head and when I turned to run away, shot me in the back twice."

"Okay, thank you... you may step down."

I got up, tears dripping down my face and nodded to Parnell as I tried to hold my head high. A bailiff let me out of the courtroom into the hall and Jaime and Tony both stood up from their seat on a nearby bench.

"You okay?" Tony asked me immediately and I nodded.

"It wasn't for Silver," I said, and let out a shuddering breath.

"Yeah, no need, we've got him dead to rights, he's already trying to make a plea," Jaime said.

"What was it for, then?" Tony asked, and I could tell his tired mind just couldn't keep up. I sniffed, and Jaime handed me his handkerchief and I wiped my eyes and blew my nose.

"Cohan, trying to indict him on murder charges, for Sami."

"Ah, yeah, son of a bitch deserves it. Do you want to wait here for the indictment?" Tony asked.

"No, I'm sure Parnell will call. Right now I want to march out that front door and tell the press where to shove it. Then I want to get you home so both of us can take a nap."

"I can't say I'm not on board with that plan, but are you sure about the press? Maybe it's not the best idea right now."

"I've never been surer in my life, and I know you're the Mick in this relationship, but this Wop girl still knows a thing or two about Irish diplomacy."

Tony laughed and Jaime frowned, "Never heard of it," he said and Tony explained.

"It's the art of telling a motherfucker to go straight to hell in such a way that they look forward to taking the trip."

"Oh, hell. That's too nice for them vultures," Jaime said.

"I don't disagree, maybe I'll just tell them to go to hell point blank."

The men laughed and we went for the front of the courthouse. I could have ducked out the back, or gone out through the garage, but I was tired, so very tired, of ducking and running, and hiding – and for what? Doing my job? Trying to put this horribleness behind me and heal in peace? I had a right to privacy and peaceful living, and these people were trampling all over that right and I was so tired, over it, and done.

We barely got down three of the old regal building's front steps when we were barraged on all sides by flashing lights, microphones, and shouting figures.

"Ms. Franco! Ms. Franco! Do you have anything to say?"

"Yes. I would very much so like for you all to leave me alone."

"Don't you think the public has a right to your story?"

"Don't you think I have a right to privacy? To not have my every step dogged by one of you?"

Another flurry and another shouted question, "What do you have to say for yourself regarding the Miranda Maguire case?"

"Excuse me? Did you really just ask me that? 'What do I have to say for myself?' How about, I did my job and an innocent woman was acquitted- but right back at you, what do you have to say for *yourself*? Because of the unwanted media attention that I have been receiving, a man is now *dead*. But I suppose *that's* just good business for you all, isn't it? If it bleeds, it leads, right? So what do you have to say for yourselves? Inquiring minds really want to know." I snorted derisively and said, "Get. Out. Of. My. Way."

Reporters, some of them shocked, parted enough for Jaime and Tony to push their way through. I followed in their wake, closely, and we made it to the curb where Jaime hailed a cab. We all three got in and pulled smoothly from the curb and into traffic.

"I just want to go home," I said tiredly, and Tony gave my hand a quick squeeze.

"We'll get you there as soon as we get to the precinct," he said.

I sighed out harshly and swallowed hard. Home... I was loved, and I knew in my heart, that I had a home with Tony if I wanted it. I mean, I think, by the way he just said it, that it was going to be a thing and I found myself asking myself if it was something I wanted. To move in with him after all of this.

My heart said 'yes' but my head was coming up with all manner of reasons as to why it may not be the best idea.

I sat in silence the entire ride to the precinct's garage, where we transferred into Tony's truck. He started it up, tiredly and I took in his profile and just about every argument my head could come up with went out the window when my heart cried, *this is where you are meant to be… with him.*

27

*T*ony…

We went home, we went to bed. No foreplay, no sex, just both of us crawling between the sheets of my bed, cuddling close and racking out *hard*. I woke before she did, relieved to find the lines of hardship and emotional strain erased from her beautiful face, everything gone slack with sleep.

I stared at her for I don't know how long, the moonlight spilling across her smooth skin from my bedroom window, before, I think, she finally sensed my staring. She sucked in a deep breath, a line furrowing her brow between her eyes that blinked open, struggling for a moment before finally fixing on my face.

"Stay with me…" I murmured and she tipped her head questioningly.

"Define, that," she whispered.

"Make it permanent, move into this place with me. Live with me for real. Take your time, find a better job, hell, never go back to work again if you don't want to, just whatever you decide to do, just *stay with me.*"

"I want to," she said and swallowed hard, and I could tell she was starting to choke up, I caressed the side of her face and breathed out knowing it was coming and supplying it for her when she couldn't make herself say it...

"But..."

"I'm so scared for you, of what could happen to you being near me. I feel like a magnet for disaster and how do I know if it's over? I mean, really over, you know?"

"Don't care if it is or not, precious." I picked up her hand and kissed the palm, breathing her in. "You belong here, with me. I need you."

She scoffed a bit of a self-deprecating laugh and said, "I think you have that backwards, Detective. I'm pretty sure it's *me* who needs *you.*"

"Fuck it, we need each other, and I love having you here. I love *you* and you said you love me, too and I believe it."

"It's a natural thing to want to protect the ones you love most above even yourself," she whispered and she pushed herself up, flinging a leg over my hips and straddling me. *God, that was so hot...*

"What're you trying to say, you want to protect me?" I asked.

"Like I've never wanted to with anyone else before... I'm not lying when I say I feel like a poison, Tony. After everything that's happened?"

"You may feel like a poison, baby," I said, sitting up abruptly and capturing her body, wrapping my arms around her and holding her to me so she couldn't slip away, "But I'm telling you, you're the cure. You make me stronger, you complete me in ways no other woman has." I winked at her then and said, "So what if you're not Irish."

She laughed then, scoffing, and leaned down, cupping my face, and whispered against my mouth, "You're sure?"

"Gonna end up with some leave time I'm gonna have to take after shooting someone... Happy to use it to help you move your shit."

"I kind of like the sound of that," she murmured. "The leave time, and spending it with me... not the whole you had to take someone's life, part."

"Hey, you're right, I'm not okay with that part but I'm sure it's going to get better, especially if I have you."

"You have me," she said and it sounded like a promise. I closed the small gap between us and pressed my mouth to hers. She kissed me back and it tasted like forever. I felt a tension I hadn't known was riding me let go, and relief flooded through me.

I made love to Chrissy in our bed, the whole time in the back of my mind putting together plans to get her moved out of that shit-hole apartment of hers and sorted out. I would have to pitch some of my shit to make way for hers, and I was okay with that. I really was.

"I love you," she whispered between panting breaths filled with ecstasy, and I loved that. I loved what I could do to her and I loved what she did for me, and I loved how we just *fit*. How she'd come in here like some kind of a refugee but she hadn't stayed that way long. How I'd come home to dinner already started some nights, or made, depending on how her arm was treating her. How I'd realized I hadn't had to clean a damned thing in a week or more because she'd already quietly taken care of it.

Hell, even my cat liked her, and she liked him, too... obviously, because she'd just sort of naturally taken over feeding him.

Everything about having her in my life made it better, and I would fight until the end of fucking days to keep her in it. That just was what it was.

I came, deep inside the condom I'd put on this time, inside her and teased her clit until she came around me, which fuck, she'd nearly been there. I held her close, and we kissed lazily, and I'd worn her out but good, because she fell asleep again, against me first. I honestly wasn't far behind her, though.

THREE DAYS LATER, I was on voluntary leave, my appointment with the department shrink had gone well, and everything was looking up for both Chrissy and I. I'd called in the rest of the McCormick boys and whoever else was available when it came to my club to help us move her into my place and had spent the better part of the last couple of days going through and packing up her apartment and pitching what couldn't be saved. Even her crazy ass drag queen nurse from the hospital was pitching in over at her place right now.

"You sure, man?" my older brother, Thomas, asked me.

"Yeah, bro. Take it. If you think Cassie could use it, by all means." We were talking about the twin bed in his old room which we were going to convert into an office for Chrissy. Cassie was my brother's oldest girl and getting ready for a big girl bed of her own.

"Yeah, can probably paint it, stencil some flowers or princesses and shit on it, I think it'll fly and it'll save me some money which is great." His ex was trying to bleed him dry on child support and alimony but he had some good lawyers and was fighting for custody of both his girls. It was an ugly and rough row to hoe, though.

"No sweat, you bring your truck like I asked?"

"Yeah."

"Cool, let's haul this to the front and drop it in and we can get moving down to Chrissy's after that."

"Cool. You uh, you're really sure about this?" he asked.

I nodded, "Yeah. Yeah I am."

"She looks pretty, from everything I saw on the news, and shit."

"Drop dead gorgeous," I affirmed.

"Well, she's gotta be some kind of special if she landed you, bro."

I laughed, "You're so full of shit!" I declared and he shook his head.

"No, man, I really mean that. I may be an engineer, but sometimes I really feel like out of the four of us, you're the only one who really went for it, you know?"

"No, I don't know," I said frowning.

"He means that out of all of us McCormick boys, you're the only one that actually made something out of yourself," Daniel, the brother next in line after me, said from behind me. I turned to see him leaning nonchalantly in the doorway, my youngest brother, Sean looking over his shoulder.

Sean asked, "So when's the wedding? Ma's gonna be thrilled."

I laughed and said, "I'll get there, little brother, just one thing at a time."

"Uh huh, so where is she?" he asked.

"Her apartment with some of the guys from the club. Like I said, one thing at a time."

"Right, so let's get to it, I'd kind of like to see Indigo City's top media sensation for myself," Daniel said and I shook my head.

"Word to the wise, buddy. Don't let her hear you call her that, and damn sure don't treat her that way."

"Oh, I saw that interview on the courthouse steps, I wouldn't want to piss her off," Thomas declared. He had the bed mostly apart and I started passing shit to our younger brothers.

"Start taking this shit out to Tommy boy's truck and let's get moving," I said.

"Yeah, sooner we're done the sooner the grill's fired up," Sean said, grinning and I had to laugh.

"Dude, you are entirely too food motivated," Danny said.

"Don't I know it, but look at me, I can't keep it on."

Sean was right, he had a metabolism like you wouldn't believe and he was already in his mid-twenties with it showing no signs of slowing down on him.

"Besides, if Reflash is cooking, I don't wanna miss that shit for the world," he called down the hall and I had to laugh.

"Pretty sure Reflash is cooking," I called back.

We hustled things out to Tommy's truck and then piled in mine for the drive into the city. We had to circle the block a few times, but finally nabbed a spot across the street from Chrissy's place. The guys already had the dumpster in the alley mostly full of broken shit, and the moving truck only had a couple of big pieces of furniture to it. Mostly her desk that'd been in the living room that looked more like an armoire. Somehow it'd managed to escape the destruction which had been good, so had her entertainment center. Not so much with what'd been on it, though.

Her television had never been recovered, her couch had already been trashed... the one lone living room chair had been slashed and had been gotten rid of a long time before this. Still, there were a lot of boxes. Mostly clothes, dishes, kitchen equipment, and shoes.

We found her standing with Backdraft, Golden, and Pasquale and she looked up from her phone, "Aw, I was trying to call you! We're all done."

"Yeah?"

"Baby," she said with a laugh, "you called in an army when I just plain didn't have an army's worth of stuff to move..."

"Yeah, well, only the best and most efficient for my girl." I pulled her against me and smacked a kiss against her lips. She laughed and sighed a bit defeated.

"Still a lot of cleaning to be done, I'm pretty much giving the deposit up for dead."

"Cleaning we can do," Danny offered up, then said, "Tony, quit being a dick, introduce us."

"Yes, please!" Pasquale echoed, he had one hand on his hip, the other up in some kind of vogue while he eyed my three brothers. "Any one of you gay?" he asked.

Tommy laughed, "No."

"Ah!" Pasquale threw his head back, melodramatically affronted and walked away, back straight, chin high. My brothers and I had to laugh, and Chrissy did, too.

"I hear you laughing at a sister!" Pasquale accused of Chrissy. "See if I *ever* go shopping with you again!"

"Oh come on, don't be like that!" Sean called and Pasquale waved him off and went and checked his lip gloss in the moving truck's side view mirror. I shook my head and ignored the queen and introduced my brothers to my woman.

"Precious, these are my three asshole brothers. That's Tommy, he's the oldest, then there's me, Danny's here and that's Sean."

"Hi," she greeted them all warmly and shook hands and said, "Well, I would *really* like to finish this and go home. I feel like I can finally really start putting some of this mess behind us by getting out of here."

We all trooped upstairs and with three and four of us to a room got the final cleaning pretty well knocked out in nothing flat.

"I'm going to catch a ride back to your place with these guys so Chrissy can ride back with you," Daniel said and I smiled, hugging him.

"Thanks, man."

"No sweat, she seems real nice."

Chrissy was right, the real work wasn't at her apartment, it was back at the house. A whole bunch of shit got shuffled around, the house almost taken apart and put back together, and that was cool. There were more furniture pieces that were headed for a consignment shop by the end of the day, and even a few more that were just plain headed for the dump.

Boxes were piled in her new office, and more in our bedroom, and those would have to be dealt with later. The rental truck was returned and by the time I got back from that, everyone was on the back deck, three picnic tables lined end to end to accommodate everyone, and Reflash was manning the grill with Skids in a support role.

I caught Chrissy and pulled her in, kissing her soundly and asking, "How you doing?"

"Really good," she said and sounded surprised.

"Yeah?"

"Yeah," she smiled and it was the lightest thing I'd seen in a minute.

I told her, "I love you," and it totally transformed her. She went from lighter than air to completely transcendent, totally angelic at the words.

"Awww! Would you look at that," Backdraft cried and there was a track of masculine laughter.

"Jealous?" I asked, not taking my eyes off my woman.

"A little," he confessed, and there was more laughter. He and Torrid had ripped each other apart and he was crashing here until he could score a new pad.

"Here, here!" Skids called, "A toast, I think this needs a toast." People fell in with their beers and sodas and Skids raised his Mexi-Coke.

"To family, both blood and chosen," he said, and he turned to Chrissy, "To a beautiful woman, and a love that lasts. Salute!"

"Excuse me, excuse me!" Pasquale cried, waving his hand until everyone had eyes on him. "That'd be *women*, you silver fox."

Laughter broke out and Skids shook his head, "I stand corrected," he said and raised the glass bottle his soft drink was in and cried, "Salute!"

"Salute," everyone echoed, and took a drink, and how could you not drink to that?

Chrissy blushed and hugged herself closer into my side and I felt like my life was pretty fucking complete.

EPILOGUE

hree months later...

Chrissy...

"Knock, knock..."

Yale and I looked up from where I was signing some final paperwork.

"Hey, you! What are you doing here?" I asked.

"Didn't think I was going to miss this moment, did you?" Tony asked and I went around my desk and reached up, my left arm only giving the barest of twinges at the back of my shoulder as I put my arms around him and hugged him hard. His arm went around me, his hand pressing to the satin of my blouse, and I breathed him in. He smelled of leather, the road, and clean air and I loved that about him.

"What moment would that be?" I asked, "Starting a new job?"

"Not just starting a new job, precious, but the day the infamous Chrissy Franco, scourge and bane of ICPD and the Indigo City's prosecutor's office *switched sides*."

I grinned at him ruefully and took a step back. The office was fairly nice, Indigo City's taxpayer's dollars at work. It was also mine. A box of my things rested on the corner of the rich, reddish wood desk, waiting for me to find them their place on the empty shelves behind it and along one wall.

"It was a long time coming, I think."

I had essentially fired myself from Reardon, Colfax & Price when I got myself a civil attorney and filed suit against them for keeping the information about the threats silent. I'd helped myself to several of their internal memos that they had stupidly also sent to my email which I then promptly printed for my own records. Memos that all but made my case for me. They were trying to settle with me now, but had yet to offer me a number that I knew would sufficiently hurt their bottom line enough to make them change their policies.

"Yeah, well, long time in coming or not, we're glad you're on our side now," Yale, I mean Mr. Parnell said, giving me a wink and shuffling the final employment papers I'd needed to sign into their legal folder.

"Thanks," I murmured.

There had been a lot to celebrate lately. Life living with Tony was good, both the man who had published my address online and the man who had kicked in my door had taken plea deals, even though the prosecution had them both dead to rights, the case against Cohan for murder and attempted murder would have been hard to prove without Silver's corroborating testimony.

Silver would be in prison for the next twenty to twenty-five years for Sami's death, while Cohan would be inside for the next twenty. I almost felt sorry for him, but then I looked down into the box with the picture of me and Sami looking out, and any pity I might have had for his actions evaporated.

Anyone who said words couldn't hurt you, obviously needed to walk a mile in my shoes.

"Soooo what's in the bag?" I asked Tony, biting my lip as he set a big paper shopping bag with those twisted paper handles onto the small round table the office had sitting by the door.

"First things first," he said pulling out a bottle of champagne and some plastic cups.

"Yale, you sticking around for this?"

"Absolutely," he said grinning, and Tony untwisted the wire cage over the cork.

He popped it over my trash can and poured three cups. Pink and sweet, it was my favorite kind. I laughed.

"To Christina Marie Franco," he said, "*prosecuting* attorney-at-law, and the love of my life."

"Here, here!" Yale said and raised his glass. We all sipped and no one complained about my girly taste in champagne.

"Mm, so what else is in the bag?" I demanded, raising an eyebrow.

"K, Yale, *now* you need to get out."

Yale nearly shot champagne out of his nose and shook his head, "I don't even want to know, she's been here five minutes. Close the door and whatever it is, don't get caught."

He left my office to peals of laughter, some of the people outside stopping to look, but then Tony shut the door and grabbed for me, pulling me close. The kiss was sweet with the taste of champagne and happiness and I smiled.

"Seriously, you're killing me, what's in the bag?" I asked.

"Jesus Christmas, you're a bitch to surprise," he said, smiling.

"Mm, I'm just a bitch period," I said sipping the bubbly liquid in my cup.

"You're definitely a bitch when you're *on* your period. The rest of the time you're pretty cool, you know, for a Wop."

I rolled my eyes and said, "You're going to be one dead Mick if you don't tell me what's in the bag."

He laughed and handed it over and it was heavy. I set it on my desk and pulled the tissue paper off the top, my frown deepening as I reached in and pulled out leather.

"What is this?" I asked as they unrolled and I gasped, looking back down into the bag. "No!"

"Figured if you were going to carpool in with me, you were gonna need the right clothes to ride."

"Does this mean..?"

"Get naked, I'll keep my hands to myself, suit up and let's go."

I squealed and threw my arms around him, excited for this new adventure. Tony wouldn't let me ride with him, he said, until a time *he* deemed me healed enough to go.

He grinned at me and it was full of mischief, "Get to it princess, I'm parked on the street and time's a wasting."

I stripped slowly, making damn sure he had a boner before I redressed slowly. I pulled on the pair of my jeans he brought me and he helped me here and there with some of the more unfamiliar things when it came to the chaps. I left my heels at the office and pulled on my brand new ladies motorcycle boots and asked nervously, "Well?"

"I need to get you home and right back out of that getup."

"I kind of like that idea."

"Mm, mm, mm, that's nice."

He handed me the last item out of the bag, a helmet, and we left the office, hand in hand, headed for the elevators.

"Keep the shiny side up, brother!" Yale called from inside his own office and Tony pointed at him with two fingers and called, "You know it!"

Down at the street, my heart palpitated with excitement as Tony told me everything he needed out of me as a passenger.

"Think you can handle that?" he asked, just about glowing with an excitement of his own.

"With you, I think I can handle anything," I said. He leaned over the machine and dragged my mouth to his, kissing me soundly.

"That's my girl," he declared.

I got on behind him once he had the bike started and off its kickstand and I held on tight. The city traffic let me get used to things and finally, *finally* we pulled onto the freeway onramp to cross the bridge.

It was beautiful, freeing, and everything I imagined it would be, the sun starting to dip behind the western horizon, the sky lit scarlet, the weather fair, and my love for the man I held onto as infinite as the sky above us.

This was living, this was life, and new as it may be, I loved it. This was everything I could have ever wished for and I was never letting go.

THE END

INDIGO KNIGHTS
MC
INDIGO CITY
NOMAD

ALSO BY A. J. DOWNEY

The Sacred Hearts MC

1. Shattered & Scarred

2. Broken & Burned

3. Cracked & Crushed

3.5 Masked & Miserable (a novella)

4. Tattered & Torn

5. Fractured and Formidable

6. Damaged & Dangerous

The Virtues

1. Cutter's Hope

2. Marlin's Faith

3. Charity for Nothing

The Sacred Brotherhood

1. Brother to Brother

2. Her Brother's Keeper

3. Brother In Arms

4. Between Brothers

Paranormal Romance (with Ryan Kells)

1. I Am The Alpha

2. Omega's Run

3. Hunter's End

ABOUT THE AUTHOR

A. J. Downey is the international bestselling author of The Sacred Hearts Motorcycle Club romance series. She is a born and raised Seatte, WA Native. She finds inspiration from her surroundings, through the people she meets and likely as a byproduct of way too much caffeine.

She has lived many places and done many things, though mostly through her own imagination... An avid reader all of her life, it's now her turn to try and give back a little, entertaining as she has been entertained.

Stalking Links

www.ajdowney.com

aj@ajdowney.com